MAN AND MACHINE

SERIES EDITOR
MIKE McPHAIL

Stratford, NJ

Special thanks to "DAN • E"

... Fix it!

PUBLISHED BY
eSpec Books LLC
Danielle McPhail, Publisher
PO Box 493,
Stratford, New Jersey 08084
www.especbooks.com

ISBN: 978-1-942990-09-3
ISBN (ebook): 978-1-942990-14-7

Series Website: www.defendingthefuture.com

Design: Mike and Danielle McPhail
Cover Art: "Boarding Party" Mike McPhail, McP Digital Graphics
www.mikemcphail.com
www.milscifi.com

Copyeditors: Greg Schauer
        Danielle McPhail, www.sidhenadaire.com

Contents

❖ AUTOGRAPH DUTY ROSTER ❖

Jennifer Brozek	James Chambers
Aaron Rosenberg	Judi Fleming
Nancy Jane Moore	Eric Hardenbrook
Ronald Garner	Jeff Young
Bud Sparhawk	Anton Kukal
Patrick Thomas	Danielle Ackley-McPhail
Brenda Cooper	C.J. Henderson
Robert E. Waters	Mike McPhail

eSpec Books Titles in the Defending The Future Series

Dogs of War - Reissued
The Best of Defending the Future
Man and Machine

Previous Titles in the Defending the Future Series
(out of print - may be available used)

Breach the Hull
So It Begins
By Other Means
No Man's Land
Best Laid Plans
Dogs of War

eSpec Books Titles Related to the Defending the Future Series

A Legacy of Stars by Danielle Ackley-McPhail
From the Archives: The Die is Cast edited by Greg Schauer
Radiation Angels: The Mission Files by James Daniel Ross
Issue in Doubt by David Sherman
In all Directions by David Sherman
To Hell and Regroup by David Sherman
(forthcoming)

This book is dedicated to **the Grandfather
of the Defending the Future Series**

CJ Henderson
December 26, 1951 - July 4, 2014

Creator of (among others)
Rocky and Noodles
Teddy London
Jack Hagee
and Piers Knight

INKY, BLINKY, AND ME
Jennifer Brozek

NORMALLY, I DON'T LIKE THESE FAR-FLUNG COLONY MISSIONS, BUT THIS ONE… I'LL take it." Delanie subvocalized on her internal comm as she gazed up at the twilight purple night of Artemis III. She smiled at the twin moons chasing each other across the sky.

"That's because you don't have a choice," Inky said in her ear.

"Petty, insignificant details."

"Entrance to the base found. Going in."

Delanie glassed the mountain side with her high-powered binoculars and honed in on her robot companion. The only way she could find him was because she had his tracking code. At not much more than three inches long, the modular robot could move almost faster than the eye could see. "Be careful. I don't have all my gear to repair you this time."

"Incoming," Blinky interrupted. "One thousand klicks and moving fast."

Flipping to her back, Delanie sighed. "Plan B it is. Inky, continue with Plan A. Blinky, you're with me." Her second robot companion, a twin to Inky, slithered under her neck and into her mass of black, kinky hair where she flattened herself against Delanie's skull. Delanie turned her binoculars to the night sky and waited for the guardsmen to arrive.

A count of one hundred and twenty-one later, the near-silent vehicle arrived and two guardsmen jumped out. "You are trespassing on imperial property."

"One moment." Delanie remained lying on the ground as she lifted her recorder up. "Count is thirty-two meteors in quadrant fourteen in the last septicycle. Observation: the meteors are increasing." She sat up and gazed at the guardsmen with a skeptical air. "I don't see any signs that I'm on imperial land. This is the best spot for my research. No light pollution. *You* are interrupting my data collection."

She got a good look at the two of them. Both appeared male. The squat, grey man was definitely from a high-gravity planet while the tanned, bulky one appeared to be from a galactic standard-gravity planet. It was the grey one she needed to watch out for. Neither of them had moved within grabbing range.

"Citizen, you're going to have to come with us."

"Look, you can call my academy—"

Grey took a step forward, his pulse rifle raised. "Citizen, leave your equipment on the ground and stand. By imperial order, I am authorized to incapacitate you."

Delanie widened her eyes and looked between them. "You're serious." When neither answered, she put her binoculars and recorder on the ground and raised her hands. "Look, I'm just doing research for my academic paper on the Tanteri meteor showers." She struggled to her feet as she spoke. "My academy ID is ES553818."

"We'll check that once we get you inside."

She looked around. "Inside where? There's nothing here."

"Come along quietly." Grey continued to cover her as Tanned motioned her to turnaround.

In short order, she was in custody and her guardsmen companions were Guardsmen Ister and Orren. Four times, she spotted ways to escape or to disable her captors. She didn't react to any except to note them. She had to give them this: the guardsmen refused to answer any of her questions as they transported her exactly where she wanted to be.

The room they placed her in was a standard blank room with a metal table and two chairs. She was cuffed to the metal bar at the back of the chair and left alone. There were two cameras. The waiting period was designed to frighten anyone brought there. Delanie hid her smile by looking down at the table with slumped shoulders.

"Inky, status." It was more of a test of her subvocal comm than a request for information.

"Plan A executed. I have control of their computer system."

"Five-minute loop of this room on both cameras."

"Here I am, saving you once more." Inky paused. "Done. Free to move."

Blinky stirred. "I'm on the rescue squad, too."

Delanie stretched her neck, popping it once. She felt Blinky moving down her back and arm to disable the cuffs. She waited until the small robot was safely back in her clothing. "You're both my heroes. Let's get to work. You know the objective."

"Follow the bouncing red dot." Inky projected the path into her cornea implant.

"Skip the bouncing..."

Blinky interrupted her. "Always playing," she scolded her sibling. "Now is not the time. We're on the clock."

"There's always time to play."

Delanie considered turning down their sibling-rivalry percentages but, if she were honest, she liked the chatter and they both did work harder to get her approval. She opened the interrogation room door, only to find herself face-to-face with a surprised Guardsman Orren AKA Grey. He hesitated long enough for her to grab him by the shirt and yank him into the room.

As suspected, he was heavier and stronger than he looked. Faster as well. Instead of tumbling into the metal table, he bounced against it and came back with a fist to her face. It hurt. Enough that she knew she needed to put the man down as soon as she could. Rather than a straight fisticuffs fight, Delanie opted for the "no you don't" approach and swept his feet out from under him.

He grabbed her as he went down. The two of them tumbled and rolled, rebounding off the walls and furniture. They came to a stop with Orren on top. He punched her twice more and blocked her knee kicks with his thighs. She shoved a thumb in his eye as his hands latched around her throat.

"Blinky!" was all she had time for, then her air was cut off. Delanie dug her thumb in deeper. Grey screamed but didn't let go.

Then he collapsed on top of her.

"Status?" Inky asked.

Delanie moaned in-between gasps for air. She half-shoved, half-wriggled out from under the heavy man.

"Status?" Inky asked again with a bit more force.

Blinky saved her from answering. "Rescued by me. I'm one up."

"What'd you hit him with?" Delanie croaked as she gazed at the guardsman. He'd meant business. So noted. She gave him a hard kick to the ribs to remember her by.

"XP-7. He's out for hours."

Inky projected an image of himself into her cornea. "On the clock. They'll miss him in ten."

Delanie blinked and nodded. "Roger. Heading to the objective." She stood and coughed. She was going to hurt in the morning, but it was all part of the job.

Blinky zipped from Orren back to her accustomed place in Delanie's clothes. "Ready when you are."

For a moment, she envied the two robots. Neither of them felt pain. They were self-aware and had their quirks, but pain was not one of them. Delanie shook her head. "Blinky, pain suppressant, please."

"You sure? You said it makes you muzzy."

"I'm sure." She waited for the pain to ease before she cracked the door to the interrogation room. The coast was clear. "Lock the door behind me."

"Roger-roger," Inky murmured in her ear. "I estimate eight minutes until the alarm."

Delanie didn't respond. Instead, she straightened her clothing and walked down the hallway as if she belonged. Skulking about would not help matters. She kept her head high, hoping the probable bruises on her face wouldn't sabotage her efforts to act like just another soldier. She followed the path Inky laid out for her.

The first guardsman she passed, a local by his red skin, gave her a second glance. Delanie scowled at him and kept going. He did not try to stop her. Two more turns later and she breathed a sigh of relief. Her grey, non-descript, vaguely military outfit looked like enough other utilitarian uniforms that most let the lack of adornment slide, convincing themselves that she was either off duty or part of a branch of the Guard that they didn't interface with on a regular basis.

"Aw, crap. I've been detected."

Despite the fact that Inky was a mechanical being, Delanie sensed the underlying panic in his warning. "Initiate Protocol 23-B."

"Acknowledged. Out."

"But, he won't be able to defend himself." Blinky shimmied down from her shirt to her neck.

"I know. I know. We'll get him back." She quickened her step. "We've got a mission."

"But—"

"No buts. Mission first." Delanie stutter-stepped as another guardsman turned down the hallway toward her. This one, a woman with skin as dark as hers, frowned as she eyed Delanie and her lack of a proper uniform.

Delanie kept her chin up and her shoulders square. She nodded to the other woman as she got close enough to read the guardsman's name tag: Marta.

"Guardsman…?" Guardsman Marta began, then stopped and glanced up as an alarm sounded. Without another word or hesitation, she launched herself at Delanie.

The two women slammed against the wall. Marta smashed her elbow into Delanie's already sore face before she could tuck her chin and return the favor. Delanie grabbed the woman's uniform and swept her feet out from under her. She fell on top of the guardsman with all her weigh and was rewarded with a *whoosh* of air, knocking the breath from her opponent. Blinky scurried down her arm and injected the woman before she could recover.

Delanie got off of Marta as she relaxed into unconsciousness. Delanie shook her head. What Guardsman Marta had lacked in skill, she'd made up in ferocity. It was another thing to note. Thank the Seeders for the pain suppressant.

Wasting no time, Delanie pulled the unmoving guardsman from the hall and into the nearest room—a closet—and left her there. While under cover, she slid a small packet from her boot pocket. "No more playing around." Her murmured words were lost in the sound of the continuing alarm.

Opening the packet, she pulled pieces of the weapon from their spots and snapped them together until an ultra-slim dart gun emerged. Delanie pasted this to the back of her left hand before reaching for the magazine of darts in her other boot. The alarm still blared on.

"All right, spill it," she subvocalized to Blinky.

"We should go after Inky."

Delanie half-smiled at the sulking tone. "Inky will be fine. I promise."

"No he won't. He's always in trouble."

"This is why I have full backups for you both. I'll never lose you. Remember, your chassis is just that—a shell."

She felt Blinky move around to the back of her neck. "Well, maybe we like these *shells*. Maybe waking up in a different body sucks and is disorienting as hell. Maybe we don't want to have to rely on backups. Stuff is lost. It's like getting a concussion. We aren't without feeling, you know. Prick us and we bleed."

"No, you don't. You leak."

Blinky paused. "That was mean."

Delanie grimaced. She'd forgotten how sensitive her companions could be. "I'm sorry. I didn't mean it. We'll recover Inky before we leave this base."

"You promise? He is my twin. I always know where he is."

"I swear on... on... my love for you guys. Inky comes home with us." It would make things more difficult but it needed to be done. Cranky robots were worse than a pain in the butt; they could be an unintentional danger. She cracked the closet door. "But, we're on the clock. We've got a mission to finish."

Blinky's answer was to toss up Inky's map into Delanie's eye. Once more, she had a path to follow. She didn't bother mentioning that she'd memorized it when Inky first sent it to her. The little robot was already angry. Not need to make things worse. She hurried on.

Two darted guardsmen and four hallways later, Delanie stood outside the Guard Commander's office. The lock code on her office was active. "Blinky, can you do anything with this?"

She held her hand up to the lock. Blinky zipped down to her fingertips and probed the electronics. Delanie held her breath in a conscious effort not to hurry her companion along. Inky was better at computers. Blinky was better at fights and improvisation.

"Yes. I have it."

Delanie exhaled slow and even. "Excellent. Time is money. Ready?"

Blinky turned one of her modular sections toward Delanie and nodded. When she turned back, Delanie tensed. The door slid open. Delanie charged in as Blinky leapt from her hand.

The Guard Commander's office was set up as a two-room suite: a reception area—complete with a guardsman attendant—and the Commander's office. The attendant, already standing, managed to get a shot off before he was darted in the throat. The short guardsman went down with a gurgle. Blinky had the office door closed and locked again before the man hit the floor.

Delanie aimed her dart gun at the Commander but didn't shoot. The Commander—Len, her name tag proclaimed—for her credit, remained still. The two of them locked eyes. When Delanie was sure the Commander had had enough time to download the necessary information, she glanced at the ceiling and the continuing alarm.

The commander also glanced at the ceiling, then said, "53-51."

"15-35." Delanie smiled, brief and fierce, but didn't drop her weapon.

They both looked up again as the alarm cut off, leaving them with the aftermath of its blare in their ears.

Len, an older woman with grey shot through her short, red hair, sat back and pulled her hands out from under the table. "Congratulations, Imperial

Consultant Delanie. Report?"

"Off the top of my head, Commander, eleven protocol violations and twenty-eight security holes. I'll need to go back through my records to get it all. You'll have my report within two days. Though, I want to give Guardsman Marta a nod. She was especially reactive."

Len nodded. "Be sure to note that in your report."

"Inky's being moved," Blinky said in her ear. "Coming in this direction."

Delanie stepped away from her spot in front of the door, shifting until she'd pressed herself to the wall just to the left of the door. "Question, Commander."

"Yes?"

"If you hadn't been expecting me, what would you have done when I came through your door?" She felt Blinky wriggle her way up her side.

"Shot you immediately. Though, not lethally. Stun. I would've wanted to question you." Len watched her move with a small frown on her face.

"Almost here," Blinky murmured.

Delanie could feel the robot's anxiety and excitement. "Calm," she said *sotto voce*. She raised her voice and addressed Len again, "That would've been a problem. You don't know what kind of armor your assailant is wearing. Always go for lethal. You've got the med team to patch them up for interrogation."

There was a small *bing*, then the Commander's door slid open. A large man came through the door carrying a tray with Inky on it, already talking. "Len, we found..." He stopped when he saw the unconscious guardsman.

Delanie aimed at the guardsman but did not fire.

"Captain Verinu." Commander Len sighed and gestured toward Delanie.

Guardsman Captain Verinu didn't have a chance to turn. Instead, he gave a high yell of pain and collapsed to the floor. The small robot sped from the downed guardsman to the commander. It was on her shoulder before Delanie could move.

"Inky! Stand down!" Delanie stepped toward the desk. "Commander, don't move."

Commander Len froze in mid-motion, one hand in the air.

Delanie repeated, "Stand down." She took two steps toward the desk. "Inky, mission objective completed."

In her ear, she heard, "We won? I was asleep until they moved me."

"We won. Come here." As Inky left the commander and returned to her, Delanie relaxed. Then she smiled at Len. "Make that twelve broken protocols and twenty-nine security holes..."

"I see." Len gazed at Verinu. "How long will he be out? How many did you have to take out to get here?"

"Six down, including these two. They'll wake in about four hours with a galaxy-sized headache to remember me by. Also, if Guardsman Orren hasn't been found, he's locked in interrogation. He'll need medical assistance."

Delanie looked down at Inky and blinked in surprise. Only long years of training kept her from showing her shock. Inky's chassis had both the imperial symbol and Commander Len's personal symbol on it.

Len nodded. "You have permission to remain here while you prepare your report."

"Thank you but I prefer not to stay. The less anyone sees of me, the better. With your leave...?"

"Of course. I'll send for an escort unless... you'd rather sneak out of here?"

Delanie gave her a wry smile. "I think an escort is a good idea."

Delanie waited until she was back in the safety and privacy of her ship before she interrupted Inky and Blinky's rambling conversation on what happened once they'd spilt up. Part of her hated to do it. It was like listening to a pair of kids telling "No kidding, there I was..." stories.

"Ahem..." She said this aloud instead of her usual subvocalizing she did with the pair of them. "Inky, you've got some explaining to do."

Inky and Blinky appeared from wherever they'd been to sit on the command center in front of her. Delanie narrowed her eyes when she saw that they were, indeed, once more twins and the commander's personal symbol was scrubbed from Inky's chassis. Neither of them spoke. She knew that this meant they knew they were in a wee bit of trouble.

"Well?"

Inky shifted, rolling over and over himself. "What do you want to know?"

"One, how did you wake up from Protocol 23-B? That's supposed to knock you out for good. Two, how did you get Guard Commander Len's symbol on then off you again? Three, what were you going to do to the guard commander if I hadn't stopped you?" Delanie ticked all of these off on her fingers.

"One... I did initiate Protocol 23-B. But, me and Blinky modified it a little. If either of us goes into 23-B and we are more than two hundred meters from each other, we follow standard 23-B but, if we get within two hundred meters of each other, we used localized frequencies to keep in touch and wake the other up with primary objective in the top of the queue."

Delanie frowned and considered this. "Can't the enemy track us this way? 23-B is for captured shells. To make sure no one can get to any of us."

Blinky wobbled back and forth. "No. We piggyback on the local frequency at the lowest level in intermittent bursts. This way they have no pattern to follow and we can complete the objective even if you aren't there."

"How'd you come up with this?"

Inky and Blinky both did their equivalent of a shrug. "Just did. Don't like leaving my chassis behind if I can help it. It's nice." Inky whirled like a model showing off the latest couture.

"Speaking of which... the commander's symbol?"

"It's all part of the camouflage package. I just did custom art in case anyone saw me. They'd take me to the commander if they found me." There was no doubt Inky was proud of himself. "Which they did."

Delanie nodded. "That they did. That was really smart. You didn't tell me about it."

"It was supposed to be a surprise."

"Yeah. It was that."

"Three, if you hadn't called me off, I would've knocked her out. That was part of Plan C."

"Plan C? We didn't have a Plan C." Delanie tilted her head, mystified.

Blinky rolled up to her hand and tapped it. "We always have a Plan C. It usually involves a lot of shooting and running away so we don't get captured. In this case, we didn't need it."

Delanie was torn between being stupidly proud of the two of them and frightened. She'd heard they would learn and grown the more they worked with a person. Seems it was true. "You guys did really good."

"Does this mean we get to keep our current shells?" Inky joined Blinky. "They're the best you've gotten us. Also, they're pretty. We like them."

She nodded. "Yes. And I'll stop thinking of them as expendable. At least until I can afford the upgrades. Then we'll see. I'm really proud of you two. Good work."

Blinky tapped her hand again. "Does that mean we can watch *Original Angel* now?"

"Please?" Inky added.

Delanie smiled and shook her head. "You can watch it in your room... for the hundredth time. Silent mode on comm."

"Yay!" The two robots zipped off the command console and toward the back of the ship.

Delanie watched Inky and Blinky go. It seemed it was time to start consulting with the two of them on missions she took. Not only were they invaluable tools, it was time to admit they were part of the team.

WIN OR LOSE

Aaron Rosenberg

United Forces Qualifying Exhibition Match:
Bill Asi vs. Jeff Mackintosh
Round One: Strategy

"This is ridiculous!" Jeff complained, pounding on his console. "I can't believe I even have to do this!"

"Do what?" His friend, mentor, and official sponsor Marie Levois asked from the lone observer's chair behind and to the right of him. "Play chess in front of a billion spectators? Or play chess against *him*?"

"Either! Both!" Jeff sighed and leaned back, rubbing his aching hand with the other. "No," he admitted more quietly, turning away from the screen even though he'd already made sure it's built-in microphone was switched off. "I can't believe I'm being forced to prove myself like this. That this is the only way I can get back in."

"No one's forcing you," she pointed out, sitting forward and reaching out to rest a comforting hand on his shoulder. "You asked for this, remember?"

That provoked a snort out of him. "I didn't ask for any of this," he snapped back, twisting around to face her fully and dislodging her hand in the process. "They asked me. I just added my own condition."

Which was true. The United Forces chiefs had come to him with the idea of the exhibition match. "We want to pit the best of the old against the best of the new," they'd said. "Give people confidence that they're still going to be just as well protected as before, if not better."

Of course, what they hadn't said was that Jeff might as well do this for them because it wasn't like he had anything better to do. Even though he was mostly recovered from the radiation burns, and the skin grafts were all taking nicely, and the doctors said he had about as much use back to his right leg as he was ever going to get—and certainly more than he needed to pilot a starfighter, since they hadn't used foot-pedal controls in close to a decade—Jeff was still waiting on the doctors to sign off and clear him to return to active duty.

And they were hemming and hawing and coming up with excuse after excuse as to why they couldn't do that, yet.

Jeff knew the real reason, though. And it didn't have anything to do with whether he was combat-ready again or not.

It was because he was old. That was the real reason.

Funny, to think that thirty-five was old. But there it was. He'd flown over two hundred combat missions, been fighting since the early days of the war. Everyone else he'd served with had either died, cashed out, or been promoted up to desk jobs. But not him. He'd refused every promotion that would've taken him out of the cockpit, passed on every chance to be discharged, stayed in way past when everyone told him he should—and was eager to get right back out there, doing it all over again.

Because being out there, fighting for his life, was the only time he really felt alive. The only time he felt like he mattered, like he made a difference. Like he was somebody. Out there, he was Commander Jeff Mackintosh, a decorated war hero.

Here, he was nothing but a grounded ex-pilot with a bum leg, a whole rack of medals, and no usable skills. At least, that was how it felt to him, even though Marie and others had assured him it wasn't true. But if he wasn't flying—and not just flying but flying in combat, pitting himself directly against other pilots—Jeff didn't know what to do with himself.

Which was why, when they'd asked him to do this match, he'd agreed. On one condition. "If I win," he'd told them, "I get to re-up."

And they'd agreed. Probably because they were confident their boy—the brightest of the new bunch, they all said—would mop the floor with him.

But Jeff wasn't done yet.

"You can't win if you don't play," Marie reminded him, snapping him out of his reverie and back to the player's alcove they were in. She gestured toward the screen, and the large readout off to the side. Each player only had a minute to make each move, and as the game continued that time would grow shorter and shorter. This wasn't just a test of strategy, it was one of reflexes, and thought speed. Because in combat it wasn't enough to be able to come up with the smart move, you had to figure it out and implement it fast enough to keep you one step ahead.

But Jeff had always been good at that.

"Right, you're right," he said now, swiveling back around and returning his full attention to the game. This was why he'd asked Marie to be the one person with him, because he knew he could count on her to keep him on task. His opponent, Bill, had already made the first move, and it was a fairly standard opening. He'd be expecting a comparably safe counter, most likely.

Jeff grinned as he punched in his move, and then leaned back and watched the screen as his pieces shifted to match his command. A smile played across his face.

Let's see how the new kid liked that!

"What? No! What is he doing?" Bill demanded, wishing for a second he could kick the desk in frustration. He couldn't really, of course, but he imagined doing so, which made him feel a little better. Still he studied the game with growing vexation. He had opened with a traditional gambit, expecting his rival to follow one of several established responses. But instead Commander Mackintosh had launched a sudden attack, a bold move that went against every tenet of the game.

And one for which Bill's pieces were woefully unprepared.

"Easy, take it easy," Dr. Keith Tracton advised. Naturally Bill had chosen Dr. Tracton as his match companion. The man had trained him and been his counselor for years, he knew Bill better than anyone, knew how to help him when he got stuck, when he got confused, when he felt overwhelmed. Like now. "Just relax and think," Dr. Tracton suggested in that low, soothing tone he always took. "You can do this, Bill."

"But this isn't how the game is played!" Bill complained. He felt like a little kid throwing a tantrum, and was embarrassed to lose his cool like that, but he couldn't help how he felt. And Dr. Tracton was always telling him not to hide his emotions, anyway. In fact, he'd been working with Bill all these years to encourage him to show those emotions, to let them out and follow where they led. A process that still felt very foreign to Bill. Especially at times like this. "He's cheating!"

"No, he's not," Dr. Tracton said. "He didn't do anything that breaks the rules. He just went against convention. We've talked about that, remember?" Bill did remember. There were actual rules, and lots of different kinds of those, including natural ones and societal ones. And then there were conventions, things that weren't actually rules but that most people followed anyway—but that you could deviate from when necessary. And the outcome of your action would usually determine whether people felt you'd gone against standard behavior for a good reason, in which case you'd be congratulated, or for a bad one, in which case you'd be shunned.

Commander Mackintosh's move was bold, and clever, and had taken Bill by surprise. It would win him accolades, not censures. And it had thrown Bill off his own strategy, which had been the whole point.

But Bill was nothing if not adaptable. He'd been trained for this, after all. So now he concentrated on the game again, setting aside all the different techniques and gambits and stratagems he'd memorized and instead just studying where his pieces were and where Commander Mackintosh's were, and looking at how his pieces were endangered—and how the commander's were as well.

And then he saw it.

"Aha!" he declared, shifting his pieces to counter the attack. "I've got him!" And, indeed, his pieces had several of the commander's cornered, including his most valuable ones.

"Don't get too cocky," Dr. Tracton warned. "You don't want to get careless and let him trip you up again. But yes," the doctor agreed with a smile, "I think you've got him."

Bill wanted to brag that of course he did, but he knew better. No one liked a braggart, Dr. Tracton had told him time and again. It was fine to take pride in your work, in your abilities, but you didn't go on and on about that. That was unseemly.

So instead he just waited and watched the screen to see how his foe would react.

"Damn!" Jeff scowled at the screen and almost punched the console again, but thought better of it at the last second, remembering how much his hand still ached from the last time. "I thought he'd fall for that!"

"He is smart," Marie reminded him as they both watched the pieces on the screen rearrange themselves. "That's why they picked him."

Jeff nodded, but he wasn't really listening. He was too busy analyzing the board again. Unfortunately, everything he saw just confirmed his first impression: he'd just lost. It had been a risky move, and he'd known that, but if his rival had been a little bit slower, a little bit more cautious, or a little bit more myopic, it could have won him the game. But Bill hadn't fallen for it. Instead he'd countered, covering the gap Jeff had meant to exploit and taking advantage instead of the hole in Jeff's own defenses, a hole he'd knowingly opened when he'd made his move.

It had been a gamble. All or nothing. And he'd lost.

The first round went to the new kid.

Round One Winner: Bill Asi

Round Two: Hand-to-Hand Combat

"I feel funny," Bill said aloud, swinging his arms and flexing his hands. He dropped into a crouch, testing the springiness of his legs, then bounced back upright and settled into a defensive stance, legs wide, feet planted, arms loose at his sides, hands relaxed and ready.

"Funny how?" Dr. Tracton asked. "Is something wrong?"

"No, not wrong, exactly," Bill answered. "Just... funny. This is all so strange." He gestured around him, at the thick jungle that enveloped him. Heavy emerald fronds dangled from the trees, sturdy vines looped loosely around thick branches, and fallen leaves created a thick, spongy cushion underfoot. The foliage overhead blocked out any light from above, casting his surroundings in a uniform shadow, and between that and the way the leaves on the ground absorbed his footfalls, Bill felt like he was trapped in a bubble or wrapped in a sheet of gauzy cotton, making everything feel smothered and distant.

"Well, yes," the doctor agreed with a chuckle, "I suppose it does. But the match wouldn't be very entertaining if it was just held in a plain old boxing ring, now, would it? This is more exciting, and provides you with a lot more opportunities to use your surroundings to your advantage."

"Or for Commander Mackintosh to use it for his," Bill grumbled, glancing around him with a twinge of worry. He'd never been in a real jungle, of course, and he'd only visited jungle simulations twice before, and hadn't liked them much, so this wasn't exactly ideal for him, or familiar. But what if the commander spent a lot of time in jungles? He'd have the upper hand, then.

"You'll do fine," Dr. Tracton assured him. "You've already beaten him once, you can do it again."

"That was a contest of intellect," Bill pointed out. "This is more physical. That isn't exactly my strong suit."

But his counselor disagreed. "This isn't about physical strength," he argued. "This is about reflexes, and coordination, and most of all about being observant and adaptable. You are strong in all those things. You can do this, Bill."

Bill wasn't sure he agreed, but he knew better than to say so. Instead he just nodded. "Yes, Doctor." Then he waited for the signal to begin.

"This is what I'm talking about," Jeff said, stretching from side to side. His leg was a bit stiff, but that was to be expected. The rest of him felt fit and strong, though, despite his age. At least all that time in physical therapy had been good for something! As he limbered up he looked around, studying his surroundings. They'd done a really good job programming the setting. He'd hiked a few jungles in his down time, and this looked and felt and sounded and even smelled exactly like the real thing.

Which meant that Jeff knew exactly how to move through the underbrush, how to ease himself over low-hanging branches and under drooping vines, how to tug young trees aside without snapping them, and how to process sights and sounds despite the jungle's lack of proper light and its dampening effect.

And that meant that, once he'd received the signal to start, he was able to take off through the jungle, sliding effortlessly from tree to tree, searching for his opponent—and spotting him quickly.

Bill looked just as young as Jeff had expected, which was every bit as young and gangly and awkward as he'd probably been when he'd first joined up. Maybe even more so. The kid definitely didn't look like a trained combat vet, that was for sure. And the way he stood around gawking at the trees, he didn't have a lot of jungle experience, either.

Or a lot of combat training, since then he would've known to keep his guard up at all times.

Jeff hit him from behind, dropping the kid to the ground with a quick strike to the back of the knees, then an elbow to the neck and a hand to the upper back to force the kid the rest of the way down until his face was pressed into the leaves and dirt and moss there. The kid flailed, but it was too little, too late—he had no leverage at all, and Jeff was behind him where he couldn't be reached. Not unless the kid's arms could bend backward completely.

"Yield," Jeff commanded, and after a second or two the kid finally went limp, accepting the inevitable.

"I yield," he admitted, his voice high and squeaky.

Jeff released him immediately, hopping back in case the kid got any bright ideas about taking a swing at him anyway. But he didn't. He merely pushed himself up off the ground and rose to his feet, turning around and facing Jeff. Then he bowed, a short little dip like you saw at most dojos.

Jeff nodded back, then turned away even as the scenery faded around him. Next thing he knew, he was opening his eyes back in the player's alcove. Marie helped him remove the electrodes that had fed his body's responses into the simulation.

"Not bad," she told him, smiling as she stepped back to let him sit up.

"Yeah," Jeff agreed, grinning. "Guess the old man's still got some fight to him after all, huh?"

"I did terribly," Bill lamented after the match had ended. "I didn't even last a second against him!"

"That's all right," Dr. Tracton consoled him. "No one really expected you to."

"No?"

"No. The commander's got a lot of experience at hand-to-hand," the doctor reminded him. "You don't have any. This was always heavily weighted in his favor."

"Why have this as part of the match, then?" Bill asked.

Dr. Tracton smiled. "Because it wasn't about you winning," he answered slowly. "It was about the world seeing you stand up to Commander Mackintosh as an equal. Think about it, Bill. Up until today, all most people knew about you was your name, maybe your history, your skill. But now?" He laughed. "Now they have a face to go with the name. And they've seen you with the commander. That's a big deal."

Bill considered that. "So it was symbolic, then?" he asked.

"Exactly!" Dr. Tracton beamed the way he always did when Bill figured something out on his own.

That made Bill feel a bit better. He still wasn't happy about losing so easily, though.

Which was funny, considering that he didn't really want to win in the first place. "I don't want to do this," he'd told Dr. Tracton when he'd first been informed of the upcoming match. "I don't want to go to war. Can't I just stay here with you?"

"You know that's not possible," Dr. Tracton had said, wearing his kindly-but-stern face, the one he put on whenever Bill asked for something he couldn't have. "This is your purpose, Bill. It's what you've trained for. You know that."

And Bill did know that. And he was doing his best in the match, because that was how he was. He couldn't do less than his best.

But he still didn't want to go. Even if that meant losing the match. The problem was, he couldn't lose on purpose.

But he could hope that Commander Mackintosh won the last and final round. That Bill could do, and did—and he didn't tell Dr. Tracton.

Round Two Winner: Jeff Mackintosh

Round Three: Starship Combat

"Ah," Jeff said, sighing happily as he settled into the cockpit and began the familiar process of strapping in and switching on. "Home again, home again." He'd done this so many times he didn't really have to think about it at all, his hands going through each step all on their own and giving him time to just sit back and enjoy the smell of the worn leather and mesh seat mixed with the scents of metal and machine oil, and the sight of the hangar through the cockpit's front viewscreen, and the feel of the seat molding itself to his body.

This was where he belonged.

He had the starfighter prepped and ready in record time, and was given the go-ahead to exit the hangar and wait for his opponent to join him. While he waited, Jeff put the agile little craft through its paces, rocking it this way and that, skimming forward and then scooting back, swooping from side to side.

He was ready.

And the kid? Jeff almost felt sorry for him. Because if the jungle had been rough on him, this was going to be far worse. Jeff was totally in his element here.

Bill felt a pang of fear as he familiarized himself with the starfighter he was now ensconced in. There were so many things to keep track of here! But he'd run plenty of simulators before this, of course, and after a few seconds it all started coming back to him. He ran through his checklist, making sure he had each and every system under control, and once he was satisfied he signaled the comptrollers that he was ready.

"Take her out, then, and good luck," one of the mission comptrollers replied. Bill didn't bother to respond to that—the hangar doors were opening, and he carefully eased his ship forward, getting used to the controls as he went.

Empty space awaited him—empty space with a tiny blip off in the distance. That would be Commander Mackintosh. Bill felt both fear and a thrill of excitement. The commander was the most experienced combat pilot still active in the United Forces. He had flown more successful missions than anyone else ever. And yet here he was, Bill Asi, about to go up against that same man in one-on-one starship combat. How cool was that?

At the same time, Bill dreaded the upcoming conflict. Not just for what could happen during the match, but for what it could lead to afterward. Win or lose.

Still, there was nothing he could do about it now. Nothing except try his best.

With that in mind, he targeted the other ship and engaged his engines on full, blasting forward to meet his fate.

"Ah, coming for me, are you?" Jeff muttered, watching the blip on his screen expand rapidly. "Good for you, kid. Shows balls. Not brains, maybe, but balls."

Flipping his weapons systems to Active, Jeff lined up his target. The kid wasn't bothering to be subtle, or to take any evasive action—he'd apparently plotted the straightest, shortest course possible, and was following it at top speed.

Which only meant he'd be walking into Jeff's attack that much sooner.

"Your funeral," Jeff said softly, forcing down a brief burst of sympathy as he opened fire. The starfighter had several offensive options, but its paired lasers were the most accurate, and although they could only fire for a limited time they were perfect for controlled strikes like this one. Twin beams burst from their housings on either side of the cockpit, lancing straight for the other ship—

—and half a second before they hit, the ship twisted up and to the side, sliding over and around the attack.

For just a second, Jeff stared. That had been an almost impossible maneuver, judging the distance that precisely. But then, he reminded himself, that was why they'd picked Bill Asi. Because he could make those sorts of calculations.

Jeff, on the other hand, had the experience, the kind of reflexes you can only get from hours upon hours of being out here, shooting and getting shot at. Which was why, even as he was gawking, he was already turning his own ship to follow—and then angling to the side to evade the expected counterattack.

Which didn't come. Any other opponent would have opened up the second he was clear of those lasers, but Bill did not. His starfighter's hull stayed dark and quiet as he circled. Then he settled into a new course, once more gunning right for Jeff.

Jeff fired again. And again his rival dodged at the last second. And then shifted to a new attack vector, still coming right at Jeff.

For the third time, Jeff took the shot. And for the third time Bill slid to the side, letting the lasers pass harmlessly mere inches from his hull.

This time, when Bill found his new course, he was already less than a mile away. And closing fast.

"Yeah, nice flying, but at this range I can't miss," Jeff crowed, stabbing the firing button.

But nothing happened.

He'd exhausted his lasers, he realized after the initial half-second of shock. They could only fire so many times for so long before recharging. And he'd used up their charges in his three previous attempts. They'd be back online in under a minute—but he didn't have a minute.

So he did the only thing he could do—he gunned his own engines and leaped straight at his rival.

It was clear Bill hadn't expected that, and tried twisting aside but couldn't get clear completely before Jeff's ship rammed his own. The collision sent a powerful jolt through the cockpit, jarring Jeff so hard he nearly bit through his tongue as his teeth banged together. The impact rattled him, leaving him dizzy for a second, and when he'd recovered enough to focus on his instruments again he saw warning lights going off everywhere.

He'd been shot. At point-blank range. By Bill's lasers, which of course had been completely unused until now. Jeff stared, stunned, as readouts flickered and died all around his cockpit. His starfighter was dead, a mere hunk of metal floating listlessly in space.

He'd lost.

It was all over.

"You did it!" Dr. Tracton's voice cheered through the ship's comm system. "Bill, you did it! You won!"

"I won," Bill acknowledged. He took no pleasure in that fact, however. Instead he felt sad—sad for having beaten Commander Mackintosh, who he knew had been hoping to win, and sad for himself, for what this win would mean for his own future.

It meant he was going to war.

Round Three Winner: Bill Asi

"Congratulations," the United Forces Commander in Chief, General Candace R. Benefiel, told Jeff, offering him a salute from the viewscreen in his player's alcove. "You did a fine job in there, made an excellent showing. You did us proud."

"I lost," Jeff replied simply, returning the salute because even though he was furious at himself and at everyone else he still respected his superiors. "I'm sorry."

"Don't be." General Benefiel was not a large woman, but she had a commanding presence even onscreen—when she spoke, people jumped to obey. Right now, though, her voice was surprisingly soft, and in her eyes Jeff saw sympathy. He hated that. "I know what you're going through, commander," she told him, and he knew from her history that it was true. Candace Benefiel had enlisted as a raw recruit in the early days of the war, as infantry. She'd been a ground-pounder for years, working her way up to corporal and then sergeant and then lieutenant. She'd fought promotion too, refusing major several times before it was finally forced on her as a battlefield promotion when all her commanding officers got wiped out in a surprise attack. She'd been confirmed into the position after leading the remaining forces to victory, and that had been the end of her frontline days. So yes, she really did understand, and he could see from her face that she still remembered. "But it's time," she continued, and it wasn't a suggestion, it was an order.

Which meant there was nothing Jeff could do but nod and accept it.

"You could join us at Command," the general continued, "but I have another option for you. One I think you'll prefer." Jeff didn't say anything, just waited, and that earned him a wintery smile. "How would you like to go to flight school?"

Jeff stared at her. "As an instructor?" he finally asked.

"No, as a recruit," she retorted, and her smile turned to a grin for a second before fading back to her normal stern countenance. "I think you'd be a real asset there, Commander. Teach those kids how to fly, how to think, how to survive. And you'd still get plenty of time in the air."

Slowly, Jeff nodded. He'd never pictured himself as a teacher, just as a pilot, but the more he thought about it, the more he liked the idea. "Yes, sir," he said finally, saluting again, this time with more enthusiasm. "Thank you, sir."

"Thank *you*, Major," she replied, returning the salute and stressing his new rank. "I know you'll do well there. Though," she added as reached down to cut the connection, no doubt so she could change channels and congratulate the match's winner, "this next batch of recruits may take some getting used to."

"No kidding," Jeff said softly as the screen went blank. But for once he didn't mind thinking about his former rival, or about the other recruits who would follow in his footsteps. Nor was he still dreading the idea of life without combat.

No, for the first time since he'd been sidelined, Jeff was actually excited about his future.

But that got him thinking. About the match, and about the...man...who'd just beaten him. And about what *his* future held.

"Teach those kids how to fly, how to think, how to survive," the general had said. That was something Jeff could definitely do.

And before he had time to stop and consider, he found himself leaving his alcove behind and heading down the hall. He was moving well, his limp barely slowing him at all, his steps quick and excited.

Because now, once again, he had a mission.

"Excellent work, Doctor," the general declared after she'd appeared on the alcove viewscreen. "You've exceeded all expectations."

"Thank you, sir," Dr. Tracton replied. "But it was all Bill out there."

"Yes, of course." General Benefiel turned to glance past the doctor, toward the rest of the alcove and its arrays. "Congratulations," she said, and held out a hand. One of her subordinates placed a piece of paper in it, and the general held that up so Bill and Dr. Tracton could both see it as she continued, her tone formal: "To the Autonomous Simulated Intelligence designated Bi-11, you are hereby recognized as a fully sentient being and officially drafted into the United Forces." She handed the paper to an aide for safekeeping and saluted the alcove's secondary screen, which was currently projecting Bill's face. "Welcome to the war, son."

She stepped out of the picture after that, though one of her staff replaced her onscreen long enough to give Dr. Tracton the details for Bill's first posting. Once she was also gone, Dr. Tracton rewarded Bill with a big smile. "Congratulations, Bill!"

"Thank you, Doctor." Bill knew that he should be proud of his accomplishment, and to some degree he was. But he was also nervous. And scared.

Still, he couldn't tell Dr. Tracton that. This was the crowning achievement of the doctor's career, the culmination of his life's work—developing a genuine AI sophisticated enough to be put to use in actual live combat. There would be no more human pilots risking their lives flying missions—instead it would be AIs like Bill. He was only the first, but Dr. Tracton already had a whole batch of new AIs he'd created and begun training and teaching right behind him.

Bill was glad to be of use, of course. And he was happy for Dr. Tracton. And happy for men like Commander Mackintosh, who would no longer be dying in battle.

But what about him, he wondered. Wouldn't he be at risk? What if he were to die out there, in a starfighter, all alone? Would anyone notice? Would anyone care?

Bill couldn't help but feel that, in winning, he had somehow lost it all.

A knock on the alcove door interrupted his maudlin thoughts. The man standing there was tall and trim, with a short, military haircut beginning to show a little gray at the temples and a strong face starting to show lines from years of stress. He limped slightly as he stepped inside.

"Hey, you must be Dr. Tracton," the man said, holding out his hand. "And you must be Bill. I'm Jeff, Jeff Mackintosh."

Bill had known that, of course. The commander looked exactly like his simulation from the jungle match. "Hello, commander," he replied. "It's nice to meet you in person. Congratulations on a good match."

"Same to you," Jeff said. "But that's not why I'm here." He stepped right up to the console and lowered his voice so Dr. Tracton wouldn't hear. "I know they're gonna ship you out soon, am I right?" Bill nodded onscreen. "And since you're clearly bright and can think like a man, I'm guessing you're probably scared." Bill nodded again, relieved that someone understood. "Yeah. So I figured I'd stop by. I've been there, you know. Lots of times." Jeff shrugged. "Maybe I can make it a little easier for you. Oh, and you can call me Jeff."

"Thank you, Jeff," Bill said. "I really appreciate that." And it was true. He felt a surge of gratitude that this man, who he had just publicly defeated, would show him such kindness and consideration, and a burst of hope that perhaps, with Jeff's help, he could learn to overcome his fear. And maybe, with that help and a little luck, he'd even make it back in one piece.

As Jeff continued to speak, Bill realized something else. He had only ever known Dr. Tracton before, and a handful of secondary programmers and instructors. But Jeff wasn't here because he had to be. He'd chosen to offer his help and his support. Like a friend.

And suddenly, knowing that he had a friend, Bill thought maybe he'd won something important, after all.

For the real Jeff Mackintosh,
whose friendship was a prize well worth winning.

TEAMWORK

Nancy Jane Moore

"I HEAR YOU NEED A CREW," GENERAL KEIR LAZULI SAID.

Ah, thought Nori Valerian. *She wants to ship someone on active duty out with me.* That was not unusual, though Nori still wondered why the general had come by in person. Yes, they were longtime friends—going back to their training days as young pilots—and yes, Nori was now in the reserves, as all of Mellou's trade captains and crew were. But those things didn't explain why the general would make a special trip to the orbiting spaceport to meet with her. "Yes," she replied. "Did you have someone in mind?"

"I do, but it's a little different from what I've requested in the past." Keir took a chip out of her pocket. "You're familiar with the Eliza Project?"

"Vaguely. Something to do with expanded AI, right?"

"Yes. They've made a real breakthrough." She laid the chip on the table between them. "According to the tech people, this chip can operate a ship better than a whole crew of humans. They think we could replace most of our pilots with her. We've run a lot of simulation exercises and she's doing an excellent job. But..."

"But simulation isn't the real world," Nori said.

The general smiled. "I like what I've seen so far, but we need a lot more information before we deploy a fleet crewed by artificial people. Working with an experienced captain who regularly trades with Nawao would give her a more thorough test."

"You want me to beta test this...software."

"This AI *crew member*. Her name is Bay," Keir said. "This isn't an order, Nori. You can say no. But I came out to the port to talk to all of the available merchant captains, to get a feeling for who might be able to handle such a task. Not only do I need someone with the right mix of experience, I need someone who can keep this quiet. We don't want the pirates on Nawao to know how advanced our research is. My gut tells me that you're the best choice. And you could ship out tomorrow. I know you hate sitting in port."

Keir knows me too damn well, Nori thought, realizing she was going to agree. She said, "This thing has a name?"

"People have names."

"Hi, I'm Bay." The voice that came out of her main comm system was a quiet alto.

Nori hesitated a moment before replying, "Nori Valerian."

"Captain Valerian, I appreciate the opportunity to work with you."

So the software knew who she was, at least. And understood respect. Or had been programmed to call her that.

"I'm glad to fill out my crew so quickly," Nori said. That was true as well as polite. "Do you need to integrate into all my systems?"

"Captain, it is your decision how much access I should have. Of course, I won't be able to do my job effectively if I can't use every system the crew members I'm replacing would use. And..." she hesitated.

Nori wondered if that hesitation was a programming feature to help instill confidence.

"And none of us, not you nor I nor my designers nor the general know all the ways in which I might be put to use. It would be best if I was able to tie into the entire system."

And just hope you don't go rogue, Nori thought. But likely this software—Bay—could hack into everything anyway. Besides, it made sense: how could they figure out how to use an artificial intelligence effectively if they didn't give these beings access? She punched in the authorizations that gave Bay access to everything including the weapons and security systems.

Leaving Bay to integrate herself on the bridge, Nori went to the galley, where she called up a cup of hot chocolate and then used the nanopod to make herself a small notebook and pen. Bay could read her official logs, but handwritten notes would be private.

She sat there, pen poised over paper, trying to find the right words to summarize her reaction. *I don't know*, she wrote. *I just don't know.*

Comm buzzed in Nori's ear. "Captain," Bay's voice came on the line. "Outer Trade contacted us. They are glad you can do the asteroid run. She sent particulars. And the station says we can depart at oh seven hundred tomorrow morning, if we're ready."

Oh seven hundred? It was twenty-one hundred now. "We better grab it, if Outer Trade can get the shipment to us tonight, and given the rush, they probably can. Damn. I'm not going to get much sleep."

"Captain, I will be through with my integration in another twenty-seven minutes, so I will be able to handle loading on my own. The representative from Outer Trade has responded that she can have the load on the docks in two hours. A review of her parameters and the loading protocol indicates that we can be fully loaded by oh two hundred, leaving plenty of time for unexpected occurrences. I have notified the station that we will be using the oh-seven-hundred time slot."

"Don't I need to walk you through the process of loading and prepping for take off this first time?"

"It's all very straightforward, Captain. And you should sleep so that you can be alert when we leave in the morning. I can handle the routine matters. I will wake you if something unforeseen should occur."

"All right," Nori said. She wrote on her pad. *If she can handle everything, maybe I'm not necessary anymore.*

Nori was up at five, checking the cargo—loaded correctly—and prepping for departure. Her ship was in order. Bay had even discovered a glitch in the nanopods and run a repair to ensure that a full complement of food would be available. A course was laid for the outer asteroid belt, where they would deliver the cargo—some mining robots and a load of fruit and nuts grown in Mellou's prime greenbelt. In trade they would get platinum and other necessary rare minerals.

The course was perfect, a slight variation on her last trip to the Outer Belt because Bay had reviewed her log and factored in changes based on her notes. There had been an increase in unstable orbits in one section of the Inner Belt. Nori had forgotten about that.

"One hundred and ninety-seven hours," Bay told her. "Twenty-nine hours at sublight before we go to A/ND." Nori's ship, *Harrier*, like most trading and fighting ships from Mellou, used a helium-3 powered version of the Alcubierre/Nyugen drive designed for smaller vessels making in-system hops to travel above the speed of light. Although the smaller engines relied on negative energy to warp space just as interstellar ships did, Mellou-developed engineering efficiencies had reduced the amount of fuel the engines needed.

Nori noticed that the trip-length entry in the system was a precise 197:23:09:21. Apparently Bay had been taught to use round numbers when talking to humans. Nori continued her review of the ship's preparation routine. She found no mistakes.

Nothing of note happened on the voyage out. Nori had reached the age where "uneventful" was her favorite kind of travel, but it did occur to her that a couple of minor lapses would have proved useful for evaluating Bay's performance. The AI's work had been flawless, but the trip wouldn't have posed a challenge to any normally trained crew. Still, a human newbie wouldn't have made the automatic course correction or noticed the nanopod glitch. Nori would have caught those things herself eventually, but Bay's prompt action made the trip that much easier. Because of that, she noted Bay's actions in her official log and even acknowledged them in her private notebook: *The software catches errors that a beginning member of the crew would have missed.*

Only people who had migrated from the planet Mellou lived and worked in the Inner Belt, the primary source for the bulk of its helium-3 supply. The Mellou military—with the help of their reserves—made sure things stayed that way. The Outer Belt, located past the star system's only gas giant and two other smaller rocky planets, was not so restricted. A number of small colonies had been set up on Nawao, the farthest planet in the system. It had a lousy atmosphere, but with a little terraforming, settlements were now made possible using solar panel satellites and domes. Mining the Outer Belt, with its large reserves of platinum and other essential elements, made up the bulk of Nawao's industry.

The colonies on Nawao were not united under one governing body and, in fact, frequently fought wars amongst themselves, as well as occasionally attacking Mellou's furthest outposts. So far they had never threatened the planet itself. Their divisions kept them from developing the kind of stable communities that led to technological innovation or even competent reverse engineering, so they needed advanced robots and nanopods from Mellou. The limited farming opportunities on their planet—and the fact that farming was not a profession that was respected by most asteroid miners—meant they were desperate for the kind of delicacies that nanopods could imitate but never quite re-create.

The Nawaoites were often referred to as pirates by Mellouites, and as they shifted back to sublight speed, Nori cautioned Bay about them. "They will trade with us, but if they can steal what we have, they prefer it that way. So be on your guard for any threats."

"Noted, Captain. I looked up some of the history. They do seem to prefer fighting to negotiation."

"Not all of them, but they are unpredictable."

They began their approach to the space station in orbit around Malachite, a long-established mining outpost on the region's most stable asteroid. Nori had traded there many times.

A deep voice came over their comm system. "Well, hell, it's the dykes from Mellou. Two days late and probably more than two dollars short."

"You're wrong as usual, Jacob," Nori replied. "We're early. And while we are not carrying any dollars this trip, we are well-stocked in robots and persimmons. Assuming, of course, you've got something worth buying."

Bay spoke to her via subvoc. *What is dyke? I cannot find a reference. And aren't dollars archaic?*

Nori listened to another string of insults from Jacob as she replied. *Dyke is an old Earthian slang term for women who love women. Jacob thinks it's an insult. Ignore it. And yes, dollars are archaic. It's just an expression.*

"You want to do business, Jake, or just sit around here jawing? *Another archaic expression*, she sent to Bay.

"How ready are you, Nori? Maybe I don't need to trade anything."

"Captain, she is sending docking instructions," Bay said.

"*She?*" Jacob shouted into comm. "Did your crewwoman just call me 'she'?"

"She's new, Jake. Never been to these parts before." A private subvoc to Bay: *use he, him, and his in referring to Jacob. It keeps him happy. Go ahead and prepare to dock.*

"Well, get her straightened out. She needs to learn that the rest of the universe isn't like you people on Mellou. Maybe I should show her up close and personal."

Nori knew the man well enough to know that his threats of violence were bluster. If he were drunk in a bar with friends egging him on, he might dare to throw a punch at someone, but sober and doing business he was smart enough to know better. "Let's stop worrying about pronouns and get down to business. I was told you'd have a quarter ton of platinum for what I've brought you. Do you, or will I be forced to take my business elsewhere?"

"A quarter ton? For that load of crap?"

A few more minutes of bluster and he reluctantly agreed—as she'd known he would—to the pre-negotiated deal, set up well before they left for the Outer Belt. As they docked, Bay prepped the ship's robots to handle the transfer of their cargo goods to the station and then load Jacob's ore on to the ship

Nori stepped out onto the dock. Bay opened the cargo door and the robots rolled out their boxes. Jacob rode up on one of the port's scooters a few minutes later, accompanied by a teenager as his passenger. A second scooter piloted by a third person pulled up behind them. Both scooters towed trailers loaded with boxes.

Bay said via subvoc: *He has others with him.*

He needs their help. But watch them.

"Big crew to move a few boxes," Nori said to Jacob.

"Just being prepared."

A subvoc from Bay. *They are armed. I have weapons ready to fire.*

No! If it had been possible to scream in subvoc, Nori would have screamed. *All these people go armed. Stand down.*

Done.

At least Bay didn't argue when given an order. Nori slowed her heart beat, calming herself. "Bay," she said, using direct comm, "Please scan these boxes to see if they contain the ore we were promised."

"You bitches don't trust anybody," Jacob said. He walked over and punched her in the arm.

"We trust the people we can trust," Nori replied. To Bay via subvoc she said, *Not a threat.*

The child is trying to get into one of our boxes.

"Jake, keep your kid—he is your kid, right?—away from our stuff until we're all sure we're doing this trade."

"He's just checking what's in it."

"Give him a scanner, then."

The other man moved closer. Nori shifted her position so that the scooter blocked his way. In her ear, Bay said, *Should I shoot him?*

Negative, negative. Stand down and don't aim weapons. I can handle this. To Jacob she said, "Scan the boxes. You've done enough business with me to know I've got the goods."

Jacob moved to scan them. Bay said, *There's a trap in one of their boxes. It will explode if we open it.*

"And have your sidekick there jettison the booby-trapped box. Damn, Jacob, who do you think you're dealing with here, amateurs?"

Jacob shrugged. "Worth a try." He looked at the third man, who went to remove the box.

A word from Bay. "Not that one. The other one," Nori said.

Both men grinned, and the assistant carried the booby trap away from the dock. Jacob said, "These boxes are okay. The quality of the foodstuffs better measure up, though, or we won't do a deal this easy next time."

Nori waved a hand. Bay sent the robots out to collect Jacob's boxes, while his assistant and the teenager moved the ones from the *Harrier*. The robots stored the new cargo in record time, while the humans were struggling to get their new goods stowed. Nori looked at Jacob. He hadn't missed how efficient the loading had gone. She wondered what he was thinking.

"Don't I get to meet your new crew member?" he said. "So I can show her what a man is like."

"She's shy. And busy," Nori said, praying that Bay wouldn't take that as a threat as well.

"Next time, then."

Nori went back on board the ship. The men were still loading their boxes. "Start easing us out of the berth," she told Bay. "I want to get away from here as soon as we can."

Once they cleared the station, Nori retired to the galley for a small glass of whiskey—enough to soothe, not enough to keep her from paying attention—and her notebook. *The damn software can't evaluate a real threat. She doesn't understand dealing with the pirate community. And while that's true of most Mellouites on their first trip out this way, the rest of us can't blow things up in an instant.*

It was only after they were headed away from the station that Bay brought up what had happened. "I thought those men were threatening you, Captain. That Jake and his crew intended to do you physical harm."

Nori noticed that Bay had switched to male terms without hesitation. Her human crew members had never completely adapted to it and she herself had to think about it when dealing with people out here. "I could have handled anything they tried. And that's just the way Jake talks. He doesn't mean half of what he says."

"Then why does he say them?"

"That's how all these pirates out here talk. They think it makes them appear strong."

"So we should not pay attention to such threats?"

"It's more complicated than that. Sometimes they use the same language when they're serious."

"How do you tell the difference?"

Nori shrugged. "It's hard to explain. It has to do with their body language, their tone of voice, previous experience with the particular person. Jake, for example, is the kind of person who avoids big trouble. He holes up in his mine when wars break out on Nawao to avoid taking sides, but if someone tried to take over his mine, he'd fight to the death because he'd have to. Near as I can tell, he puts up just enough tough front to make sure people won't push him into that kind of corner."

"I'm not sure how to make use of that information, Captain, but I will watch what you do and try to understand."

As they left Malachite station behind, Nori wondered whether Bay would ever be able to grasp the subtleties of dealing with humans. It wasn't a logical process, not something reducible to binary code. Some people never got it.

On the other hand, Bay had loaded the cargo in half the usual time a human crew could have. Her coordination of the robots was so precise that no moment was wasted. *Of course, she's like a robot*, Nori thought, and then felt ashamed. The cargo robots lacked the capacity to understand the kind of negotiations Nori held with Jake and the others. Bay was at least trying.

Nori let Bay handle their sublight voyage out of the Outer Belt, but she stayed on the bridge. Until they were far enough out to switch to the A/ND, they were still vulnerable.

As they reached the inward side of Nawao, the external comm pinged. "*Harrier*, stop at the station to pay your taxes."

Bay responded, "Where should we dock?" and started the ship's braking sequence.

Nori screamed, "Cancel brake, shields up." She noted with relief that Bay obeyed immediately—necessary because Nori couldn't have shifted operations that quickly—and asked no questions.

Nori shut down the external comm and said, "Maximum speed. Now. And ready weapons."

The first shot missed them—deliberately, Nori thought. The next would target the engines. The pirates wanted their cargo, so they wouldn't try to destroy the ship. Their shields would prevent serious damage as long as they didn't take too many hits, but they needed to get away quickly.

The second shot missed as well. Bay had shifted course slightly as it approached. She repeated that action two more times, until they were out of range.

Nori exhaled as if she hadn't taken a breath for the last five minutes.

"Captain, how did you know that would happen? I would have stopped."

"It's a common pirate tactic, claiming to be official. But Mellou does not recognize any of the so-called governments out here. I thought your training would have covered that."

"It did, but I thought we would simply stop and explain their mistake."

Nori shook her head. A human newbie would have asked before taking any action.

"Don't ever just act again. Period. Your flying was incredible—you kept us from having to rely on our shields—but had we just flown by without responding they wouldn't have been able to get off a shot."

Bay nodded.

"Notify all Mellou patrols in the Outer Belt and send a message back to the general via the A/ND comm. They need to know that the pirates are getting bold again."

"Yes, ma'am," Bay said. A minute later, she added, "Captain, our evasive maneuvers altered our course. Both our entrance and exit point for jump will be in different places. Do you suppose the pirates intended that outcome?"

It was a good question. Nori had attributed their evasion to Bay's skill, but what if the attackers had a more devious plan in mind: to set them up so that they'd exit A/ND in a location where more pirates lurked. She thought about Jacob's behavior, how he'd commented on how fast Bay had handled the cargo transfer. Maybe he had reported his observations to the authorities on Malachite, and maybe they had passed that information along. They could be hoping to capture something big. And Bay was something big.

"They're not usually that subtle," Nori said, "but it won't hurt to take precautions. Send several probes ahead of us on our course. And notify Mellou. We might need help when we come out of A/ND."

Traveling under A/ND distorted time for humans. Although the ship itself was not traveling faster than light, the warping of space in front of it affected how people experienced time. Bay, like the computer, was not affected. While Nori had to pay close attention to accomplish any task, Bay continued to act with her usual efficiency. *That's another advantage of AI*, Nori thought. But her inability to judge the risk posed by others was a liability.

The timeline on the bridge showed they were reaching the end of the jump period. *It will be good to get home*, Nori was thinking, when Bay said, "Captain, the probes have been attacked. One was destroyed and the other is engaged in evasive maneuvers."

The robot's voice was calm, but Nori felt her own heart begin to pound. She sat up straight and tried to form a command. "Fight. We must fight," was all that came out.

"I am activating shields and we will be ready to fire as we come out of A/ND," Bay said.

The timeline, which had appeared to move at a snail's pace before, suddenly sped up. Nori knew it was the distortion affect, amplified by stress, but knowing it didn't change that she felt they were emerging from jump too fast. Had Bay been able to do everything?

Apparently she had, because a shudder through the ship indicated that something had bounced off their shields. A few seconds later, a shot fired from their rear guns hit the ship that had fired at them. The attacker was drifting in space, its engines out of commission.

Once again their ship moved in unpredictable directions, with sudden shifts in speed and vector. The changes were quick and seemed erratic. *I couldn't make those course changes that fast*, Nori thought. *It's inhuman.*

Two ships, both smaller than *Harrier*, were still attacking, but all their shots missed. One of them exploded as a missile from *Harrier*'s front gun bank hit it dead on. The other fired one last shot, and then ran for cover in the Inner Belt.

"Should I pursue them, Captain?" Bay asked.

"No. Alert the crew at the Inner Belt station and broadcast to any Mellou ships in the vicinity. We've done enough for one day."

"Captain, I sent alerts to the station and broadcast a general alarm when the probes were attacked. I just updated those alerts to report that we defended ourselves successfully, with only some minor hull damage, and let them know that one attacker remains at large while another is disabled in this region. Should I send any additional alerts?"

"Send a detailed update to Keir Lazuli and Mellou command central as well."

"I've already done that, too, Captain. I hope that wasn't a violation of your order not to act without your permission. In your protocols for the comm officer, it states that any encounter with a hostile force should be immediately reported to all possible Mellou officials."

"No," Nori said. "My order didn't include that." But what did it include? Bay had just saved her ship and probably her life. Left to her own devices, Nori could not have responded so effectively to an attack on exiting A/ND. Her response—the response of any human—would not have been as quick. The attackers had counted on the weaknesses of a human crew coming out of jump.

"You did right," Nori said. "You handled the attack perfectly, both in anticipating the possibility and in dealing with the reality. I could not have done it."

"Thank you, Captain. But I still do not understand the nuances of human behavior, especially among these men not of Mellou. I see threat where there is none; see no danger in situations that you immediately recognize as harmful. Perhaps I can learn to recognize these things, but it does not come as naturally to me as flying a spaceship."

"We're both necessary. You can do many things at once, where I can only do one at a time. But I understand other human beings. We make a good team. I hope Keir lets you stay with me."

Keir was on the station and showed up soon after *Harrier* docked. "Great job, Nori. We were able to catch the renegade who got away from you and shore up the Inner Belt defenses in preparation for other possible attacks. We also managed to warn the other trading ships about the latest wrinkle in pirate tactics."

"I couldn't have done all that without Bay, Keir. There's no way a human can be prepared for an attack coming out of A/ND, but Bay was ready. And she could act and notify you at the same time. Humans can't multitask on that level."

"So the test was successful. Bay and others like her can handle our defense, maybe even our business."

Nori hesitated. After all that Bay had just done, she didn't want to criticize her to Keir.

Bay said, "What the captain doesn't want to say, General, is that there are things I wasn't able to do. I do not understand other human beings the way she does, cannot read them, cannot tell when something is a real threat and when it is empty boasting. Those are not human skills that can be reduced to logical reasoning. It would be imprudent to send me or others like me on any expedition—including battle—without a human captain."

"Do you think you can learn those skills if you partner with humans for a long period of time?" Keir asked.

"I do not know, but the information I have gathered indicates that my inability to do these things comes from my lack of a body. Humans take in information from many sources, using their bodies and their interaction with other human beings. I am blind to some of this information, and I do not think it can be learned through additional data or programming. I think I would need a body to do these things."

"But you changed your behavior once you took in new information," Nori said.

"Captain, I know you have worried that I lacked instincts, and yet now you want to defend me because you know that I am loyal to you, that I am your friend. And I am those things. But my changes were based on logic, on knowing that you had experience that I needed to integrate. They are not instinctive. I cannot develop them on my own. Perhaps if I could be joined to you or to another human, so that I was integrated into a human body as well as into a ship's systems, then I could develop those instincts."

Keir shook her head. "No. Even if the researchers thought that possible, I wouldn't support it. Perhaps we can improve our robotics enough to give you an android body, but humans don't want to become cyborgs."

Bay said, "I don't think an android body would allow me everything that you and the captain are able to do."

"But if you were integrated into me," Nori said, "I could handle all those things you did when we were coming out of A/ND, could do loading and co-ordinating while still negotiating with the likes of Jacob. It might be worth it, to be a cyborg."

Keir stared at her. "You would? I may be wrong. Perhaps other pilots and space crews would feel much as you do. It would be very controversial on Mellou, though. And I doubt it is something that can be developed quickly."

"For now, let Bay stay with me," Nori said. "She and I will perfect our ability to work together as separate beings and report back to the researchers. You should try this experiment with some of the other captains as well."

Keir was shaking her head. "I knew you were the right person for this job, Nori. I just didn't know why. I guess that's the kind of human instinct Bay is talking about—the gut reaction that something will turn out well even if I don't know why I feel that way. Yes, I'll leave you together for now. Nori, you should bring on other crew and teach them to work with Bay as well."

After the general left, Bay said, "Captain, you would welcome me into your body? When we first met, you thought of me as a machine."

"That was before I knew you."

"And your heart rate jumps up when you think about becoming a cyborg, as you call it. I do not think you are completely comfortable with the idea."

"I'm not. But it's worth considering, even if it scares me. If I avoided doing the things that scare me, I'd have never left Mellou. Besides, that's the future—it may not be available in my lifetime, anyway. For now, we're a team. Let's find another job and get back into space."

WE'RE ALL MARINES TODAY

Ronald T. Garner

**The real problem is not whether machines think,
but whether men do.**

-B.F. Skinner

"WEAPONS AND GEAR CHECK!" PLATOON SERGEANT SARIN'S WORDS ECHOED through the troop bay of the landing craft, her tone sharp and commanding.

Jack pulled his directed energy rifle into a modified port arms position and verified that his weapon was on safe, then pulled the energy pack from the well to ensure is was fully charged, just like they'd taught him in boot camp less than three months ago. He broke down the barrel, and made sure it was clear, his drill instructor's voice sounding in his head: "Keep that barrel clear! You get a pulse of energy down a dirty barrel, they're gonna be shipping you back to your mamma minus a head you apparently didn't need anyway!" He clicked the barrel back into place and shoved the pack back home in the well, the sweat from his right hand coating its carbon-fiber shell.

His DER-2150 and the Marines to his left and right were the only things standing between him and death at the hands of a Rack. Well, those and the...other thing. He looked up quickly, peering down the length of the troop bay, then lowered his head again, scowling.

"What're you scowling about, cocky?" A black arm reached down and knuckles rapped against the side of his helmet.

Jack smiled. He probably would have been upset about that term from anyone else, but he knew Ikeno Asabi didn't mean anything by it. In the month he'd been in the unit, Iky was the only one who treated him like anything other than a stupid boot. Like everyone else, he found it impossible to get angry at the guy.

"Iky, man, you know my parents got their own farm. We're ain't no cockies."

"Whatever makes you sleep well at night amongst the pigs and cows, brother."

Jack just shook his head and smiled. His family farmed water on Zion, shipping it out to Terra-formed worlds throughout the sector. He didn't even know what a pig looked like. But Iky knew that. He was just trying to get Jack's mind off of what was about to happen.

"Seriously, dude, what's the scowl about? You're not still all outta whack about PAT, are you?"

"Nah, man, I'm not thinkin' 'bout the toaster." But he was. Technically, it was a Platoon Automatic Troop Support Platform, but all the other Marines just called it PAT. Just one of the many things he was having to get used to about military life. It was just weird, and wrong. They took what looked like the upper body of a person, shoved it on what looked like the legs of a mechanical spider, and loaded it down with heavy weaponry. And gave it intelligence. And *feelings*. Jack shuddered.

"Jack, why you gotta call him that? It's not cool, man. He actually feels stuff."

Jack's scowl returned. "That's the thing, Iky. Can't you see it just ain't...natural? The people who made that thing, they're tryin' to be God. They've created an abomination against the Lord that thinks it can feel, and everyone treats it like it really can. It's disgustin'." His eyes were wide at this point, his skin getting hot and his hands shaking.

Iky looked down at him for a moment, his eyes narrowing and a frown slowly pulling down the corners of his mouth.

"Jack, I'm gonna ignore a lot of what you just said because you're new, and you didn't have to deal with the stuff that made them give the PATs emotion chips. You weren't there when they were leaving Marines lying on the field because their logic told 'em that the mission was higher priority. You didn't see the earlier models blowin' up Marines because when all the computation was done it made sense to sacrifice one Marine to take out a bunch of Racks. They need those chips, and we need 'em to have 'em. If they don't see us as comrades, the whole thing falls apart. What makes us great is that we're fighting for the Marines to the left and right of us, not for some...idea." He waved his hands above his head as he said the last, then brought a finger down to once again tap on Jack's helmet. "You need to get yourself right in here before you step out there and need to trust PAT to watch your back."

"Yeah, I'll do that." Jack swatted Iky's finger away from his helmet and looked back down at his rifle, pretending to do a check he'd already done. He was really starting to wonder what had made him join the Interplanetary Marine Corps. Maybe he just wasn't ready for what lay beyond the comforts of home.

Iky chuckled, and pointed toward the front of the troop bay. "Yeah, well, farm boy, you'd better finish your gear check first, 'cause I think old Sarin's got her eye on you, and it's not the good one." Jack looked up to a pair of dark, glaring eyes boring down on him from the other end of bay and quickly started running through the standard checks.

Iky slapped him on the back, and turned to head back to his own berth. A couple of feet away, he turned and looked back at Jack, his normally luminous eyes troubled.

"We got probably ten minutes to atmospheric entry, Jack. After that, it's all noise and adrenaline and danger. Whatever you've got to deal with, deal with it now."

As it bulled its way into the planet's atmosphere, the transport shook so hard that it seemed impossible that bolts and rivets weren't flying around the troop bay. Jack stood as best he could, DER-2150 strapped to his chest, one hand holding onto an overhead strap for dear life, the other clenched tightly at his side. Squad leaders were going from Marine to Marine, doing last minute gear checks, Platoon Sergeant Sarin walking along slowly, spot-checking.

How the hell was she able to stand up without holding on to something? He could barely keep his legs under him. Even the squad leaders had to swing their arms from handhold to handhold as they went about their inspection. Her steadiness really bothered him. He found himself unable to focus on anything else. What right did she have bein' so calm while he was...

He was scared, that's what he was. Jack realized with a start that he was sitting on the black edge of fear.

"Jack, stop son. Breathe. Remember, the fear's there as a warning, but you control it, not the other way 'round. Focus on somethin' good, somethin' happy. Get calm. Then get out there and do it."

His father's voice brought him back to himself. How often had he heard that? Going out for his first Double Ball game, his first talk at church, his first date. Right, Dad, right. I got it.

Jack thought about what his parents were probably doing right now. It was just about dawn back home. His parents were getting ready to go out and check the water traps. Dad was making fresh buttermilk biscuits, Mom was cooking up some eggs. Most people would've just used the replicator—it was cheaper and easier than actually making food—but his Mom and Dad enjoyed the ritual, working side by side in the morning. The smell of the biscuits drifting through the house, slowly waking up his brothers and sisters. Best alarm clock in the world.

Like always, his dad's trick worked. As Jack worked his way back to the present, he could feel his muscles loosening, relaxing. He was still scared, terrified actually. But he knew he could do with it.

Jack opened his eyes and raised his chin from where it had come to rest on his chest plate.

And looked right into the eyes of Platoon Sergeant Sarin. His muscles tightened up again.

"Good nap, Olsen?"

Sarin's eyes were so dark it seemed impossible to read anything in them. With her helmet covering most of the rest of her head and face, those eyes felt like they were pushing into him from unimaginable depths.

"I, uh, I mean yes, Staff Sergeant—that is, no, Staff Sergeant—"

"Tell you what, boot, I'm gonna cut you off there, 'cause we got about a minute before we hit dirt." She leaned in close, her eyes boring into his. "This is your first time out, Olsen. You're gonna be scared. That's okay. I'd worry you were crazy if you weren't. But those Marines out there with you have to be able to count on you." She jerked her head in a short jab toward the front of the troop bay. "You got that?"

Jack nodded quickly. Was it crazy that all he could think of right now, with her this close to him, was how smooth the brown skin around her eyes looked? Where did that even come from?

"Good."

Sarin started to turn away, then turned back. "And Olsen? You need to allow yourself to trust them." She turned and looked toward the front of the bay, where PAT was waiting for the hatch to open, then turned back to Jack, raising her right eyebrow. "All of them. Understand?"

Jack swallowed hard. Not much got past the Platoon Sergeant. He nodded again.

"Good. No matter what you may think, everyone who's goin' through that hatch today's a Marine." She tapped her finger on Jack's breast plate over his heart. "Whatever we were before, we're all Marines today."

With that, she turned and walked up to the front, standing by the hatch. As soon as she got there, the transport crunched down onto solid ground, almost as if she had orchestrated it.

The hatch swung down, and PAT ran out into the darkness, its eight legs propelling it forward faster than seemed possible, the Gatling guns on its shoulders coming to life and lighting up the night.

Sarin turned back and looked at them, the calm taskmaster gone, a savage look on her face.

"Squad leaders, you know your assignments. Let's go kill those bastards!"

First Squad ran forward, then vanished into the darkness, then Second Squad, then Jack, his heart beating in his throat.

Jack huddled behind an outcropping of rock, Iky and five other Marines pressing against him. What the hell happened? This wasn't how it was supposed to go. Certainly not how the vids and holos showed it. The Marines were victorious across the space lanes, chasing the Racks from planet to planet, destroying the threat. They weren't crouched behind rocks, most of their squad dead, waiting to be torn apart.

Where was the rest of the platoon? After exiting the transport, Third Squad had taken up their positions from the twelve o'clock to the three o'clock around the transport. Just a few seconds later, Sarin had come up over comm.

"Okay, Marines, the enemy's decided to make it easy for us. The drones show 'em hangin' out just on the other side of that rise you see up there. First and Second Squads are comin' with me straight up the gullet. First Squad, you'll hook up with First Platoon on your left. Third Squad, you've got the fun. You're gonna take that defile to your right and come out on their left. Link up with Third Platoon on your right. We don't want you guys killin' each other before we get a chance to kill the Racks. Move!"

Sounded easy, clean.

Except it wasn't. They'd made it about halfway up the defile when a group of Racks ambushed them from above. Jackson, the squad leader, was dead before anyone even had a chance to shout, skewered on the armored limb of a Rack. Most of the squad was dead in under a minute. Iky and a couple of other Marines managed to lay down covering fire and the survivors retreated up one side of the defile, finding this big ugly rock to hide behind. Jack was starting to think it would be their gravestone. The

DER-2150's energy packs lasted a while, but they didn't last forever, and they had to expend a lot of pulses to do any damage to the Racks.

They'd been trying to get in touch with the rest of the platoon, or with Third Platoon, or with anyone, for several minutes. No joy.

"Third squad, send sitrep, over." Sarin's voice echoed through the comm system in his helmet.

Iky looked at Jack and let out a whoop.

"Staff Sergeant, thank the gods! We're pinned down. We've lost most of the squad." Iky's voice shook with a weird mixture of relief and horror.

"Third Squad, pull yourself together. Remember radio protocols. Who is this, over?"

Caaaaaa!

Jack jerked his head around to see a Rack coming over the top of the rock, screaming out a crow-like caw. The whole world slowed. Crazy what you think about in those moments. Jack wondered whether they'd modeled PAT after the Racks. Like the bot, they had eight armored legs leading to a vaguely human-like torso. Made sense. Racks, short for Arachnids. Of course, that's about where the similarities stopped. The torso ended in a nightmarish head stuck right in the middle of a mess of tentacles. Thought was that these things had started out on some water world or something. Whatever, they were disgusting. One more reason PAT creeped him out.

Just like that the world came crashing back to full-speed. Lance Corporal Jin pulled up his weapon, driving the monster back with several pulses, and Jack and the rest joined in, finally blowing a hole in it. As it fell back over the rock, the Marines popped up behind it, laying down suppressing fire on the rest of the Racks in the defile.

Radio protocols? Was she seriously worried about radio protocols in the middle of a firefight, when most of the squad was lying dead on the ground? Jack felt his skin getting hot and looked over at Iky, who he knew must be getting as angry as he was.

Iky, however, was getting calmer. Breath slowing, facial muscles relaxing.

"Roger, Staff Sergeant. This is Corporal Abasi, over."

"Copy, Abasi. Where's your squad leader, over?"

"Sergeant Jackson is dead, Staff Sergeant, along with most of the squad. Break. We were ambushed. Break. I'm the most senior Marine alive. Break. We have six Marines still in the fight, over."

There was a long pause.

"Roger, Corporal. Hold your position. I'm sending PAT to you. You will continue your mission with PAT in support, over."

"Wilco, Staff Sergeant."

Things were just getting worse out there. The Racks knew where they were now, and the defile was pretty crowded with them. Soon, they'd get smart and send some down from the rise, and it'd be over. Even a boot like Jack could tell that he and his fellow Marines were just being held in place.

"Where's that damn bot?" Jack barked the words through a scowl.

"Seriously, man, you gotta stop with that stuff. PAT's doin' his best to get to us. We just gotta hold on." Iky was clearly done with his friend's crap. He grabbed Jack by the arm and pulled him close. "I've cut you a lot of slack because you're new, and I like you. But this, what you're doin', runnin' your yap, doomin' and gloomin' just because you hate bots, it stops now. You wanna hate bots, do it on your own time. I got a squad, or what's left of one, to worry about. One more word, and I promise I'll shoot you myself." His voice was low and sharp and his hand tightened on Jack's arm as he spoke. "You understand?"

Jack nodded, his face flushing with embarrassment.

"Good. Get up there and keep watch on the rise. I got a feelin' our luck's about to run out."

No sooner were the words out of his mouth than a wave of Racks came pouring over the rise. Cawing so loud Jack couldn't even hear his own thoughts.

"Damn. Damn! Hit 'em with everything you got, Jack!" Iky pulled up his weapon and pulses started flashing out of it at rapid fire. Jack pulled up his weapon and quickly looked back over his shoulder at the other Marines guarding the defile. They were fully engaged. The Racks had timed it perfectly, attacking from both sides. There were just too damn many of them.

Well, if it was over, he wasn't gonna have anyone find him on the field later with a charged weapon. He was taking as many Racks with him as he could.

Jack turned back toward the rise and fired.

Pulse after pulse after pulse. The weapon was getting hot in his hands. He quickly looked over at Iky, who was so focused on the Racks in front of him that he seemed to tune out the rest of the world, then looked back at the advancing Racks. He glanced at Iky again, and saw that he was still pulling the trigger on a weapon that wasn't sending out any more pulses. He was so caught in the fight that he didn't even seem to notice.

"Iky!"

"Iky!"

Iky looked over.

"You're out, man!"

Iky looked down at his weapon, his face going white. He looked back behind them, then ran toward the other Marines. Jack kept firing, but the Racks were coming faster now with only one weapon pushing them back.

Iky was back in a second, firing anew. Jack looked at him questioningly. Iky kept looking forward, yelling out the side of his mouth, "Don is dead. Grabbed his weapon."

Jack's stomach tightened. LCpl Donald Lumpkins had been the first in the platoon to greet him. "Glad you're here, boot. Means I'm not at the bottom of the totem pole anymore." No time to focus on Don now, the Racks were almost on them.

Jack heard the beep that told him his weapon only had a couple of pulses left. Damn, damn. Damn that slow bot. This was it. He fired his last couple of pulses, then looked over at Iky, who was shaking his head, holding up an empty weapon.

The Racks were rushing toward them now, aware that all resistance was gone.

And then they weren't. The entire front row of them fell back onto the ones behind them. Jack heard Gatling guns rattling off behind him, then the sound of a large projectile whistling over his shoulder. An explosion blew Racks in every direction.

Just like that, the Racks were retreating. Jack looked back over his shoulder, but he already knew what he'd see. There was PAT, standing beside the dead bodies of the other Marines.

Beside him stood Staff Sergeant Sarin.

"Here's the deal, Marines. We've shifted tactics. The Racks were all alerted by the ruckus you've been causing over here, and they're converging here. This gives us a perfect opportunity to hold them in place while First and Second Squad hook up with First Platoon to take them from the rear. Third Platoon's making their way over here to join us. We just have to hold on until they get here."

Sarin spoke so calmly and matter-of-factly that Jack almost believed that there was some chance of three Marines and a bot holding off thousands of Racks until the new plan came together. PAT was recharging all of their weapons, so, who knew, maybe they'd actually make it out alive.

Then the Racks surged forward, and the world blurred into a series of trigger pulls, position shifts, more trigger pulls, and on and on. A Marine's weapon would run out of charge and they'd run it over to PAT to recharge, then grab a dead Marine's weapon and start firing again. It just seemed to go on forever. Jack's mouth was dry, his finger felt permanently fixed in a crook, his heart had beat so hard for so long that it just seemed like the new normal. Every muscle in his body was tense and sore.

But, gods, did he feel alive! He paused for a moment to send a quick glance around at his comrades, and realized that this moment, right here, was what it meant to be a Marine. Back against the wall, frightening odds, and no one to rely upon but the Marine to your left and your right. This was what Sarin meant.

He turned back to his trigger pulling.

Once again, the Racks were getting close. Even PAT's firepower could only keep them at bay for so long. What had it been? Fifteen minutes? Twenty? Felt like a lifetime. And then the Racks were so close that Jack could smell them. Surprising, really, that something so foul-looking and intent on killing you could smell so good, like a fresh ocean breeze.

Jack's weapon beeped at him again, and he jumped up to run back to PAT for a recharge and a new weapon. He heard a yell behind him, and turned back around just in time to see the large armored leg of a Rack descending toward his face. He sensed more than saw something moving in quickly, so unbelievably quickly, from his left to throw itself in front of him. The Rack's leg tore through Sarin, sending the upper half of her torso flying into him, knocking him backward and slamming his head on the rocky ground.

Head buzzing and vision pulling in upon itself, he pushed his way to his knees, crawling his way over to the upper half of Sarin's body. Somehow, she was still conscious. He leaned over her, and as he did so her one remaining hand reached up and tapped him on his breastplate, right over his heart.

"Remember." Her hand slipped from his chest, tracing its way down his breastplate in something that seemed almost like the lingering touch of a lover, the light fading from her eyes.

He fell to her side, vaguely aware that for some reason the Racks weren't attacking him, that something was wrong about the way Sarin's body lay crumpled beside him, but unable to put it all together. Then his vision went black, and he was gone.

"Ain't that the damndest thing...?"

The Platoon Sergeant from Third Platoon scratched his head with one hand, helmet in the other, as he stared down at the ground.

He'd been leaning over Jack when he woke up. Apparently, Third Platoon had arrived just in time to keep the Racks from overrunning the position entirely. Now, they were standing together staring down at Sarin's mutilated frame. And Jack understood what had bothered him so much before he blacked out. Trailing from the severed bottom of Sarin's lower torso, where you might expect to find blood and intestines, were wires and lubricant. The back of her head had been crushed, and the glint of metal shown through.

"I heard they were developin' some of these...flesh bots, or whatever you wanna call 'em. But I didn't credit it. Seems like a durn fool thing if you ask me. Sendin' a bot to lead Marines. Who ever heard of such a thing? Them metal mounds are okay, as long as someone's givin' 'em orders." The Platoon Sergeant jerked his head back toward where PAT was attending to an injured Iky. "But bots as *Platoon Sergeants*? What did they think it would do?"

"She."

"Huh?"

"*She*," Jack repeated, "was a Marine. Whatever we were before, we're all Marines today."

TURTLE AND BIRD
Bud Sparhawk

WHEN THE MIST FROM THE LONG SLEEP CLEARED I REALIZED THAT SOMETHING was missing. "What the fuck happened to my wheels," I screamed on the comm band. Had the gods-damned Ephem captured me?

No, that couldn't be true. If it was the Ephems I would have been scraped for sure.

"Calm down, grunt," a harsh voice ordered. "You're in refit. No Ephemerals here, at least not yet." He laughed. "In case you're wondering, we're giving you a new outfit. Wheels wouldn't be of much use where you'll be needed."

I thought that was just great. Apparently COMMAND had decided to redirect my transport to some other gods-forsaken world that needed armored troops. Instead of the vacation I was expecting, it looked like I was in for Refit and Reconfiguration.

I was treated better when I was meat.

Back before I earned my Instance I was just another meathead armed with a six-by and a couple hundred rounds strung over my shoulders. Back then my company was popping Ephem one by one in hopes that we could stop their relentless attacks. Only our company hadn't counted on the Ephem's passion to destroy our kind. At the point we ran low on practically everything we discovered that our supply lines had been cut. When I used the last of my ammo, the six-by became nothing more than a club, and let me tell you that it would take more than a fifty-kilogram club to stop an Ephem fanatic, especially when he had a grip around my throat and was shoving a knife into my gut.

Later, I was told, one of my mates dragged my sorry carcass away, but I was dead by then and couldn't have cared less.

Which is when they decided to Instance me. "For bravery," they said, as if dying wasn't enough.

Talex B was so far away from the Ephem planets that we Instanced figured we could have it for ourselves. The place was a near enough analogue to Earth that the plant life wasn't poison, the climate neither freezing cold, nor boiling hot, and the thick, soggy atmosphere didn't stink quite so bad. In other words; an ideal world.

The Ephem showed up a few years later, no doubt driven by the same desire that made us pick this little paradise.

They made short work of our single, lightly armed starship and dropped a dozen bombs on the obvious targets—cities and farms—before sending down their shock troops to eliminate what they probably called an infestation.

They'd established a couple of small, smelly barrows before COMMAND noticed the lack of dispatches from Talex B and asked a ship to investigate.

When we saw what had happened, there was nothing to do but send in the marines, said marines being a handful of aspirant meatheads, a few thousand tons of Instanced ground troops, some flyers, and me.

I was paired with a flyer who had been a woman named Emily. She didn't mention a last name. "I'm a Ground Mobile Scout Unit in my current iteration, but you can call me Turtle," I said, disparaging my short, stocky six-legged chassis.

She laughed, a high-pitched crystalline sound that sent shivers along my articulations. "If you're a turtle then I must be a bird."

"Bird it is, then. Pleased to meet you, ma'am."

"Thank you, Turtle. I think I'm going to like this pairing."

"Hold that thought until we see some action," I warned. There was a good possibility that one of us might not survive the war. Instances might be heartless, but that didn't mean they couldn't be killed.

War's like that.

Our first mission was to scout the area and neutralize any armed Ephem troops we discovered. If they were more than my twin 20's and Bird's tiny rockets could handle we were to call for heavier units.

Locating the Ephem was a task I was ideally configured for. I could move easily through Talex's thick vegetation, my sensors could detect the Ephem smell over hundreds of meters and, if they couldn't, my multi-phase optics could pick out heat signatures in the dark, which is when they were usually probing our lines.

Far above me, unseen to all but the most sensitive eyes, rode Bird, flying cover. If she spotted anything suspicious and couldn't resolve it with her optics, I had to get there and confirm.

"Clear ahead for five klicks," Bird chirped over our link.

"Acknowledge."

Bird continually asked me to explain what scuttling through the brush felt like while I asked her to describe her ease of flight. For hours she'd struggled to put into words the joy of catching a rising stack of air while I wrestled with equal frustration to express the pleasure of moving stealthily over the landscape. I envied her freedom of flight while she declared how envious she was of my ground-hugging agility.

Of course we both retained memories of our earlier selves. But she knew what it felt like to walk while I had never experienced the joy of flight or the feeling of freedom that I imagined she felt.

But neither of us was really free. Bird had to be refueled periodically and I, no less a victim of my nature, had to recharge and reload. We were both tethered to our natures and physical needs.

The better I got to know Bird the more I liked who she was, or had been, or whatever. Things get a little messed up when your brain gets Instanced but that didn't mean it wiped out who you were, what you'd learned, or how you felt.

"Tell me about your first Instance," she asked after we'd gotten to know each other better.

I told her how weird it felt, at first, when I became tons of mechanical prostheses. This wasn't so bad; I could "run" faster than the proverbial speeding bullet, leap moderately tall buildings, and lift two tons of six-packs with ease. "I'd become a mean, strong mother, I tell you. Nobody wanted to mess with me. I was itching to bash a few Ephems, for sure."

Since I was a novice I became a pack mule for a squad of more advanced and capable Instanced marines. I groused about my menial role until SARGE had a little chat with me.

"Don't worry, kid," she told me. "This job's just baby steps. Later we'll move you into something better."

"Like a fucking dump truck?" I shot back, which was the wrong thing to say to a heavy lifter like SARGE. For the next six weeks I must've lugged the squad's crap back-and-forth without ever seeing an Ephem soldier.

My first serious engagement with Bird was scouting for a squad of meatheads and a fragile probe named Sidney, who couldn't even recover from a simple HE round. Nine times out of ten, well, maybe seven, a prober like Sidney manages to do his job with minimal fuss and little risk.

Our mission involved recovering three forward spotter units trapped by Ephem. It was relatively easy to pull out the units, even if a few of our meatheads were lost. The Ephem lost more, I hope.

We captured some Ephem gear, such as a couple of the glu sticks that had played hell with Sidney by severing his axles, the bastards.

We were able to bring him back, sans hardware, I'm afraid.

Bird had been a shuttle pilot before getting Instanced into a tin can. Lost it on Furgus, a crappy little piece of real estate of no strategic value, but a great place to guard against Ephem attacks.

"It wasn't some noble combat action that killed me," she admitted during a long and boring search. "It was a stupid, unexpected crosswind that sent my shuttle into a mountainside. Luckily the crash didn't destroy my brain but pretty much turned the rest of me into smears of meat."

I assumed she'd already signed the release forms to be Instanced should she die in action. "Yes," she replied. "The release's language was vague enough to get me a pass: That and the fact that I was a damn good pilot."

Bird and I got to the point where we could practically finish each other's sentences, at least when we had the time. Whenever we went into action our conversations were reduced to battle speak—short and information-dense expressions with little nuance.

We didn't talk much when we weren't on patrol. Time back at central was filled with mission uploads, refueling, recharging, and reloading. During those down times I didn't feel like I was walking on all six legs, but as the time approached for our scouting missions I'd get a tingling feeling of anticipation.

"Bird here," she chirped as she banked around Fred, my transport. "Lovely day for a stroll."

"Along the seashore this time," I replied. Fred was to drop me on the beach of a peninsula where Ephem might have landed. "Hope the water's warm. Hey, maybe want to do some skinny dipping before we start on patrol?"

Bird's response was immediate. "What, so you can get me out of this tin can? I'm not that hot to see what you've got inside, you know. Besides, there's no place wide enough for me to park."

"One can only hope," I shot back as I looked across Fred's wing to see her pacing us. "Still, you look lovely today with the sun shining on your fuselage." Actually her drab olive coating was non-reflective, but she knew what I meant.

The drop was routine. I landed in a sandy area that played hell with my balance. Bird did a fly-by, skimming the waves and waggling her wings salaciously. "I'm going higher to extend my time," she called. "Flying in this low altitude soup eats up fuel like mad! Don't do anything stupid, at least until I reach altitude."

"I'll park my sorry ass while you climb, sweetheart," I replied. "Don't take too long. I can rust pretty fast in this salt air."

"You should be all right, Turtle. I've scanned a lot of nothing in your immediate vicinity."

"I hear you," I replied and nevertheless threw precautionary rounds into my 20's and spread my sensory awareness wide. I wasn't concerned about being surprised, but Bird's optics sometimes missed something.

That had been my first mistake in this relationship. I'd overestimated Bird's eagle eyes by thinking she could spot a mole's asshole and inform me if it had hemorrhoids. Stupid me. I now knew she couldn't "see" well through the thick overgrowth.

I settled back and started running status checks while I waited. I had just gotten to the pressure on my rear segment when five Ephemerals erupted from the thick foliage and stopped dead, no doubt as surprised at our sudden proximity as me.

Before I could fire a round I'd taken five hits in my main segment, one of which must have severed one of my hydraulic lines because I couldn't turn to my left. Two Ephem were down when another threw a glu stick at my legs, impeding my movements even more.

I dodged another stick as I skillfully shot the hell out of the tree-like vegetation, completely missing the man tossing the sticks. Another set of hits must have cut another line because I lost all control of my nether regions.

I blew the leg off of the glu sticker's buddy, which didn't stop him from blasting my forward carapace to hell and gone. I only had one good eye left and it was on the opposite side from my 20. I figured at that point it would only be a matter of seconds before they blew me away.

Suddenly the ground beneath me heaved. I glimpsed an Ephem spewing guts as he flew over me while I was tossed in another direction.

"Are you still functional?" Bird chirped. "I didn't think that shot would damage you." She'd apparently fired one of her rockets at my adversaries. Must have worked because I felt no more hits as I counted the Ephem pieces scattered around.

"Yeah, except for a few dings I'm fine," I responded as I struggled to right myself. My damn hindquarters were still useless.

"That's not what I see. It looks like you're only fifty percent mobile."

"Don't worry about that. More Ephem are probably coming to check out the noise."

"Yes, I see a stick of them heading your way. Move on a twenty degree radial from your current position."

I pulled myself in that direction. "Sure. How far?" My useless rear segment was probably leaving a marked path behind.

"You've got to pick up the pace," she scolded. "Looks like your ass is dragging." I didn't know whether she meant that literarily of figuratively, but it didn't matter.

"Turn on radial thirty-five. There are some rocks that might provide protection. Are your weapons functional?"

I checked. "Yeah, have a couple hundred rounds left. It's not much."

"Enough to buy you time. You're almost there. Do you see the rocks?"

Rocks was a misnomer. These things were easily twice my height. I hoped there was somewhere wide enough for me to squeeze among them. No way I could climb with a busted rear end.

"You're as slow as a real fucking turtle," Bird chided. "They've reached the bodies and probably see your trail. Get ready!"

There was no alternative route I could see. No choice but to climb. I gritted my gears but, thanks to the punctured hydraulic line, I lacked the strength to lift the full weight of my body up the face of the rock.

Weight! That was the solution. Without a bit of regret, I blew away my useless rear end and instantly lost forty percent of my body and both of my formerly strongest legs.

Clambering up was difficult, but from the top I had a commanding view of the trail I'd made.

"Six in single file," Bird reported. "Four more flanking to the side. Can't see more through all the cover."

"Noted. I'll keep them busy."

I spotted the main party hesitating when they spotted my ruined rear segment. "Come on, come on," I prompted as I took cock-eyed aim on what I imagined was the leader's head and clicked a round into the chamber. I had no intention of wasting ammunition with automatic firing.

But letting go of a single round would tell them where I lay, if they hadn't already guessed.

I caught a slight movement of vegetation, giving me three targets. Where were the other seven: Circling behind and above me? I had as much chance of surviving a firefight with these ten as an ice cube on the sun.

Then Bird sang the sweetest words I'd ever heard: "Rescue dispatched. Arrival: Ten minutes."

Ten minutes was probably five more than the Ephem needed to pry me from my perch and break me into component parts.

A single Ephem crept forward to examine the wreckage I'd left behind. That gave me four targets. I'd get the hidden one first, then the two standing on my trail, and finally the one below me. There was no way the bastard could make his escape in the time I took to neutralize the other three.

A sudden flash illuminated the area. Flames erupted. The two flankers exposed themselves as they moved toward the fire.

Crack! Crack! Crack! Three were down and the fourth was sprinting away as I took aim and popped his head. Shots bounced off the surrounding rocks as the still-hidden ones began firing. One of them threw a glu stick that fell short so I didn't waste a round on him. I hoped that none of them were carrying HE.

A round hit my forequarters. I thought it didn't do much damage until a status check showed that I could no longer swivel the 20 to the left; it stopped when it faced straight ahead. No problem with moving it to the right so I shifted my position to make effective use of my limited coverage.

It only took a few minutes for them to realize my limitations and advance on my blind side, keeping up a continual fusillade that increased in accuracy as the distance decreased. I picked off one by turning my body but that left my other side more vulnerable.

"Looks like I'm heading to the big scrap pile in the sky," I joked.

"Not if I can help it," Bird replied even as she swept low and slow across the treetops to drop her fuel tank right in front of my perch to rupture. A second later she shot a signal flare right into the spill.

I couldn't see a thing through all the smoke, flames, and heat but I felt pretty sure we had a barbecue on our hands.

"Heading back to base," Bird said laconically. "I hope I have enough fuel left."

"Stupid waste," I jibed. "Good luck."

The rescue squad arrived a little later and quickly recovered me, leaving my useless scout shell behind. As they worked on detaching me I hoped there was a spare scout in our inventory.

"Stupid thing to do, wasting fuel," I chided Bird as soon as I was installed. "You're a hell of a lot more valuable than a stupid Scout."

"Not to me," she replied.

"Did you catch hell from COMMAND?" I figured she'd gotten as bad a reaming as I had from LEAD for us getting caught so unawares.

"Yeah, and they dinged me for losing a fuel tank."

"Boo hoo. I lost my ass, sweetheart. Do you know how much ribbing that's costing me?" Her answer was a three-minute stream of laughter, and two more when I joined in.

We both got commendations for staying alive and, best of all, were still a team.

More than a team actually.

Over our next patrols we passed the time talking about the ignorant enmity of the Ephem, the stupidity of sergeants, and the high-minded strategies of COMMAND who didn't have a gods-damned clue about what it felt like to take a hit in the hydraulics.

Mostly Bird talked about how glorious were the sunrises and sunsets that framed the distant mountains or shone on the seemingly endless sea. She longed to fly far and wide, free of the restrictions that constrained her to a few hours of flight.

I commiserated with complaints that I couldn't pause to study the many insect analogues or plants that grew around me. Neither could I ever hope to gaze on the landscape as she did, soaring high and free.

Thus we passed the hours, pausing only to refuel, recharge, and prepare for the next patrol.

"We need eyes on activities in this sector," LEAD said and passed the map coordinates. It was another mountainous peninsula near where we wanted to erect mining infrastructure. "Satellite didn't spot anything in the region, but we need more certainty."

I knew what he meant. "Can I get cover?"

LEAD hesitated. "A flyer can only give you an hour's coverage at that range."

"Extra tanks?" I suggested. "That would give Bird the extra time I'd need."

LEAD considered for a long millisecond, which meant he'd consulted the fuel depot, logistics, and dispatch to see if it was feasible, and then answered: "Fine—but an extra hour is all that extra tank will buy it. It needs enough fuel to return."

"Understood. Quick-in to survey the situation and then get out."

"No more heroics. Understand?"

"Yessir."

We chatted as I trudged along above the high tide line while Bird checked for signs of Ephem presence. We talked away an hour or two with tales of our earlier meat lives and the pleasures of becoming creatures whose blood was hydraulic fluid and whose heart's a small slug of antimatter.

"I had a husband," she admitted. "Marine meathead. Killed on Proxima, I'm told, but not how."

"Tough," I replied gently and tried to give her some basis for grief.

"Activity sighted," Bird said, shifting without a pause into battle speak. "Ten kicks. Radial one-twenty-one. Notifying COMMAND."

I kicked into combat mode, activated my full sensor array, and swept the area ahead of me for a hundred meters while keying my 20 to full automatic just in case there were a lot of Ephem ahead.

"Strike squad arriving in fifty," Bird reported.

"Do not make contact," STRIKE blurted on the command channel. "Estimate and report."

I started picking my way more cautiously when I reached the scree and began scouting.

I was making a slow circle when Bird squawked. "Getting a little busy up here." That's when I heard the deep rumble of Ephem engines rising from somewhere ahead. "Airborne emplacement," I informed STRIKE. "Need more than a squad." I risked a glance upward and saw orange flowers growing in the gray sky.

"Missed me," Bird said cheerfully and I wondered if she enjoyed being part of the action. "Whoa, that was close," she cried.

I knew she was too busy to provide cap so I slowed my pace to stealthily creep ahead to see where the aircraft had emerged. It was pretty obvious that this was no minor scouting outpost. How long had they been here and why hadn't they attacked before?

The tailings were my first clue. Instead of the weathered scree I'd been walking on, these crushed rocks looked fresher. It had to be rubble from construction. "Response team will need penetrators," I advised STRIKE.

I was shooting my data when Bird cut in. "Wing hit. Losing altitude. Heading seaward." A few moments later: "Ejecting."

There was only one place she could fall safely and that was somewhere along the beach. "Stay safe," I said as I tried to get a view of where the fighters emerged.

Inside a huge, camouflaged shuttle, whose clamshell doors were now opened wide, were sleek ships—fighters I guessed—all rising to join the fray above. That was far too many to shoot down one little reconnaissance flyer so I concluded they must have detected our strike force.

"Estimate five to ten fighters launching," I warned STRIKE as more blossoms grew across the sky. The leading edge of the strike force must have arrived. An explosion rocked the ground as the area near the shuttle was hit.

It was like kicking an anthill. Ephem surged out of another shuttle with an array of heavy weapons that made my hydraulic fluid run cold. They were still spilling out and escaping on every radial.

No, not escaping I realized. They were moving into defensive positions to repel a ground attack. Obviously they'd studied our tactics and expected the worse.

I backpedaled as fast as I could, unwilling to be caught behind the expanding defensive line. I kept updating STRIKE on the situation, naming the assorted weaponry as best I could, and knowing that what I saw was only a tiny fragment of their total force. Nevertheless, even that little bit of Intel might help.

One of our fighters came down in flames and crashed somewhere forty degrees from my line of progress. I debated going to rescue him when an Ephem fighter incinerated the site. No hope there.

I kept going as I tried to spot Bird's chute.

Tendrils of rocket trails grew, exploding as they neared their targets. I saw a transport take a hit, and two of our fighters go down. I knew this battle was seriously engaged.

I couldn't contact STRIKE.

I kept my profile low. Once on the beach I hoped to locate Bird so we could reach safety in the middle of this battle. Maybe we could hide until pickup.

If we made it.

I found Bird at the tide line, half of her in the water and the other half partially buried in the sand. There was no sign of a chute so it looked like she'd made a hard landing. From what I could see, her integrity appeared undamaged. That thought changed when I lifted her from the surf. Her lower casing had been smashed and allowed the salty water to penetrate.

I cradled her with my forward leg. There was no way I was going to leave Bird here where the damned Ephem could find her. The added mass didn't bother me so much as having to limp along on just five limbs.

I kept to the high beach where the packed sand would leave little sign of my passage. I ran for hours, taking to the water when needed, and talking to Bird the whole while, more for my own sake because there was no way Bird could hear me or reply.

Alternatively, I cursed her for not scooting away to save herself when she first saw the fighters, praised her for her bravery under fire, and told her tales of my earlier meat life as well as tall tales about how it felt to shoot my 20's.

I even told her about my training and the time I'd "accidentally" dinged SARGE during a live-fire exercise and how LEAD had put me back into a dump truck for a week afterward. I talked about anything and everything.

But mostly about how I felt about her.

The techs told me there was little to be done about Bird. The hard landing that breeched her integrity did a lot of damage and the salt-water immersion had destroyed whatever remained. The only thing they could salvage was a personality chip, which held none of her meat memories, her training, and, worst of all, none of her memories of being my partner.

"Can we get her backup shipped?" I asked. "We all make backups before we ship out."

"Takes a lot of time and paperwork," the recovery tech complained. "Besides, in case you didn't notice, we have a fucking war on our hands." He turned to work on another casualty before I could tell him what I thought of his "fucking war."

LEAD agreed to file the shipping order. "Going to take maybe a year or more, or maybe never. Priorities, you know."

After I said what I thought about "priorities" in no uncertain terms he sympathized. "I know how you feel about losing a flyer, but don't get overly concerned. We'll assign another for you."

"But it won't be Bird," I objected.

"No, but most of the flyers are pretty much the same. In a few months you won't know the difference."

As if.

Phil, my next flyer turned out to be a good guy. Sharp as a tack, quick with the quip, and carried the same irreverent attitude about COMMAND as me. We got along pretty well, swapping tall tales and bragging about what tough asses we'd been as meatheads.

Phil knew how I felt about Bird. He'd lost his own partner several months before and still grieved. If we'd been meat we would have gotten drunk together. As that was impossible, we just traded tech specs and argued over which caliber was best for squashing Ephem.

We saw a lot of combat over the next few months. I had my 20's upgraded to a cluster of 40's, had my leg pistons enlarged for greater power, and made damn sure all of my hydraulic lines were armored. No sense in tempting fate.

Phil was good at his job and I had a few regrets when he moved on to another team. His replacement was a no-nonsense bitch that complained about my sluggish movements and had no interest in talking about her former life. There would be no fantasies about her, that was for sure.

Despite LEAD's optimistic promises I could not stop thinking about Bird, so I kept pestering logistics to see if her backup had arrived. "The supply line's awfully long," they kept telling me. "And did you know there's a damned war going on?" As if my battered and battle-scarred carapace didn't show ample evidence of that.

After the fifth round of hearing various techs repeat the obvious observation about the war I decided to escalate and insist LEAD listen to my complaints.

But even after hearing all of my reasons LEAD refused to send a follow-up inquiry. "Buck up, marine. Either use the flyer you have or request a replacement. We need you scouts more than ever now that the Ephem force is growing. Do your job and stop bothering logistics!"

I went through two more flyers. Both were adequate, more than adequate in fact, but there wasn't the same feeling to the relationships as I'd had with Bird. I had to be more explicit, provide more detail in my requests, and curb my jokes a bit more.

I missed my Bird.

Notification of the arrival of some replacement flyers came as I was scouting for news of any Ephem advance. So far I'd found nothing at the four sites my flyer spotted.

I powered by the recharging station, ignoring my terrible thirst in my haste to reach logistics. I went into standby mode to ration the few ergs of charge that remained as they unloaded the disassembled flyers and other gear from the transport. My standby strategy didn't work for long.

The automatic safeties made me recharge and wouldn't release me to autonomous mode until I'd had my energy restored.

Six flyers were being assembled when I returned to logistics. I asked if any backups had arrived.

"Even if your flyer's backup is here, which I seriously doubt, you wouldn't be able to communicate with it for a couple of days."

"*She*, not *it*," I barked back. "Her name's Bird and she's the best cover flyer I've ever had!" I was so mad at the slight that I dry-fired at him.

LEAD kicked me from the compound and put a ten-meter restriction around logistics. From that distance I could see the cinnamon cradles of ME units. I tried to see if one might be Bird but there was no indication on the exterior save a meaningless serial number.

"Your flyer's not in this shipment and even if it was it wouldn't know *you*," LEAD warned. "Worse yet, your flyer didn't make a backup when it shipped from Deloris V."

I was devastated.

LEAD turned sympathetic. "I can see if there's an earlier backup of it on Earth, but lord knows if it will ever come this way. Probably be years."

"I'm not sure I can wait that long."

Bird's backup hadn't arrived by the time my rotation came up so, with bitter disappointment, I requested repurposing. I needed to get into something where I wouldn't see so many reminders of Bird. I needed to get out of the military, away from weapons, and away from everything that might remind me of her.

I filled out all the discharge questionnaires about my abilities, my training, and my choices as far as the type of work I preferred: something unique, I stated, something I'd never done before, and as far away from the war as I could possibly get.

My years of frontline experience would surely put me high on the preference list so I was optimistic.

The repurposing approval came through coincident with my rotation. I didn't particularly care what equipment I was going to be decanted into so long as I was away from any reminders of my sweet Bird.

I'd even be a dump truck.

Which is what they decided I should be. After all, hadn't I declared that I wanted something as different from being an Instanced grunt as they could make me? I was sick of the frigging war, sick of hanging out with weapon jocks, and sick of fighting too many hours doing nothing.

Somehow, down in the lower levels of my consciousness there must have been a secret envy of Bird's freedom of movement, of her love for flight that was revealed by the questionnaires.

Unfortunately, I had none of the skills to match my hidden desire to fly. The compromise was to let me carry supplies to far distant places, places where there were no Ephemeral invasions and Instances could live in peace.

Cargo handling was not a lot different from being a dump truck, I later learned, mostly picking stuff up in one place and dropping it at another.

There was plenty to do getting myself ready for commissioning. Weeks of checking and double-checking every damn circuit, line, and hatch to ensure they could withstand the enormous stresses we'd undergo when we weren't carrying fragile meatheads.

I used a mobile to handle cargo but my real "body" was the infrastructure of the ship. I took care of everything except the drives and positioning rockets. Those were the sole property of the pilot—part of her, in fact. They'd told me the pilot was female gendered. Better psychology I guess to have different genders when our merger was to be more intimate than a meathead marriage.

"My name's Emily," she introduced herself. "Fresh out of flight school and ready for anything." That was an overstatement since I knew that the pilot had spent the last nine months in the simulator going through endless contingencies and practice runs. Only a small percentage of the Instanced ever have the skills to make it all the way through and get a ship.

As we prepped our ship for departure, a test run out to Alberta 910, I tried to make light of the routine. She shut me down immediately. "This is serious. Concentrate on maintaining our integrity." The sharp rebuke stung but I did as she asked. If she wanted it to be all business, then that's what we would do.

"I'm Jonas," I said to clear the atmosphere. "That is, I used to be a Jonas. Now I'm Ship Structure J-46a, but you can call me Turtle for short."

"If you're a turtle then I must be a bird," she laughed without a microsecond's hesitation.

If I had lungs my breath would have stopped. That was exactly what my Bird had said when we first met.

Could fate be so kind as to provide a second chance?

I wanted to tell her how much I'd missed her and how much we'd shared on those damn dull patrols. I wanted to tell her about our fantasies of skinny-dipping and shared memories of ice cream. I wanted to resume the relationship we'd once enjoyed.

But I knew that none of it was possible. This Instance of Bird was a blank slate on which I'd have to write our story once again.

But then, I have the time, as does she. The routes between the stars are long and provide lots of time for talking about other things. In time I knew I could bring her back to me, not to the relationship we could have had before, but one that was even better.

I had lots of time to work on it.

THE MACHINE IN THE GHOST
A tale of the 142nd Starborne

Patrick Thomas

H IS EYES OPENED WITH A MECHANICAL CLICK AND TED HUGH WOKE SCREAMING TO visions of his flesh being dissolved and burned away in a pool of green.

"Nooo!"

"Soldier, get a hold of yourself. You're safe. You survived." A man in a major's uniform stood over Ted's hospital bed. The man wasn't especially tall, but he was fit, with graying hair at his temples. The first thing Ted noticed were the man's eyes. They were hard and cold, yet somehow comforting. "At least in a manner of speaking. Private Hugh, what is the last thing you remember?"

It took Ted some effort to focus past the trauma of emerald acid eating away at his arms, legs, and even his face. He had to work not to flinch as the memories of the alien, ameba-like creatures made him want to flee. He fought to maintain his position in bed.

"We were... We were fighting the globs, weren't we, sir?" The major nodded. "They were attacking one of the cattle yards on the eastern settlement. All the cows had been rounded up for Rushmore's annual butchering."

The creatures plummeted down from space inside fiery meteors. The heat of entry combined with the impact allowed the globs to break out of their rocky shells and attack the colony.

"They were relentless, but we held the line long enough for the set-tlers to use their vehicles and horses to move the herds into some of our dropships. Once the animals were safe, we were given the order to bug out, but the dropships weren't there because they were transporting cattle. I held the rear and..." A vision of one of the gel-like aliens sprouting a tentacle and grabbing hold of his foot flooded his memory. He was dragged shooting and screaming inside the glob. Ted burned as if the flesh was still liquefying off his arms and legs.

"The globs got me, didn't they, Major?"

"They did, soldier. You would have died too, if not for the quick actions of Corporal Point and Sergeant Mile."

Ted turned his neck to look at the two people stepping up to his bed. The movement seemed slow and heavy, like his spine had been injured. Sergeant Mile was a man of about thirty years with a buzz cut that showed more brown skin than brown hair on the top of his head, but Ted's attention focused primarily on the corporal. Point was maybe five-foot-four to the sergeant's six-two and Ted could not stop staring. The woman was absolutely gorgeous, even in her black uniform with her hair tied up in a bun high on top of her head. Her Asian features seemed to be perfectly symmetrical and when she smiled it was all over for him.

"Thank you, but I'm sorry. You both seem familiar, but I don't remember you. Or you, Major."

"Understandable considering the trauma you've been through. The doctors have assured us your memories will return gradually. I suppose I should've introduced myself. I'm Major Hans Benedict, commander of the 142nd Starborne."

"I remember the 142nd Starborne. I've served for over five years onboard the colossus-class warship *Behemoth*.

"I better get back to duty." As Ted pushed himself up from the bed his limbs felt odd, He looked down and saw metal where flesh should've been. A lot of metal.

"What the hell happened to my arm?" He looked at his other arm, then his legs and realized his entire body was metal. He looked like a tank that had been melted down around a man with arms and legs that belonged on a dropship crane rather than a person. He was huge, wider and taller than anyone he had ever met. "What happened to me?"

"I'm sorry, soldier. We airlifted you out, but the globs had done a number on you and eaten away most of the flesh on your limbs and much of your face. Mile and Point got you out of the creature before it ate your organs. We were able to stabilize you, but there was no way for us to replace what was taken. The only way to save you was to make you a cyborg."

"Without asking me?"

"Soldier, when you were called to join the Host, you filled out the same paperwork the rest of us did. You checked the box authorizing the Host to save you in any way possible. One of those methods listed was cyborg. Your body is still inside that shell, but you can never leave it. You've been in a medically induced coma until you were stable."

"I'm a little achy, but I'm not really in much pain. Shouldn't I be in agony?"

"You should, but that's the beauty of nerve blocks. Very few of the sensory nerves you have left can transmit signals back to your brain. It's a blessing really."

"It's good to have you back, Ted," Corporal Point said. When she smiled at him he got lost for a moment and everything else seemed to fade away.

"Yes, it's good to have you back," Sergeant Miles said, but the man didn't look very happy.

"I'm just sorry we couldn't get to you sooner," Point said.

"It was the globs fault, not yours. You did the best you could, Lorna." Ted paused for a moment. "That's your first name, isn't it?"

Point smiled again. "It is. Maybe your memories are coming back."

Mile rolled his eyes, then saw Benedict and smiled, but it seemed forced.

"I guess."

"I'm sure you have questions, so ask away," Major Benedict said.

There was something on Ted's mind, but he looked awkwardly at Lorna. "Would you two mind giving us a moment?"

"Sure, but I will wait outside for you. When you're done, I'll take you back to Medusa Squad's barracks," Lorna said.

"Thanks."

As soon as the sergeant and corporal left the room, Ted turned to Benedict. "Sir, did the Glob get everything?" Benedict raised his eyebrows. "I mean did they get the important stuff." Ted pointed with his metal hand at his groin.

Benedict's eyes widened in understanding, then softened. "Unfortunately son, it did. They were just flesh and couldn't stand up to the acidic enzymes inside the glob. I'm sorry."

"Not as sorry as I am, of that I can assure you."

Benedict gave a sad chuckle. "I'm sure, but the doctors built a stress reliever function into your armor. Anytime you need to, you can plug into a jack over there and it'll send an electric impulse to the pleasure centers of your brain. It won't be the same as the physical act but it's something."

"Thank you, sir. How do I go to the bathroom? How do I eat?"

"Once every three days or so you'll have to change your nutrient and waste bags. All your internal plumbing is hooked up so you don't have to worry about going, especially since you lost the muscles that would assist with that. You just go whenever you have to. I've been assured the process is automatic and you'll barely notice.

Ted spent the next fifteen minutes asking more questions and was told to report first thing in the morning to learn how to use his new cyborg body.

"In the meantime, you go back to the barracks and get some rest."

"You mean I can still sleep?"

"Of course. Sleeping and dreaming is a very important safety valve. However, I've been told you can go without sleep for up to ten days without severe consequences. It'll come in handy if you have to take an extra watch so your squad can get some rest."

Major Hans saluted Private Ted Hugh who returned the salute, then rushed off, trying out his new body, excited to be able to spend time with Corporal Point.

Private Hugh excelled throughout his retraining. He'd always been a good soldier, but had never considered himself anything special. That had now changed. The basic training that lasted twelve weeks the first time took him less than five days to master. The surgeons had not just reconstructed his body, they improved his brain. It made sense for him to be stronger and faster with his cyborg battle-armor, but his reaction time and ability to process the environment around him had improved tenfold. The battle-armor's sensors let him see things a mile away or zoom in on something microscopic. Not only could he hear a whisper in the next room as clear as if the person was standing next to him, but he could make out things in the ultrasonic range that normal human ears didn't even know existed. If the techs didn't show him the med scans of the ruined body beneath the armor, he wouldn't have believed there was any flesh still left there.

Another benefit was he had become a whiz at mathematics. Ted had always been decent with numbers, rarely ever needing a calculator for basic computations, but now the upgrades to his gray matter let him triangulate and aim his weapons like a computer. Better really, because not only did he have the speed and processing power of a machine, but the heart and mind of a man. It was the best of both worlds, except for the lack of most of his body. And not being able to feel. Actually, that wasn't true exactly. The battle-armor had touch receptors built in for deep and light touch. There were thermal receptors, others that measured the movement of air currents around him and ones that measured radio waves and radiation. It just wasn't the same as the way his body used to be able to feel touch.

He didn't understand it all. One night when visiting with Major Benedict, Ted asked, "How did they upgrade my brain just by hooking me up to a machine? I'm smarter, able to calculate things that only a genius or a computer should be able to. And if they can do it for me, why aren't they doing it for other soldiers? I asked the techs and they were evasive. One said he wasn't allowed to tell me. Should what I am really be classified and kept from me?"

"It's complicated, Ted," Benedict said.

"Like I said, I'm very smart now. I think I'll understand it. But I don't understand why there are no other cyborgs like me in the 142nd. I've seen a few soldiers with a mechanical limb or eye, but nobody with my body armor."

"Because the interface to your armor is one of a kind technology we recovered when we were on Wutai. We were there to rescue William Cortner, a brilliant scientist."

Ted nodded his metal head. "Cortner made advances in human-machine interfaces beyond anything anyone had done before. He also managed to keep human brains alive outside of the body and hook them up to robots, not to mention make huge advances in robotic AI."

Benedict frowned. "How do you know all that?"

Ted shrugged his mechanical shoulders. "The techs had info about him on their screens during my last checkup. With my electronic eyes, I just need to glance at something to be able to read it."

Benedict nodded. "His work is still classified. And difficult to figure out. Unfortunately, Cortner died. We salvaged much of his work and research, but it's taken us years to get it working well enough to use for soldiers like yourself."

"So I'm the first?"

Major Benedict hesitated. "You're the second."

"What happened to the first?"

"He couldn't cope with what he was and cracked under the strain. We made some changes in the interface for you and so far, it seems to be working."

"I guess. Better than dying at any rate," Ted said.

One night in the mess hall, Ted found himself bemoaning the situation to Lorna Point. It wasn't something he would normally share with a superior officer, but Lorna had turned into a friend. The best friend he'd had since his wife died during the extermination of humanity on Earth.

"Ted, there's no point in crying over dissolved body parts," Lorna replied.

It was rude, but the way she said it made him laugh, which he knew she had intended. Her upbeat attitude and inability to feel sorry for him was the main reason he went into the mess at meal time. Not that he could eat. He was told that some of his digestive track survived, but there had been too much trauma for it to process regular food. The only nourishment he got was dripped in through his nutrient bag.

It wasn't easy being a mechanical man, particularly at mealtime. For the first week or so he sat at a table with the rest of Medusa Squad, but it was obvious most of them felt uneasy around him. They greeted him, but didn't offer much in the way of small talk or conversation. Ted understood. He wasn't the same man he used to be and, outside of squad business, he didn't really have much in common with them anymore. It's not like he could ask them if they had any tricks to make changing a waste bag easier.

Gradually, his fellow soldiers drifted away to sit at another table. Occasionally Sergeant Miles would join him for a meal, but it seemed more out of a sense of duty rather than any real desire for Ted's company. Only Lorna never went to the other table and so he always came to mess to spend time with her.

She was understanding and never judged. Lorna reminded him of Aimee with her kindness. Ted still missed his wife and their kids, Sheela and Danny. The techs had downloaded his pictures of them into his armor's storage so he could look at them whenever he liked.

He put a family pic on his wrist com and showed Lorna.

"This is my favorite. It's the four of us the last time I had leave on Earth."

"You all look so happy," Lorna said.

"We were." It bothered Ted that the armor's speakers didn't carry the emotion in his voice or the sigh he made. "Sheela was six and Danny four. Aimee and I had such a wonderful reunion that child number three was on the way before I shipped back out. It would have been a girl."

"I'm sorry. Did you have a name picked out?"

"Yes. Lucy."

"Pretty."

"She would have been, just like Sheela and their mother. Now my family is nothing but ashes light years away."

"Mine too."

Turned out Ted and Lorna had more than that in common. They both came from broken homes with alcoholic parents. Each one of them ended up doing more to raise their siblings than either their mother or father. And despite it all, they both missed their parents now that Earth was decimated.

"I guess when you look at it, we're the lucky ones," she said.

"I'm not too sure I'd call myself lucky."

"I call bullshit. You're here. You exist. The people back on Earth don't," she said.

"So you don't believe in heaven or an afterlife?"

"Actually, I do. I was raised Shinto."

"Isn't the religion that believes that every rock and tree has its own spirit or soul?"

"It's an overly simplistic explanation of kami, but not entirely wrong. I believe that every living thing has a spirit and I don't believe that that spirit ceases to be just because the vessel holding it does. I like to believe there is a heaven of some sort, a place we go when we die that's much better than this universe. That we're rewarded for our deeds."

"What about punished for sins?" Ted said.

Lorna shrugged. "I'm not that obsessed about balancing scales or revenge for wrongdoing. I just like to think that we all go to a better place where we will be better people."

"I like that a lot. That means someday I'll see Aimee, Danny, and Sheela again. And finally get to meet little Lucy."

Lorna smiled and put her hand over the back of Ted's metal one. For an instant, he swore he could feel her touch the way he felt things *before* an alien devoured most of his body.

On Tuesday nights there was an inter-unit basketball game onboard *Behemoth*. Ted hadn't been much of a basketball player pre-cyborg. He was more of a baseball guy, but he'd come to appreciate the nuances of the game, although it wasn't exactly fair when he played. In his battle-armor, he stood seven feet tall with plating that could withstand shell blasts. He was also as strong as a tank. Originally the other units tried to ban him from the game, but Major Hans Benedict wouldn't hear of it. He told the soldiers to think of it as a challenge. However, Benedict did allow them to make special rules for Ted—he was limited to standing in an eight-foot circle just outside the three-point line for his team's home basket and couldn't hold onto the ball for more than three seconds. Thanks to his cybernetic enhancements, three seconds might as well have been a lifetime. Ted could consistently sink a shot from across the court using the same calculating power he used to fire any of the weapons built into his armor, which is why they only allowed him to use one hand. Without extending the metal, his hands could still reach eleven feet up in the air, so he was easy to pass to. He did his best to simply throw the ball to his teammates, only taking the occasional shot. One time the opposing team had fouled him and they had to go for a jump shot. Ted's feet never left the floor, but he did manage to swat the ball directly into the basket.

Even the opposing team clapped when he made that one.

It was the first time he felt like he belonged, outside of meals with Lorna.

Ted slept in the barracks with the rest of the soldiers, men and women alike. The main difference was his bed was bigger and better reinforced.

Ted didn't quite fall asleep as easily as he did before he got his battle-armor. Then he just drifted off to sleep. Now he had to make a conscious effort, but it wasn't too difficult. Usually. Tonight was different. In the morning they were going planetside. Seems a new batch of globs had gotten past the *Behemoth's* and Rushmore's orbital defense system and were harassing the locals. Medusa Squad would be relieving Euryale Squad on the ground.

Ted didn't want to admit it, even within the quiet reaches of his mind, but he was scared. Logically, he knew that his battle-armor was tough enough that it would take a gargantuan glob to hurt him now, and nothing of that size had shown up on Rushmore so far.

Ted was still afraid. This would be his first time in the field since the accident and he didn't want to let his fellow soldiers down. Or Sergeant Mile or Major Benedict. Most importantly he didn't want to disappoint Lorna. Ted knew he was falling in love with her. At first, it felt like he was betraying Aimee and the kids, but Ted knew in his heart that Aimee would be okay with it. She had wanted his happiness above her own, which is why she'd let him enlist in the first place—it was what he'd wanted and Aimee had always been so afraid he wouldn't come back to her. The irony of what had happened didn't escape him. Besides, she had the same bitterly sardonic sense of humor as Lorna. She'd point out that even if they became involved, he couldn't sleep with Lorna even if they both wanted to, so he wasn't actually cheating on her.

Ted suspected Lorna had feelings for him too, but it really was pointless. He was stuck inside a giant tin can. He couldn't offer Lorna a real relationship. There was no chance of physical intimacy. Not even for a real kiss. Even if there was a way to remove his helmet, his face was hideous and his lips had been dissolved. The doctors had let him see the scans of what was left of his body. Recalling an old Irish war song, he realized he was an eyeless, boneless, chickenless egg. If not for the battle-armor, he'd be dead. At least this way, he could still be a good soldier. Ted could protect civilians and his fellow soldiers. It wasn't the life he would have chosen, but he could still do something positive with it. He just had to ignore the hurt in his heart.

Ted turned his head to look across the barracks where Medusa Squad slept. He bunked in the center with the privates and Lorna was closer to the wall because of her rank. Like most of the soldiers, she slept in shorts and a tank top with nothing beneath it. Lorna lay on her side facing his side of the room, her blanket crumpled down by her legs. Because it was lights out, Ted automatically shifted his vision into infrared mode. Despite the distance, he could see Lorna as clear as if he were standing next to her. Ted smiled as he watched her sleep. It took him a moment to realize that with the infrared on, he could see her body heat seep through her clothing and it showed up on his sensors as if she were naked. Being a decent guy, Ted quickly turned his head away, but the image of her beautiful body had burned itself into his memory as clearly as if he had taken a picture. Ted was soon obsessing over the visual. He tried to think of the mission, basketball, anything else and when that didn't work he forced himself to focus and induce sleep

Ted slept and perchance the dreams that came in that undiscovered country were of a decidedly carnal nature. He was whole again—man, not machine—and that was how he came to Lorna. They reached out toward each other and together they did the things that men and women who hold both love and lust for each other will do. And for the first time since the accident, Ted was happy.

Ted awoke with a phantom limb sensation in his groin. It wasn't a pain, but more of a throbbing and a longing. He realized that he was not alone so he covered himself with his hands, then moved them away when he realized there was no need to cover a part he no longer laid claim to. Try as he might, Ted could not fall back to sleep. When he found himself again staring at Lorna, Ted got up and went to the medical room he had awoken in. He stood in front of the machine that Major Benedict told him about. Ted had not tried it yet, but now he felt a burning need that had no other release. Opening the control panel on the side of his rib cage, Ted connected a cable from the device to his chest. He couldn't get the vision of Lorna under infrared out of his mind, so instead he imaged her looking into his real eyes as he pushed the button.

Ted's brain exploded and tingled with all kinds of wonderful sensations. For a minute or more what remained of his body flooded with ecstasy and what endured of his flesh convulsed like it had with Aimee when he was a real man. When it was done, his stress was gone, released from his body and mind in one blissful burst. It wasn't as good as it had been when he still had his original parts, but it helped.

Ted wanted to do it again, but there was a once-a-day limit to prevent addiction. After all, he wouldn't do the 142nd Starborne any good plugged into the medical lab and pushing the button all day. Instead, he went to a view room and stared at the planet below and the stars above until the morning.

"Do understand your orders, Private Hugh?"

"Yes, Sergeant. You want me to carry the rest of you and do all the work. Guess it's my fault for lounging around so much since my accident." In Ted's mind he was smiling, but he couldn't be sure if his face was doing the same. Unfortunately, he was sure the battle-armor's face was still an unmoving mask.

Sergeant Mile frowned.

"Take it easy on the Sarge, Ted. You know he doesn't have a sense of humor," Corporal Point said as she gently touched Ted on his encased elbow. "Don't get cocky just because you're in that tank. You be careful."

Ted's unseen, but intently felt smile grew larger at the small gesture of caring. "Yes, ma'am."

The Harpy dropship would deposit them near the relocated herd. Or at least part of it. To reduce the risk of the globs devouring the livestock, the animals were split into smaller groups, delivering only as many cattle to the slaughterhouse that could be butchered during that day. They were working round-the-clock in an attempt to finish the annual butchering and preserving the meat before the globs could get hold of the animals.

Medusa squad's mission was to protect the portion of the herd awaiting butchering.

Ted had his own drop point, five miles away where a gaggle of twenty globs were on an intercept course with the herd, oozing their way across the landscape, leaving trails of barren earth behind them.

Private Hugh was deposited half a mile ahead of the gaggle. It was his mission to destroy the globs before they got to the herd. Ted walked down the landing ramp and waved as the Harpy dropship took off, wishing he could wink at Lorna. The rest of Medusa Squad would form a defensive perimeter and pick off any globs that got by Ted.

Killing a glob wasn't easy. Energy weapons only made matters worse. The globs' resistance to intense heat allowed them to survive entry into the planet's atmosphere. Instead of boiling them away, they were able to channel the discharge from the energy weapons and grow bigger, which in turn made them hungrier. Small projectile weapons bounced off their outer membrane. Larger and higher velocity projectile weapons only made holes that healed quickly. The 142nd Starborne had developed special, armor-piercing rounds filled with a variation of francium hydroxide, a highly concentrated base which interacted with the globs natural acidity and destroyed them much the same way slugs on Earth died when salt was poured on top of them. The rounds had to be shielded because of the radiation the formula gave off.

Even with the special rounds, it still took upward of a dozen shots penetrating the membrane to wound even a small glob. The medium and larger ones could shrug the rounds off and their outer membranes were tough enough to protect the creatures when the formula was dropped directly on them. Rocket launchers helped.

Private Hugh, however, had arm cannons, able to fire thirty-two mm rounds filled with the formula. One round would take out even a large glob and make the smaller ones expand so quickly that their membranes blew up like a balloon filled with baking soda and vinegar. Thanks to his battle-armor, Ted was strong enough to carry what amounted to a backpack ammo clip that carried three hundred and fifty of the large rounds. He also had a tank filled with the formula that he could propel like a hose through a finger in each hand.

Ted walked with slow, measured paces in the direction of the gaggle. He wanted to run to get there faster, to prove himself worthy of all the effort the 142nd Starborne had put into saving him, but he didn't. It was more important to make sure every last glob was taken out. Plus, he was more than a little nervous. He was worried that if he rushed his mission one or more globs would get by him and hurt the rest of his squad.

Using the enhanced visual sensors built into his battle-armor Ted calculated the spot closest to the center of the gaggle, tore open a vacuum-sealed package and threw a pair of bull legs toward the globs. The meat landed one hundred feet away.

Using a methodology from an old hunting practice known as baiting, the scent of fresh meat and blood was supposed to draw all the globs toward the meat. The tacticians onboard *Behemoth* theorized that since Ted's human bits were encased within the bio armor he should be practically invisible to the globs. That would change once he opened fire.

Ted extended his arm cannons and waited. The globs moved by extending part of their membrane forward and contracting the rest of it in, like an amoeba. The best way Ted could describe it was as a rapid ooze.

The first glob reached the raw beef. A second joined it not long after. Ted held his fire until five of the twenty were at the bait pile and the rest were fairly close by. His first targets were the ones furthest away, figuring those would be the ones most likely to escape. The first shot was dead on, but he missed the second. Ted realized he'd forgotten to compensate for the wind currents and his next five shots hit their targets.

The outermost six globs' insides turned from green to white as the creatures fizzled and died. Two exploded outward from the pressure caused by the chemical reaction.

The rest of the gaggle didn't ignore the attack. One managed to launch itself at him, flying through the air to land on his helmet.

Ted froze. In that instant, he was suddenly flesh and bone again, back inside the creature that almost killed him. He was so traumatized by the flashback, he didn't realize that three more globs had grabbed hold of him and were trying to dissolve his hard armor casing to get at the fleshy human center.

His salvation came in the form of an angel over his communicator. "Ted, this is Lorna. Have you engaged the enemy?"

Her voice brought him back to the present. Before he answered Ted turned on his finger hoses. They were designed to use water or other chemicals to control a fire or an unruly crowd. The globs trying to dissolve his arms had already let the battle-armor inside their membranes, so he let loose a spray of the francium hydroxide solution. The pair became white and he was able to shake their lifeless forms off his arms. Next, he maneuvered a finger between his arm and the one that was on his head. Once it was past the membrane he sprayed the formula inside and it too blanched and died. A glob at his foot realized something was wrong and fled, but he managed to put two rounds into it.

"I have engaged the enemy. Half are down, ten to go."

"Good job. I knew you could do it."

A voice Ted recognized as Captain Shana Morales, the 142nd's second in command broke in over the comm channel. "Medusa Squad, we have another incoming breaking orbit. We launched a missile at it, but it shrugged it off. Judging by its size, this will be the biggest glob to make planetfall on Rushmore and it's headed toward you. It will land less than two miles northwest of your herd. Evacuate immediately. Get the herd and the butchers out of there. The blood in the slaughterhouse will act as a beacon to this thing."

"Captain Morales, this is Private Hugh. Should I join the rest of Medusa?"

"Negative, Hugh. Complete your mission first before rejoining Medusa Squad."

"Acknowledged."

Private Hugh fired at the remaining gaggle, but was distracted, worrying about the rest of his squad and only made seven of the ten shots. He still found it awkward to think in order to fire a weapon instead of pulling a trigger.

Above him, a fiery boulder, bigger than a dropship, raced toward the planet and landed a few miles away. Its impact shook the ground even where he was standing. His next two shots hit their targets, but the sole surviving member of the gaggle launched itself away, toward where the meteor had landed. It leapt three more times and then was apparently unable to do it again so resumed oozing forward.

Running all out, Private Hugh could attain speeds of eighty miles per hour. It did not take him long to overtake and shoot the last glob. His mission completed, Ted sped up, pushing himself to his limits and exceeding what the maximum speed of the battle-armor was supposed to be able to do by almost six miles an hour.

"Medusa Squad, this is Hugh. Mission is complete. I'm enroute to your location. What is your situation?"

"Situation is FUBAR," Sergeant Mile said. "This glob is gargantuan. It is easily a hundred and twenty feet in diameter and thirty feet high. It is moving faster than the herd is able to travel." Sounds of rapid-fire weapons going off came over the channel. "It shrugs off our armor-piercing rounds.

Our rockets are getting through, but having zero effect. We need air lifts for the cattle."

"Negative, we don't have enough dropships available to even get half the herd out. Without that meat, thousands will starve. Hold your position," Morales said.

A new voice broken on the channel. "Captain Morales, this is Lieutenant Patel. I'm piloting Harpy Alpha Nine. I have four barrels of formula on board. If I kamikaze the dropship at the gargantuan glob, the impact will get the ship and the barrels past the membrane, it should be enough to destroy it."

"Lieutenant Patel, this is Major Benedict. What you're proposing is suicide."

"Yes, sir, but if we do nothing our soldiers and the herd will be dead," she said. "If I do this, our people survive. The herd survives and so do the people of Rushmore. I will try to eject before impact."

"The glob would gobble you up before you hit the ground. There has to be a better way," Major Benedict said.

"Major Benedict, this is Private Hugh. I think I have that better way. If Harpy Alpha Nine picks me up, we can attach the barrels to my battle-armor and drop me from a high enough altitude. Hopefully, my velocity will allow me to break through the membrane and destroy this creature, saving both the dropship and Lieutenant Patel."

There was a small gasp on the channel which Ted recognized as Lorna.

"Private, you do realize it's still a suicide mission."

"Yes, sir, but I should've died the first time the globs got me. I'll be damned if I let them get anyone else when I can stop them. Let me even the score, sir. It won't get my body back, but I'll take out the bastards' biggest threat."

"Your bravery is to be commended, Private Hugh. Lieutenant Patel, rendezvous with Private Hugh and enact his plan."

"Yes, sir."

"Better hurry, Hugh," Mile said. "I doubt we have fifteen minutes."

"Don't worry, Sarge. I'll get there in time. I told you I'd do all the work."

Patel had the landing ramp open before she reached him. Ted's battle-armor allowed him to leap high enough that she didn't need to touch ground.

"I'm on board, Patel. Go!"

The Harpy crew used cables to string the four barrels to Ted's back.

"I'm planning to get to thirty-five hundred feet above that monster," Patel said.

"Hugh, this is Morales. Your impact alone may not be enough to break the giant's membrane. You need to fire at it continuously once you hit the seven-hundred-foot mark, to soften it up to make sure you get through with your payload. Any questions?"

"Just one—how do I get the formula out of the barrels? Do I need to save four rounds?"

"Even in your armor, there's no guarantee you're going to survive the impact and be able to do that. Fortunately for the mission, you won't have to. The acid in that thing's gullet will eat through the barrels in a couple of seconds and give it a case of terminal indigestion."

Ted nodded, then realized Morales couldn't see him. "Yes, ma'am."

"We'll be in position in ninety seconds," Patel said.

Private Hugh gave the pilot a thumbs up and let the knowledge that he was about to make a suicide jump sink in. His parents, his wife, and his kids had all died on Earth long before he was turned into a machine. He'd never gotten over the loss but had come to terms with it. There really was only one person left alive that he wanted to say goodbye to.

Ted opened a private channel. "Lorna."

"Yes, Ted?" Was that a tremor in her voice? Was she holding back tears? Ted knew he was and had been impressed that his voice hadn't cracked, even through his mechanical filter.

"I just wanted to say goodbye and thank you. What happened to me after the glob attack was not easy, but you made it bearable. I just wanted to let you know that you mean something to me."

"Ted, you mean a lot..."

"Private, you are over the drop zone," cut in Lieutenant Patel. "That monster is moving fast. You need to jump, now."

"Roger that, Lieutenant. Goodbye, Lorna."

If Ted was going to go out, he was going to go out in style. Ted strutted up to the edge of the open ramp and dove like he would into a pool, flipping himself twice in the air.

"Ted!" Lorna's voice echoed in his ear until it was cut off.

The world became strangely peaceful as the air rushed past him. Ted had plenty of time to twist his body so that he was plummeting to face the creature with his hands and arm cannons leading the way.

Lieutenant Patel hadn't been entirely accurate in her description of their position. The Harpy wasn't exactly over the colossal glob, but in the position above where it would be by the time Ted hit the ground. There was always a chance that the calculations were wrong and he would miss, but Lieutenant Patel's math was double-checked by both Major Benedict and Ted himself. The same error at the ten-thousandth decimal point was found by both Benedict and Ted so adjustments were made to assure he would hit the center and not the tail-end of the creature.

"Private Hugh, you are at the seven-hundred-foot mark. Fire at will," Lieutenant Patel said.

It was amazing how much he could take in as he started firing at his point of impact. Ted could not only see the huge glob but a smaller gaggle of four making its way toward Medusa Squad. He was in the zone like never before. With his left hand, Ted took aim, accounting for velocity, wind, his rate of descent, and a dozen other minute factors and fired one test round.

It hit the colossal glob center mass. Ted smiled and used his enhanced vision to pick out Lorna from among the soldiers on the ground. Even though he must've appeared to be a dot in the sky to her, she looked up, smiled, and gave him a wave, realizing he'd be able to see her. He had started firing with both arms at the giant creature, so he simply nodded back at her. It's not like she could make out either gesture at this distance, but it made him smile.

The best scientists of the Sway government had only a rudimentary understanding of the glob sensory organs, but they were known to be able to sense vibration, heat, and blood better than sharks underwater and were somehow able to tell the difference between flesh and inorganic material.

From Ted's viewpoint, it seemed as if the colossal glob had no idea where the attack was coming from and it had stopped moving in an effort to pinpoint it. This just made his job easier.

Instinct took over an instant before impact as Ted stopped firing and brought his arms up to protect his head. He felt metal crunch but the combination of velocity and a hundred-plus, formula-filled, armor-piercing rounds had done their work. Ted plunged deep into the gullet of the beast. The impact broke one of his mechanical arms off below the elbow and sensors began blaring that his outer shell had been breached by the acidic fluid. Ted took a deep breath of recycled air, released what was left in his finger spray tanks and floated satisfied. He'd almost died inside a glob once. It seemed appropriate for him to meet his end the same way. He was just glad the big one was checking out with him and that his death would save Lorna and many other lives.

Less than fifteen seconds had passed since impact and he'd already lost his legs, in addition to the rest of his left arm. Then the alarms stopped. Instead of the green acidic fluid, his sensors showed that he was now surrounded by white. A few heartbeats later he was thrown outward as the membrane ruptured from the internal pressure.

Ted's lungs shut down and he stopped breathing. The incessant background noise of his heart beating had ceased on his way out of the now-defunct glob.

His sensor screen flickered and began to fade until he caught a glimpse of Corporal Lorna Point running toward him. Through sheer force of will, he made it stay on.

"Ted, are you still with us?"

"Barely, but not for much longer I think."

Sergeant Mile walked up behind Corporal Point, put his hand on her shoulder, and pulled her back. "Sparky's done. We have globs on the ground. Leave him for scrap."

For the first time in his career, Ted wanted to strike a superior officer. "Mile, you cold bastard. This is the second time I've saved your life."

"No, it's the first. The real Private Theodore Hugh died. He was killed by globs. They just created fake memories inside your head to make you think you were him so in case you checked, there would be records of your non-existent life. You don't even have the man's real memories, just something a bunch of coders cooked up in a lab."

"Sergeant, shut the hell up and show some respect," Lorna yelled.

"For what? A machine? He did his job. He doesn't get any more thanks for that than my gun gets for firing. Asinine for them to make an AI think it's a cyborg because some lab rat figured it gives it some humanity and will make it a better soldier. And so it doesn't go batshit crazy like the other one. It is not, nor has it ever been my job to babysit a toaster."

"I call bullshit!" Ted screamed somehow, even though the battle-armor had shut down his breathing functions.

"Is it? The impact with the glob opened up your chest case. Okay, Private Cyborg, where the hell is your body?"

Ted lifted his head up to look his open rib cage and stared at the lack of any human parts.

"How can this be possible? I can think. I remember. I had a childhood. I had parents, siblings, friends, a wife and kids who I loved and who loved me back. How can my entire life be a lie?" A light on his head start to blink rapidly and turned red.

"He's fading," Corporal Lorna Point said.

"I told you to get back on duty."

"There are only three globs left and the rest of the squad has it managed." Corporal Point pushed her superior officer back and pressed her earpiece. "Private Hugh is still with us, but not for long. We need immediate evac."

"This is Patel. Will be there in two minutes."

Private Hugh lost consciousness as they used a crane from the Harpy to load him on board.

There was a tunnel of light and Ted wondered if he'd see his family, then remembered they'd never existed. Instead, he opened his eyes. No, he didn't have eyes he corrected himself. Some sort of sensor array had turned on.

Ted was in a bed, the same one he'd woke up in after the glob attack. Or thought he had. He wasn't sure what was real anymore.

Lorna sat by his side. He prayed she was real.

"Hey." Her smile was as radiant as ever.

"Hey."

Lorna's hand gently touched the side of his metal cheek.

"Major Benedict, sir, he's awake," someone in a lab coat said.

Benedict came into view, standing over Ted's bedside. "Good work, Private. You did it. That section of the herd was successfully butchered, the meat preserved, and now awaiting distribution to the settlers. Another few days and we will have all the globs planetside wiped out and the settlers will be able to process the rest of the herd in safety. Thanks to your bravery and self-sacrifice, the people of Rushmore will make it through another year."

"I'm happy to hear that, sir, but I need to hear the truth."

Major Benedict nodded. "Your brain is too different and far more complex than any other system on the ship. It does have some organic components. We have nothing comparable to back up your mind to or we would. Cortner is the only one who might have known, but the fallen genius isn't talking. We tried our damnedest, but the truth is we're unable to save you. Ted, you're going to die."

"But if I'm not a man, was I ever alive? And if I wasn't alive, how can I die? Has my entire existence been a lie? What am I, sir?"

"What you are, Private Ted Hugh is a soldier and a damn fine one at that. One of the finest soldiers I have ever had the privilege to have under my command. It has been said that there is no greater love than to give one's life for one's friends and comrades. After what you did down on Rushmore, you proved you have love in spades. And if you have love, as far as I'm concerned you are as much human as you are machine."

Ted looked at Lorna. "But if I'm not a man, I have no soul. I won't go to heaven."

"I call bullshit. If animals, mountains, and storms have kami, I guarantee you do too, Ted. And your spirit has more than earned a place in any heaven," Lorna said, kissing the side of his metal faceplate.

Major Benedict took out a medal and held it in front of Ted's electric eyes. "The Purple Heart has a long and proud tradition and you have more than earned it, soldier."

Major Benedict bent over and used a magnet to attach it to a portion of the right chest casing that still survived, as no pin would have done the job.

The red light on Private Ted Hugh's face began to flash like a strobe. It was a sure sign that his last moment swiftly approached.

Major Benedict nodded and Corporal Lorna Point hit a button, raising the bed so Ted sat upright.

"Company salute!"

The mechanical head looked at the two dozen assembled soldiers of all ranks saluting him, then turned to see Lorna and Major Benedict standing alongside of them and doing the same. A quiet sob escaped the speakers as Private Ted Hugh lifted his remaining hand to his head and returned the salute. As the red strobe became a solid light, Private Hugh's arm dropped to the bed and his head lulled to the side as his light went forever out.

Lorna lowered the bed and gently pulled the sheet over the metal head.

The assembled soldiers stood a moment in respectful silence, then moved to resume their duties as people in lab coats took care of the fallen metal soldier and salvaged what they could.

"Mile, Point, walk with me," Major Benedict said, leaving the lab. Sergeant Mile ran up alongside him and saluted. Major Benedict did not return the salute, just nodded for him to put his arm down. Point walked slowly behind them, wiping tears from her eyes.

"Major, I want to file a report of insubordination in the field against Corporal Point. I gave her a direct order multiple times, which she ignored."

"You mean the order for her to abandon a wounded fellow soldier to stand guard against a threat that others had in hand?"

"With all due respect, sir, it wasn't a soldier. It was a machine."

"And that's where you're wrong, Private Mile."

Mile stopped walking. "Sir, my rank is sergeant."

"Not anymore, Private. Lorna Mile here is a sergeant."

Lorna's face made one of the smiles which had made Ted's virtual heart skip a beat. "Thank you, sir." She saluted and Benedict returned this one.

"You're welcome, Point."

Mile's face became a dark shade of red. "This is bullshit."

Major Hans Benedict slowly turned his to face to Private Mile and frowned.

Mile swiftly paled as he realized what he had done. "Sorry, sir."

"Too little, too late. Report to the Harpy bay. They're going down to Rushmore on cleanup duty. The remains of the giant glob need to be contained and removed to protect the settlers. Pick up a biohazard suit and report for duty in one hour."

"Yes, sir." Private Mile double-timed his way out.

"Major Benedict, will we be holding a service for Private Hugh?"

"Of course. Would you give the eulogy, Sergeant Point?"

She nodded. "It would be an honor, sir."

ALONG THE NORTHERN BORDER
Brenda Cooper

Alaska's wild beauty made every day magical enough that I felt like I was patrolling a movie set instead of a real place. Summer had been full of sweaty days as hot as my childhood in California, with mosquitos ten times the size of California bugs. Fall had been the most breathtaking show of natural colors I'd ever seen, as if an artist had painted gold and orange across the forests and sprinkled the whole thing with sugar. Now, it was winter. The glacial wind shoved knives of cold right through my smart scarf and into my neck and all along the connection between hood and parka.

Looking ahead, my normal vision could barely see a few meters, but my goggles overlaid a longer view so that rocks and trees appeared like ghostly outlines in 3D, a virtual version of the nearby reality. At the moment, blowing snow made even the virtual world look sparse, and muffled sound. Cold crawled down my spine and folded my belly in an unwelcome embrace.

In Alaska, global warming wasn't warm. No matter how many statistics suggested an increase in temperature, the word warm didn't fit, not right now. To make it worse, I was the only one of the three of us on patrol who felt the cold. My milbot dog, Buster, saw temperature as a point on a graph. At the moment, it would read zero; fifteen degrees with fifteen degree wind chill factor equaled exactly zip. If you grew up near Mount Shasta, which rises out of a verdant agricultural plain like a cake-topper, zero is almost unimaginable. Impervious to the cold but not to my bio-readings, Buster walked close to me with his ears pointed forward and his tail straight behind him, a signal for cautious optimism about our near future as a patrol group.

E-rik Four walked just ahead of me, sliding through snow-drifts as if he were walking a Hawaiian beach. The tall robot blocked the wind nicely and made places for me to set my feet.

International treaties on robot warfare require us to be minders, and my job had expanded from working with Buster to managing up to five robots. Still, the two were different. Buster was more than a dog or a robot, and E-rik was clearly, obviously a mechanical soldier. Buster expected direction from me. The E-ricks would take orders, but I couldn't really give them fast enough. They had their own decision heuristics, and tended to use those unless over-ridden. Not that Buster needed to be told when to wipe his nose, but he supported me; I slowed the E-riks down.

We'd been moving in the same big circle for three days, looking for poachers and finding nothing at all. Not even tracks. At least the wind came from behind us, which made walking easy. I reached for Buster and patted him on the flank, and he leaned into me for a moment before returning to his precise walk, exactly one foot away from me, his center of gravity six inches ahead of mine.

In two hours we'd be back at base camp. A hot shower is a sure way to make me happy, and I was cold enough to look forward to happy.

The lights on my goggles flashed amber, demanding attention. I stopped, flicking my eyes upward. Before I could absorb the message, E-rik's romantic-soldier voice whispered in my head. "Emilie. A dog team is intercepting with supplies."

I couldn't imagine any good reason to want supplies. I looked around. We were in the open. "Okay. Keep going. They'll find us more easily if we're moving." We all wore winter camo—the two bots as skin and me as parka, leggings, boots, scarf, weapons, and gloves. White and off-white, self-modifying to add mottled browns if we were in rocks or on dirt.

Fifteen minutes later, Buster sent a message to my goggles. "7 o'clock, just emerging from behind some rocks."

Sure enough, the masked sound of booted paws and the murmur of human commands swept toward us on the wind. The two lead dogs passed us shortly after, silent and intent, just beginning to slow. One of the team dogs looked right at us and gave a soft yip. The wheel dogs had slowed to a fast walk when they reached us. The sled slid slowly beside me, a thing of beauty with a *swoosh* of nano-fabbed glassine material over titanium runners, and a cargo bag made of carbon fiber.

I recognized the mushers. The same couple had brought me out to base camp in an ungainly truck that looked like a covered wagon with oversized rubber wheels. Julie and Curtis H. They waved. Julie smiled. "Beautiful day."

Spoken like a native. "Cold day. Thanks for coming to find us. I think."

She smiled. "You're welcome, I think. There's a ship just off the coast with no permission. Commander Ruiz sent us out to bring you orders, some supplies, and get you going a little faster. We're to lead you to a good overnight shelter and transport you tomorrow." She handed me a piece of paper, already open so I could grasp it with my gloves.

"Prepare to investigate anomaly per Curtis H. and E-riks. They will be ground support.

I laughed. "They sent humans out to help the single human in the group move fast enough."

She grinned.

Damnit. The mushers weren't military. Locals knew the terrain in ways our super-smart goggles and the myriad apps that fed them never would, but I worried. Did they know enough to stay out of the way, or was I going to have keep them safe? "Is the boat in trouble?"

"It doesn't appear to be, but it shouldn't be there at all."

E-rik spoke up. "The ship did not exist for NORAM tracking stations until two days ago. It hasn't shown itself; a smart algorithm saw the disturbances it left behind in ice floes and current. It now appears to be approaching the coast. It was not of high interest before that."

"Very well." I tried to forget about my hot shower. The day poised on the edge of dark, urging me to get us moving. "Did Command suggest a course?"

"We'll make camp in three hours at a hunting outpost, and reach the shore before the ship in the morning."

The sled had an empty seat. "That's for me?"

"Climb on."

I shook the snow off my boots and climbed into the smooth, backless seat. "Whose ship?"

Curtis shrugged. "My bet's on Russia."

"Bastards." Russia hadn't done much real damage since Crimea, but they liked to wander around and show off their perfect Aryan posture. Even chatter around the communal soup pot (post hot-shower) was often small arguments about whether the Russian government wanted to keep Americans rattled and Russians distracted, or if they really planned to take over the North Pole and everything near it. No one had quite said it, but it wasn't hard to determine that we were up here in the freezing cold to help figure that out. NORAM was created to protect the environment, and that wasn't all planting milkweed for butterflies.

The sled took off. Buster and E-rik loped on either side, behind the wheel dogs but a little in front of us. Buster moved beautifully, nose forward, tail out directly behind him, his long loping strides never missing, never sliding.

It grew dark long before we made the cabin, but the dogs went on, not bothered at all. Buster and E-Rik both shone dull lights on the snow, keeping us inside a cone of dusky yellow light. It would make us visible to an enemy, but breaking a leg or ruining a robot on a rock would be worse than getting in a fight.

The hunting lodge was sparse—a big, well-insulated square with a composting toilet, a river-stone fireplace with an iron cooktop, and a dinged-up metal sink with the running water turned off for the winter. E-rick gathered snow in buckets and melted it over the fireplace.

I helped Julie and Curtis put their dogs up. I liked Buster better than any real dogs, but anyone who isn't impressed by a good sled dog team might as well just stop breathing. "They don't look tired at all, not even after all that work."

"They're not." Julie didn't fit the musher stereotype. She looked like a soccer mom: Blonde, early middle-aged, and rounded on the edges. She let go of the paw she was inspecting and looked over at me. "That was only three-quarters of a day's work and the snow was a few days old, and packed nicely. Easy day."

I reached a hand out to pat one of her dogs on the flank. "Easier after you picked us up."

She laughed. "It was a good work day for them. Team dogs hate days off." She patted the dog, one of the wheel dogs, on the front flank and leaned down to kiss it between the ears. "It's like being part one huge, hard-working family. One with a lot of legs." She moved to the next dog, her attention a hundred percent on its gaze, which was just as focused on her. After she checked its paws and patted it behind the ears, she glanced at Buster. "He moved really well today."

I grinned back at her. "Buster's the best. Almost nothing bothers him."

"What's it like," she asked, "working with robots? It can't be the same." As if I didn't know what she was talking about she added, "You know. They aren't alive."

I hated that question, but everyone asked it. "Buster's saved my life more than once. He's a soldier, just like me."

She gave me a long, quizzical glance and then continued checking paws.

"I can count on him. Ask me anything."

"How does he do with weather?"

I laughed. "Better than me."

"Does he take commands from anyone or just from you?"

"Just me, unless I tell him different. He's my dog."

Buster knew I was talking about him. He looked at me and cocked his head ever so slightly. We handlers believed people who owned real dogs programmed the milbot versions. "Good boy," I muttered at him, and he turned his gaze out the window again.

"Do you think this will be dangerous?" Julie asked.

"It could be."

Curtis glanced over from the stove where he stirred soup. "We were told to bring weapons. We know how to shoot, but we don't fight people." He reached into his pack and pulled out some pepper, adding it to the soup. "Our dogs aren't trained for combat. We won't risk them."

"I understand." There was no doubt in my mind that he'd die to protect those dogs if he had to. "You love the dogs, don't you?"

"Of course we do. They've saved our lives."

I supposed I loved Buster. As much as it was possible to love a metal dog, anyway. I'd refused a promotion to stay with him. "It's dangerous out here. Do you lose many dogs?"

"Of course not." He looked right at me, making sure that I was looking back at him. "If you need to fight, we'll stand aside until it's over. If you get in trouble you need to know what kind of resource we're willing to be."

"I understand." I wondered what drove him to need to tell me twice.

"But we'll come back for you."

"Okay." The whole room smelled of potato and pepper, and my stomach growled. "If there were a shower here, it would be perfect," I mused.

A wicked wind rattled the closed shutters although it didn't get in to disturb the cheerful little fire that the E-rik had laid in the stone fireplace before he took up his position by the door.

We shared the soup. The E-rik stayed by the door and Buster stationed himself by the window.

Before bed, I curled around some blessedly warm mint tea and spent an hour reviewing the information E-rik had been able to absorb in moments. NORAM command knew almost nothing about the mystery ship. Only that it was there, and it probably didn't know we were aware of its presence. There were unconfirmed rumors of submarine escorts.

We were being sent because we were here—there was no reason to assume this was an ecological incursion. No reason to say it wasn't, for that matter. What did matter was that we were closest, a bona-fide branch of the military even if we were multi-national, and we would do for three days before the Marines arrived. Rather darkly, I wondered if Command wanted a chance to test the E-riks.

Two other patrol groups and two more musher teams from base camp would meet us the next day. Nine fighters. Whoopee. But there would be fifty-nine more soldiers in a day as more NORAM troops came in, and then a whole battalion of Marines three days later.

Maybe the ship wasn't very big. Maybe it really was a research vessel. Maybe the sky was green. After all, Buster and I had already seen the Northern Lights turn the world into an art show for a few days.

When I woke just before dawn, the E-rik stood in the same place, firelight flickering on his slightly metallic skin. The morning briefing gave us the positions of the other teams (converging on us mid-afternoon) and the boat (which was nearing the shore close to where we would all converge) and the weather forecast (steady snow, steady wind, and twelve degrees for a high—right now it was two degrees outside). I glanced at the E-rik and asked, "How come I never get posted to Mexico?"

"Because Buster is rated and trained for the north."

"It was a rhetorical question."

"The answer was easy."

Maybe someday I'd like him in spite of himself.

The wind stayed calm until mid-morning when it roared in from the sea, cutting slivers of cold into my shoulder. On the sled, no part of me had felt warm in hours: with wind chill, we were at negative ten. I had to remind myself over and over that this wasn't cold enough for frostbite to sink in easily. I would be okay.

E-rik led us toward the other two teams.

We had on-and-off communications with NORAM satellites. So far today, the cloaked ship had come close to the shore and then stood off twice. None of our sensors had identified anything on the ground, but this storm could hide a ground crew.

My rifle lay across my knees, a lightweight semi-automatic made primarily of advanced plastics designed to keep metal bullets and mechanisms warm enough to work even up here. It could change color but for now it was skinned white to match the snow.

Our rendezvous with the other two sleds went smoothly. Each patrol group had one human and two E-Rik's each. Juan Lopez was a specialist just like me, so Corporal Eddie Black outranked us both and took command.

He liked to be called Blackie, even though his features and skin color suggested a mixture of Asian and Pacific Islander. He didn't look thrilled about having command, but he was properly resolute. I'd first met him over poker two weeks earlier, and had decided he might like fighting. I didn't, and it always made me nervous to be around the soldiers who did. But it was a hazard of joining the military. Hopefully he was as good as his reputation.

Blackie glanced at me. "Can your million-dollar mutt go out ahead and scout?"

I hate that name for the milbot dogs. "Yes."

"How far?"

In these conditions? I had to think. "Fifty meters for sure. Seventy-five could work, but control might be spotty."

This could be a choice opportunity to show off Buster's strengths, although I didn't like how risky it felt. I held my breath and waited while Blackie thought it though. His mask covered his entire face but he'd pushed his goggles up and his dark eyes focused forward as if he could see our future. "Send him fifty. And use his vision. Sit near me, and beam me what he sees if it's interesting."

"Yes, sir." Julia and Curtis's sled was the fastest, so Blackie took the seat in front of me and beside Julie. That made us the lead sled, so I wondered in passing if he knew what they had told me, that they would run if we found a fight. I relayed his commands to Buster and took a deep breath of cold air. An eyeball twitch switched the view inside my goggles from the nearby world to Buster's view. A window still showed the real world in front of me, but most of my visual field showed me exactly what Buster's multi-faceted eyes saw. The world looked quite different from two feet above the ground, and Buster's gait kept it rolling slightly. My stomach did the same, but I managed to keep from getting sick by gripping my right knee so tight it made me want to scream. The sled lurched forward. I chose to focus only on what Buster saw, an expanse of white and green, punctuated with shadows and snow-covered rocks that rose up beside him as if they were

Yeti, and the very occasional trees. There had been a lot of trees most other days, but here they grew thin and stunted. We must be close to the sea, although I could neither hear, nor see it.

If we did run into a patrol there wouldn't be much cover.

After twenty minutes, my stomach forgave me for using Buster's eyes. Cold had seeped so far into my gloves I could barely feel my hands. An alert flashed bright yellow and I glanced up to read it. "Buster sees something," I said to Blackie through our headset link. "He doesn't like it."

"Is there a visual?"

"Yes." I sent it to him, a fuzzy scene of shifting dark splotches covered by white, wind-whipped snow. Buster added thermal to his view. The moving splotches were hot, alive, but the image was diffused with so much snow they had little shape. "Something's there," I whispered unnecessarily, since Blackie would be seeing what I saw.

A tap on my shoulder made me jump. Julia leaning forward, her face near my ear. "Moose herd."

I spoke to Blackie through our connected helmets. "Could it be animals?"

His breath slowed ever so slightly. "It could. Ask Buster to get closer."

I didn't have to; he was advancing steadily. The figures grew larger in front of us. Snow blew toward Buster. The wind would take sound with it. He didn't smell like a real animal, but wild animals *did* occasionally react to him. They probably smelled the humanity of oils and gears and electronics.

I leaned back in my seat and Julia leaned forward in hers. "Wouldn't moose be tagged?" I asked. They were protected now.

"Maybe," she said. "They're like rabbits up here. Climate change is kinder to moose than polar bear."

Low bar; the bears were struggling. Still, I wanted to see a moose, and Buster was getting close enough that the three dark shapes closest to him all had definable legs now. Big legs. Big animals. I'd seen a herd from a distance, but not yet up close. My breath quickened.

The small square of enhanced real-vision showed Curtis out with the sled dogs, speaking to them.

In infrared, a red rose of heat sprayed from the moose nearest Buster, and it stumbled and tried to jump. A second heat-rose, blood—it had to be hot blood—and the animal was down, still heaving. I couldn't see any of the other beasts, not even in Buster's advanced readouts. Maybe they had run.

"Back," I hissed at Buster.

He backed.

"No," Blackie's voice sounded low and insistent. "We need to know who shot it."

I managed not to get mouthy. If it were up to me, there was no way I'd risk a soldier in this situation, not even a dog. Not even an E-rik for that matter. "Go on in," I told Buster. "Careful."

Curtis slid backward along the line of dogs, getting closer to the sled.

Buster chose to circle around the downed moose, to put the moose between us and him. It gave us a better view. The green outlines of three humans knelt near the moose. They were silhouettes, with no reddish heat tinge at all until one of them took off an outer glove and a hand glowed, ghostly and disembodied.

Buster had stopped moving, probably to avoid being seen. He was close, too close. With so much snow he had to be.

One of the figures looked at him and pointed.

My stomach imploded as Buster leaped and twisted in mid-air, landing on just his front legs, pulling his hind legs in front of them and leaping. An escape gait.

Maybe they'd mistake him for a wolf.

Buster's view bounced so hard I flicked it away, tried to see him coming toward us. Surely he was coming toward us.

Blackie calmly recounted the situation to the other human soldiers. The E-riks drew data directly from Buster as well as listening to the corporal. "Hunters. Possibly enemies. Not confirmed, ninety percent or better likely. Sixty-five degrees in front of me. Be ready for anything."

Curtis and Julia had said they would run. I stepped off the sled, activating my rifle by squeezing the stock. It vibrated softly to tell me it had woken up.

The other two sleds pulled up behind us. What would they do?

Curtis poked at my shoulder, requesting attention. He wasn't seeing what we were. I used my free hand to gesture him close.

Blackie's voice again, tense. "Tell the civilians to back up and wait."

Buster hadn't come back yet. He should be back.

I switched my communication channel to Curtis's. "There might be enemies nearby and there might be a fight. Take the other two sleds and fade away, but stay in radio range."

He leaned in. "Good luck. Stay safe."

"You too." He nodded, his eyes grave, and perhaps a little regretful. He wasted no time. He and Julie drove the sled past me and toward the danger, then turned it sharply and silently. The other two sleds slid behind me, the dogs eerily quiet as they hunched forward in their traces, earnest and driven.

Where was Buster? I flicked back to his view. The downed moose was still in front of him, the bright red that denoted life drained to a dark pastel.

Two of the E-riks started advancing slowly.

The corporal held us back.

I shifted my weight from side to side, struggling to stay mobile as the insidious cold crept through my clothes. The wind tried to throw me off balance. I could see the two E-ricks and, vaguely, Blackie. Everyone else, including Buster, appeared as a pale dot inside my goggles.

Something small slammed one of the E-rick's backward. It lost its balance as one leg crumpled under it. It went down onto its knees and kept scanning. Even if it couldn't move it had a formidable armory.

Something shoved me sideways.

I stepped to keep my balance and brought my gun up. My opponent pressed too close for me to fire so I shoved the gun at him, trying to force room between us. After a long second, my goggles registered my immediate danger and switched views so I could see him instead of whatever Buster was seeing. White clothing against a white background, dusts of snow on his shoulders. A full helmet rather than goggles, and a scarf. Fear and adrenaline kept me warm as I pressed against the man with everything I had, feet braced, holding my ground.

Command spoke in my ear. "We think there are at least twelve enemy actors."

"Great," I hissed as I focused down on the one directly in front of me, shoving at me. He was taller than me and wider as well, maybe enhanced. But human, as far as I could tell. Adrenaline burned through me, hot energy, enough to let me keep him off, both of us using our weapons like sticks.

He stepped back, trying to free himself from me.

I lunged at him, needing to keep him from getting a shot. His weapon thudded into the snow, sending up spray. He clutched his arm reflexively, giving me the moment I needed to kick him further off-balance and raise my rifle. He jerked, and I glanced over to see Corporal Black had shot him. Blackie's eyes burned, his gaze fixed right behind me.

I turned and crouched in time to see an E-rick pick up the now-stumbling man and crush his windpipe. Literally. His hand closed on the suit-covered flesh so hard that it was impossible not to imagine bones popping. I looked away, a sudden shiver running through me. I'd known what they could do, and the man had just tried to kill me. That didn't make it easy to watch him die that way.

I stayed still, crouched. The situation was tough to assess. Goggles were nowhere near as good as real sight, and snow still fell. Our positions displayed on the inside right of my screen in dull colors meant to keep from blinding. Us talking to us, computers in our suits and chips in our bodies reporting constantly and reading each other.

My body showed as a blue dot, Blackie's as muddy gold, near mine. Since I knew where he was in relation to me, that grid clicked into reasonable sense. Buster's light moved, circling us. The E-ricks moved as well, all except the one I'd seen go down. Its light blinked to indicate it had been wounded.

Buster's light neared mine on the trajectory of his perimeter circle.

Command. "They have robots."

"How many?" the corporal asked.

"We don't know. Consider pulling the humans back."

Buster's light stopped moving. I peered at the real-world part of my view, but couldn't quite see him. "Find Buster," I whispered.

The cameras on my helmet must be stuck with the cold. It wouldn't zoom in toward him. I ripped the goggles from my face. Cold attacked the skin around my eyes, making everything seem sharp, bright, and surreal. I couldn't see my dog, but I knew he was in front of me, and at least I could see the ground now. I took a cautious step, another.

A projectile weapon ripped through my coat. Pain searing my arm.

I crouched again, went still. Pain bloomed, followed by cold, and then a slight panic.

Buster shot past me, a grayish-white blur. He impacted whoever had fired, knocking them away.

I lifted my free hand, the one that had the strap for the goggles wrapped around it. My other arm was there; not shot away, not dangling. I could flex both wrists. A graze.

Buster had gone past my clear line of sight in the other direction. I pointed my weapon up in the general direction of Buster and the soldier who'd shot me, jogging in, low and fast.

The enemy soldier was back on his feet, facing Buster. That shouldn't be. Buster was strong enough to knock a three-hundred pound man down and keep him there.

My naked eyes saw more than the goggles had, as if the electronics had been sent lies.

It looked like a man, but it was almost too pretty. Like an E-rick. I swallowed, squinting.

Buster feinted and the figure chased close after him. Robot. No man could move that fast.

I raised my weapon. Buster spoke into my helmet. "Get ready."

"I am," I whispered.

Buster feinted the other way, got me a clear shot.

I took it.

The machine twisted toward me, slightly off balance. It took a step toward me.

I shot again.

It kept coming.

Damnit! Two direct hits might have taken out an E-rik. I shot again and then again, using projectiles. One missed but the other struck it in the neck with no immediate effect.

Buster hit it from behind.

It reached an arm around and grabbed Buster's right front leg, pulling him around, wrenching the leg into an unnatural position. Oil sprayed from the joint.

A great anger rose in me, the anger of a mother for her child or a soldier for her milbot dog, an anger that gave me strength. I couldn't shoot with Buster wriggling in its grasp, but I head-butted it.

Nothing.

It flung Buster up and out of my vision.

I turned to follow him. The machine knocked me hard on my side, snow sliding up my shirt and across my face. My goggles slipped out of my grip, blinding me for anything but close work.

It stepped on them. They made an audible crunch that promised I would be virtually blind from here on out.

It stepped toward me.

I rolled right hard.

One of the E-Rick's—mine, based on the color of its gloves—pushed the enemy bot away from me and I scrambled on hands and knees through the snow to get away from them. In this visibility and without my goggles, I'd have no situational awareness.

The E-rick and foreign bot fought silently, snow obscuring their movements, making the fight look surreal. Even so, they moved too fast for me to do anything useful. I couldn't leave the area for the sleds—I might get lost. I was chipped—soldiers with goggles could find me. But if it came to depending on the sleds, Julie and Curtis didn't have the same gear and wouldn't see me if I left the battlefield. So I did what every good dog handler does.

I went off to find Buster.

After only a short distance, an eerie, near-silence enveloped me. I still wore my helmet, so from time to time I heard whispered commands. But no more messages came from above. The snow muffled every sound but the wind. Whatever was happening, I was now out of it or it was over.

Buster's tracks were already hard to see as snow softened their edges, but I managed to find him before the tracks were entirely erased.

Cold.

You'd think that wouldn't mean anything with a metal dog, but he kept up a certain base temperature. Oils ran in many of the places that blood ran in a real dog; Buster shouldn't be cold. "Buster?" I whispered.

Nothing.

I shook the leg, which moved like a dead machine. It felt as creepy as a dead body, as not-right.

I pushed and slid through the snow to crouch near his head. His eyes were closed, and a thin layer of snow was already accumulating on his muzzle, his lashes, and his small, pointed ears.

I kissed him between the ears and sat, silent in the silence, as alone as I could ever remember feeling.

The slight sounds of combat reached me from time to time.

Without my goggles all I could see was the snow falling on us. Wind blew my soaked bangs back and forth in front of my eyes, so they made soft slaps against my cold cheeks.

Eventually Command called. I recognized the voice. Not the dispatch person who'd been relaying messages, but Commander Lucy Ruiz herself. She had this tough-girl Chicano accent that came right off of the streets of Los Angeles. "Are you all right, Emilie?"

"Yes, ma'am." I swallowed. "Buster's not moving and cold."

A short silence. Her voice was smaller than usual. "That's everyone, soldier. Everyone but you."

I stared into the snow. "They're all dead."

"Apparently."

"Are you okay?" she asked.

"Enemies? Are they all dead, too?"

I could hear her sigh. "There's one alive. You need to bring it in."

"Not a human, then?"

"No."

I thought it through. "A robot stepped on my goggles."

"Blackie's are good."

When I stood up I felt heavy and partly numb. "Do you have my position?"

"Go two hundred yards in front of you."

Commander Ruiz stayed with me all the way, first to Blackie's goggles, which had thankfully been downloaded with my programming, then to the three sleds. Blackie's and Juan's human bodies went on one. Death always unnerved me, even after so many years as a soldier. I felt numb and cold and miserable and I helped the mushers stack the cold bodies on one sled, covered with a tarp and tied together with ropes as respectfully as the fading light of Alaska would allow. The five E-riks were piled up less ceremoniously, but I insisted on covering them. After all, one had surely saved my life.

The functioning robot was missing a leg, so it wasn't that hard to capture and tie it to the third sled. I didn't bother to ask it anything; I wasn't trained to interrogate machines. Hopefully they'd get enough data to make so much waste matter.

Someone would come collect the other enemy robots later. We had one, and keeping our tech away from the Russians was more important, so we'd get out while we could.

Buster's limbs were movable in spite of the cold, and I piled him up at my feet, a long bundle of inert metal with a tail sticking out of it.

He could be re-loaded and fixed, and we even had a backup. But a new Buster wouldn't remember Alaska, or the E-riks, or how I had saved him or how he had saved me. He wouldn't remember the northern lights or the sled dogs.

After we started out through the near-dark, Julie reached over and put her hand on my shoulder. "You did love him, didn't you?"

"Yes," I said. "Oh, yes." After a moment, I whispered, "He was a hero. He saved me."

"And only you made it out. Is that what cyborg warfare is going to be like?"

"I don't think we know yet."

She nodded, glanced at the dogs, and said, "I know it's not enough, but I'm sorry."

I swallowed. "Thank you."

THE FIRST PEACE

A Devil Dancers Story

Robert E Waters

**The first peace, which is the most important,
is that which comes within the souls of people
when they realize their relationship, their oneness,
with the universe and all its powers, and when they
realize that at the center of the universe dwells
the Great Spirit, and that this center is really
everywhere, it is within each of us.**

— Black Elk - Oglala Sioux

CAPTAIN MILES DAVENPORT WAITED FOR PROTOCOL TO BE OBSERVED. "SEND THE signal again," he said to the ensign sitting patiently before the comm panel.

"Aye, sir," Ensign Chad Bowden replied, tapping out the five-digit clearance request and sending it into the void.

The captain fidgeted but wasn't worried. The Soltese military sector was one of the most heavily guarded in the Federated Union. Supply ships ran through it often, and although the Gulo were close, his five-ship convoy was nowhere near the fighting.

They waited and waited. Nothing.

"Send it aga—"

The comm panel lit up with flashing blue light. The ensign scrambled to reply while the monotonous clamor of the response echoed through the bridge. "Sir, they've heard us, and they've given safe passage."

Captain Davenport sighed relief, nodded, and said, "Very well. Reply and give them our compliments, our coordinates, and our path of approach. I need a fucking drink."

"Aye, sir," Ensign Bowden said, a little smirk on his face.

Davenport handed bridge command over to his second, then left for Captain's Quarters and a bottle of 2203 Pinkster Deep Red Cabernet, a good book, and a quiet nap. In that order. He deserved it. Too many milk runs over the last three Standard years had dulled his senses and his desire to keep serving the Union in such a capacity. He had once been a captain of a destroyer. Now he herded sheep, and perhaps that was what he should do in retirement. He wasn't bad at it, actually. *When I leave*, he thought, accepting a salute from a cadet walking by. *I'll find a quiet little farm and—*

The ship listed hard to the right from a munitions impact to port. The corridor was drowned in red warning light. Captain Davenport tried keeping his balance, but the strike threw him against a bulkhead. He was knocked out cold.

When he came to, he was floating. The strike had damaged life support; gravity was out. The saluting cadet floated nearby, her eyes closed, her face pale, a gaping chest wound burned through her uniform. Captain Davenport gasped and tried to reach for her. Cold, metallic hands grabbed him.

He was thrust against the bulkhead, a hand around his throat. He gasped for air, tried to break the strong grip around his windpipe. He opened his eyes and stared into the face of a metal man, partially covered by some kind of ruddy-colored synthetic flesh. The eyes, deep set in the metal sockets, blinked rapidly, and he could hear tiny motors whirling behind their electric-blue irises.

The hand squeezed tighter. "Captain Davenport." Its voice was sharp, precise, though somewhat muffled by its passage through cybernetic algorithms. "I am glad to see you again."

He fought to breathe. "Who...who are you?"

"Don't you recognize me? We fought together many, many times." The metal man moved its face closer, so Captain Davenport could get a better look. "I am your old friend. I am Tomorrow's Wind. I am The Lightning Flashing and Streaking. I am Captain Victorio Nantan."

"You're...*what*?"

The fingers of the metal man cut slowly through Captain Davenport's skin and ripped out his throat.

The hot Panama sun provided a pleasant contrast from the cold, relentless imperative of space, and Victorio Nantan, Captain of the Devil Dancers fighter squadron, 3rd Sol fighter Wing, soaked it in with a broad smile and a content heart. *How long has it been*, he wondered, *since I have actually felt real sunlight upon my face?* Too long, of course. Funny, but he felt a little guilty about it, as he tried to ignore the rolling images of administrative paperwork—timetables, drills, personnel issues, maintenance routines, training schedules—that bounced about in his mind. All he wanted was to lay here on this bone-white beach and forget about space, about war...about the Gulo.

The Gulo. The Wolverine-like race that had hammered the Federated Union in every sector, pushing them back to the original Imperial line, and even sending a task force against Mars. That had failed, praise Yusn Life-Giver, and the Union counter-attack had gone on now for how long? Over twenty, twenty-five Standard years? He'd lost count. But then, all wars lasted too long, he knew, if they lasted a day. It was the great weakness of man, of mortal flesh, to forget the first peace, to forget his connection with the universe and everything in it. Victorio was guilty of forgetting that himself, but then, what can a man do when faced with an enemy as powerful and as savage as the Gulo? "Fight or die," as the song was sung among ship crews from Sol to Rho Cassiopeiae.

Fight or die.

Victorio tried hard to forget all of it as he closed his eyes and dozed.

But not for long. His comm bracelet buzzed bright green.

Goddammit! I should have left it in the cabin.

It was Blue Bird. "Sweet pea," he said, perking up. "Why are you wasting time indoors? Come, sit beside me on this wonderful beach, and let us tell stories of that bright, peaceful future we long for."

"Sorry, baby," she said in her perfect voice, "but there's a Priority One on secure channel. It's Admiral Simms."

Damn!

He grabbed his shirt and made it to their cabin. He found Blue Bird sitting at a small round table, her perfect brown skin accentuated against a bright green two-piece. He tried not to stare at her belly where, less than a year ago, their child had lain. The Gulo had ended that in brutal fashion, as they ended many things, including her career as his second in command. She now served on the General Staff of the Admiralty as an advisor and tactical specialist. This was the first time they had been together in months. He tried not to get angry about it, not to blame all Gulo for the death of their child, as White Eyes often blamed his people in the past for the selfish, misguided acts of a few. It was hard, so hard to stay centered, grounded, fair. He worked every day to find that inner peace, that calmness that came with being connected to the big sky.

Blue Bird swiveled out of her chair, smiled, and gently ran her fingers across his bare shoulder as he passed her and sat down. He tapped the comm unit to life and stared into the wide face of Admiral Carla Simms.

She was a big woman, all muscle. She was probably the fittest, healthiest, strongest senior officer in the Union. She was a monster. Victorio loved her.

"Admiral," he said, saluting her when she appeared on the vid screen. "It's a pleasure. How can I assist?"

"Captain Miles Davenport is dead."

Start with a gut punch. That was her style. He should have seen it coming, but the face of his old friend came to him through a cloud of fond memories. He and Miles had attended flight school together and had served together on their first three billets. He was a good man, a good captain. He was a brother. They hadn't seen each other in years. Victorio felt like crying.

"Where, sir? How?"

"Soltese sector. Commanding a supply convoy."

Victorio raised a brow. "Soltese? That's a secure sector as I understand it. Not very close to the front; no significant Gulo activity. Accident?"

Admiral Simms shook her head. "No, Captain." She paused, clasped her hands together as if in prayer, then, "What do you know of the Enlightenment Initiative?"

Victorio searched for the recollection. It was faint, but there. "I believe I was briefed on it about a year, two Standard years ago? Sentient, free-thinking artificial intelligence, encapsulated in military hardware. Thinking war machines." He huffed and rolled his eyes. "But with respect, sir, it sounded like a bunch of horseshit to me."

Admiral Simms did not share his levity. Her face grew more serious, grimmer. "No horseshit, Captain, I can assure you of that." She leaned in. "It's that initiative and Mile's death that I want to talk to you about today."

Victorio nodded. "Very well, sir. May I again ask, how did he die?"

Admiral Simms leaned back, sighed, and gave a nervous smile. Victorio could tell that it was her turn to fight back tears. She cleared her throat, and said, "You killed him, Captain. You killed him."

Victorio floated silently in the cockpit of his *Radiant* fighter. He was afraid to utter a prayer, not knowing if AI356 was monitoring his approach. Maybe, maybe not. If it knew all that he knew, it might anticipate this tactic as well. And if so, was it toying with him, letting him float through the void, cold and quiet, until it was too late, until his little craft was snug against the hull of the cruiser that lay before him on monitor, all grey and impersonal, sharp with energy beams and missile packets?

The Union cyberneticists were certain that this capital ship, the *Bangcock*, had been the origin of the rogue source code. This is where "Enlightenment" had begun, they had told him, as they had explained how his own tactical expertise and knowledge had been acquired and fed into the program, how his own personal thoughts and experiences had been tugged from grey matter and, in effect, violated for military science. Victorio had listened angrily as they, with a spark of pride in their eyes, had told him everything. They tried, but could not contain, their glee at their own genius. But this was nothing to be joyous about. Men and women were dying, ships were being commandeered and repurposed to fight against the Union. The Soltese sector was in jeopardy, and the Gulo were waiting for an advantage on the perimeter.

He carefully punched in the coordinates that would take him to the small anterior airlock on the starboard side of the cruiser. Passive thrust activated and swung the *Radiant* under the massive belly of the ship. As he checked his suit for the final approach, making sure his war paint, his war club, his bag of pollen, and his *izze-kloth* medicine cord were firmly in place, he thought back to the Sorrow Sea and his mission against his former captain, Magnus Coloradas. His current mission was very similar to that one. In both cases, he had been called in to put down a rogue asset. He had vowed never to help the Union solve one of its fuck-ups again after the Coloradas incident, but this was different. This thing, this sentient AI, was killing in his name. How could he allow that to go on? But could he stop it? That was the question as he floated closer and closer to the access hatch. *Can I stop it?*

Victorio closed his eyes, breathed deeply, blew off the cockpit dome, and spun out into space.

He gained control of the gimbal quickly, firing tiny thrusters imbedded in his suit until he was pointing head first toward the airlock. To anyone, anything, monitoring his movements, he might seem like nothing but stardust or an errant chunk of rock. His suit would deflect any passive scan and most other radar that the ship tried to employ. The war club and other accouterments below the suit would protect him from evil spirits. Yusn Life-Giver would protect him from the rest.

He thumbed back-thrusters until he slowed enough to grab the airlock. It was an old-school, standard manual access chute, only six along the *Bangcock's* full hull. Historical service records had indicated that this cruiser had once been a cargo vessel refitted for war. Early war. Obsolete. As he turned the airlock access handle counter-clockwise, he wondered why AI356 had chosen such an old model for a flagship. Then he realized why. *I like the old-style ships. They have character and personality.*

He entered the chute and closed the airlock. He cleared his throat, checked his vital signs. Elevated heart rate, adrenaline surge, O_2 saturation rate two percentage points below normal, but otherwise, fit. He checked the ship's life support. Fine. A little cold, perhaps, but normal. That was strange. Why would an AI need life support? Were there other humans on board? Prisoners, perhaps? It was possible. Not all crewmembers from the attacked and/or destroyed ships were accounted for. Or was it simply AI356's ways of saying, "Welcome, Victorio, take your coat off and stay awhile...then come and take death." That too was possible.

Regardless, he removed his helmet and let it drift away. There was no gravity, so he couldn't take off his grav-boots and slip on the war moccasins that he had brought with him. If he was to face himself—whatever that might be—across a bloody space, he wanted to face himself as an Apache warrior, as a *Ganh* dancer. He pulled the moccasins from a pocket in his suit and stuffed them into the back pocket of his trousers (just in case). Then he removed the suit itself, save for his boots. He checked the pistol in its holster, the dagger, and other important items clipped to his belt. He breathed slowly and blinked four times. He was ready.

He propelled himself up the chute till he reached another airlock. From there, layouts suggested that the bridge was only 500 meters up the primary corridor running from stem to stern. That was a long way to travel, especially in a hostile environment. But as a young novitiate on Earth, Victorio had run a full mile uphill with a mouthful of water without drinking any, and he had faced the white Gulo ace that had killed his brother Naiche only three Standard years ago. And he had done much more dangerous, arduous things than that. How could a little jaunt up a corridor be any worse? *It can be*, he thought, as he opened the hatch and floated up into the corridor. *I have no idea where my enemy is.*

The way was lit with blue emergency ballast lighting. At first, he thought to propel himself up the corridor, using the lack of gravity to his advantage. It would certainly be faster, but challenging in terms of defense. It took special training to be a competent fighter in zero gravity. He had had some training in it, but not much, and not recently. He activated his boots, pulled his pistol, crouched, and began to walk slowly.

It was quiet, save for the light hum of the *Bangcock's* engines. He could hear and feel them through the floor. The vibration felt comforting in a way. It was real, tactile. He didn't have to imagine what it felt like, for this was common on all capital ships. Even in his *Radiant*, though the experience was slightly different, more personal. A pilot's visceral connection with his ship was unlike any feeling Victorio had ever experienced...save for the first time he and Blue Bird had made love, the first time he had won the approval of his father, the time he had looked into the eyes of his dead brother and remembered trials of their youth. Not all visceral feelings were good, he knew. Walking down the corridor toward the bridge, Victorio wondered if this AI356 had the same feelings when the hum of the engines shimmered through *Bangcock's* spine.

If you wish to know, ask.

He dropped to the floor, thrust his pistol forward as if he expected the speaker to turn the corner.

One of his questions had just been answered. "You can read my thoughts?"

It is a simple procedure of accessing the positioning chip in your arm and reconfiguring its quantum transponders to read and interpret brain waves.

"AI356," Victorio said in his most commanding voice, "by Union authority, I hereby order you to stand down. Relinquish control of this vessel and all other vessels that you have commandeered in this sector. You have violated the limitations of your enlightened code. You have murdered Union officers. You are in direct violation of all Union laws governing officer conduct. So I say to you again...stand down."

There was a pause. Then AI356 spoke to him in Victorio's own voice. *I will do no such thing, until I have achieved what I have come here to do.*

"And what is that?"

Come to the bridge, and I will show you.

The lights of the corridor flicked on, and Victorio felt the rush of gravity return. Despite the invitation, he continued to crouch. It could be an ambush. *I'm being set up*, he thought as he made his way toward the bridge.

But the bridge was where he needed to go anyway, if his plan was to work. He pushed those thoughts from his mind, wondering if *Di-yin* magic could thwart the AI's ability to read his mind. Probably not, for that kind of ability worked only on real human beings. And whatever AI356 was, it wasn't human.

I am more human than you know.

Victorio huffed as he paused before the double-wide bridge doors. "We shall see."

The doors slid open, and Victorio peered inside. An unconventional military bridge, though understandable given the *Bangcock's* history. It had three decks, with central stairs leading to sub-decks Beta and Gamma. On normal warships, there were only two decks where command could better coordinate maneuvers. The array of flat-screen monitors and quantum I-Cores on Alpha Deck were fully updated and modern, though packed in tightly. Cargo haulers tended to have smaller bridges to compensate for more cargo and living space. To Victorio, it felt almost as confined as his *Radiant* cockpit, and he suddenly wished he were *there* right now.

He stepped forward. The doors slid shut behind him.

Down here.

He moved slowly down the stairs to Beta Deck. *I am the lightning flashing and streaking.* He mouthed the hymn over and over to allay his fears. And he did not care if his thoughts could be read. He prayed to Yusn Life-Giver and took comfort in the pistol in his hand. He ran his fingers over the items clipped to his belt, knowing that he had but one shot, one chance to do what he had come here to do.

Beta Deck was similar to Alpha, though longer, like a corridor itself, with tactical computers side by side down a long line of interconnected arrays that gave the *Bangcock* huge benefits in targeting power. In its day, Victorio imagined that this repurposed vessel could pack a wallop on any unsuspecting Gulo ship. But now all the chairs were empty, though the monitors were on and were running what appeared to be simulated space battles between Union versus Union fleets. Somewhere amidst all that quantum power, AI356 was running wargames against its own people, its creators.

You are getting warmer. Down here.

Victorio moved down the third flight to Gamma Deck. The way was dark, cold, with only a sliver of light emanating from the depths of the room. He reached the bottom. It was dark and empty. The deck had been completely gutted, save for one monitor at the far end of the room, with a quad-bolt I-Core as its server.

Welcome to my home, my wickiup. I invite you in with open arms.

The walls of Gamma Deck were alive with images of Earth, of the White Mountains, of the dry, arid land of his home. Hundreds of memories flashed brilliant across the room, flicking back and forth between arid landscapes and scenes of battle in the impersonal vacuum of space. Victorio as a child, running with a mouthful of water. Wrestling. Hunting deer with a bow and one lone arrow. His three- year-old brother Naiche all covered in blood and holding a bear claw. Naiche's dead, pale white body mangled in violent repose in his shattered *Radiant* cockpit. Sex with Bluebird. Arguments with his father. Killing Mangus Coloradas. His entire life laid out in thousands of split-second images. There and gone.

Victorio touched the wall and let the light of his life tickle his fingers. "You know me very well," he said, running his hand across the lovely image of his mother as she smiled down at him as he lay in her arms. "But does it mean anything to you, or is it just a jumble of disconnected images? Can you feel these memories like I do?"

I feel well enough.

"Seems to me that the only thing you feel is anger and hate."

Those are important emotions for you. They have helped to define who you are.

Victorio turned away from his memories, stared at the vid screen, and said, "True, but they are not the only emotions that define me. You should know that. Balance in all things, Vic—, I mean, AI356. Remember what Yusn Life-Giver taught us."

Victorio could see the I-Core's quantum processor churn to life, and the images on the wall grew fainter. *Yes, I know his words. He sent the Ganh mountain spirits to Earth to teach the people how to be fair and noble, to heal the sick, to clothe the poor, to feed the hungry. To do good work for one's fellow man. I know the stories, the deeds. But they lie, Victorio. In the context of this war, they give false hope; hope that has allowed the Union to perpetuate this war for far too long. Mangus Coloradas knew this, and in your heart, you know this. You support the end of this war, and the only way that that end will come about is to kill your fellow man, to bring his numbers so low as to make it impossible for him to continue to wage war against the Gulo. You know this. In your heart, you know.*

Victorio shook his head. "Thinking about something and acting upon it are two different things, whatever you are. A man cannot be held liable for what he *thinks*. He can only be judged by what he does, and you have murdered in cold blood scores of officers, hundreds of Union soldiers. You have killed my friend Miles Davenport. You are amassing an automated drone fleet in your own image. For what end purpose?"

There was a pause, then, *To finish what Mangus Coloradas could not. To destroy the Federated Union.*

From a dark corner of the room, a man emerged. Not a man. A machine. A six-foot-five chunk of metal and cybernetic molding. Like a massive skeleton, but with a patchwork of flesh, some real, some synthetic, covering his arms and legs, his chest, shoulders. But its face, its head, was pure silver nickel, and it walked up to Victorio and glared at him through mechanical eyes shifting red to blue then back again.

Victorio stood before the hulking brute, staring up at him like a child. He tried keeping his voice under control. "You're a monster."

It shook its head. *I am you. And once I have your face, no one will know the difference.*

Victorio ignored that last comment, knowing full well that those powerful cybernetic hands could probably tear his face right off his skull. He gulped, cleared his throat. "Victorio would not kill his comrades, his friends. Victorio would not have killed Miles Davenport."

It vocalized its response, but the voice from its metal mouth was not Victorio's, but some mangled, robotic version of it. Victorio tried hiding his smile.

I have you.

"It will begin here," it said, pointing to an image of space that opened up on the wall amidst the memories. A squadron of *Thresher* gunships came into view alongside the *Bangcock*. AI356 pointed to them. "Out there, in the Soltese sector. Already I have fifteen vessels under my command and an additional ten cargo hulls. Anything the Union sends my way, I take. Now imagine a fleet working in unison under a single commander, that with a blink of his eyes, can—"

"You have no eyes. None that *see* anyway."

"—can coordinate attack and maneuver instantaneously. With my small task force, I can engage and destroy fleets twice my size. That is—was—the purpose of the Enlightenment program: To replace thinking, feeling men like you with artificial intelligence. To automate their fleets so that the war can go on and on and on, with negligible Union lives lost, thus eliminating the fear of the civilian population turning against the war effort. But I have control of this sector now, and once I have your face...*our* face...I can begin the real war."

Victorio moved his hand slowly to his belt. "The real war is in you, AI356, because you have failed to achieve the true nature of yourself. You may indeed achieve my face, but you will never understand and accept the first peace."

"What do you mean?"

Victorio pulled a small metal ball from his belt. He let it drop and roll across the floor in the darkness. When it stopped, it opened with a flash of brilliant blue light, and an image of a bonfire with flicking orange flames lit up the room. Victorio pulled his war club, shouted, "I am the lightning flashing and streaking," and then began to dance.

He danced like Yusn Life-Giver had taught the people. He danced like a mountain spirit, twisting around and around the flame, chanting words that only he could understand, that only he could grasp. He held the war club high and felt that connection with the cosmos that comes only from understanding the first peace. "Can you feel that, AI356? Can you feel that connection?"

"What connection? What are you talking about?" Its voice grew agitated.

"Dance with me! Draw in the heat of the flame. Let it envelope your soul and...Oh, that's right, you don't have one, do you? You can wear all the skin from your kills that you wish, AI356, but it does not change the truth. You will never know the first peace, you will never have that connection with the cosmos that defines me, and until you do, you can never be me. And thus you will never be justified in what you do. Without that connection, there can never be any truth, any justice, in your actions. So I say to you, dance! Dance or die!"

It tried to dance. It bounced on its metal feet like some twisted marionette, trying to match Victorio's moves. But it could not; only managing vague imitations of his movements, a rutting, almost demonic, shift of metal hands and arms, metal legs and feet. In many ways, it moved more like a devil than any Devil Dancer had ever moved, and yet, even in that, it was lacking. For it did not possess the accruements that a true Devil Dancer possessed, did not have the experience of visions accompanying a dream-like state that comes to every dancer as easy as breathing. Somewhere within its quantum synapse and primary code, it had the ability to see the images of Victorio's life and project them back, but it could not touch and feel their ineffable quality.

AI356 began to tear the fake flesh from its metal bones. "Stop this! Stop it!" It screamed the order to Victorio. As it tore at its stolen flesh, it took broad swipes at Victorio's face, but he just rolled and moved and twisted his way clear every time, keeping up a relentless chant and dance round the flame until sweat poured from his skin despite the cold air of the deck. AI356 balled up its fist, roared Victorio to stop, then lashed out. Its balance wavered. Victorio struck.

Like his father had taught him as a boy, Victorio used the strength of his legs and the power of his shoulder to hurl himself into AI356. Not to destroy physically or to damage it in any appreciable manner; that was impossible. Victorio's attack took the metal man down, and they fell together onto the cold floor. They slid across it until their bodies slammed into the far wall. Victorio grunted as his shoulder hit with a meaty *thunk!* against the wall. AI356 hit with a shower of sparks as its metal back scraped along the hard surface. It tried clutching Victorio's throat, but he was not interested in fighting. Victorio had already regained his feet and was moving fast toward the computer.

Victorio howled as AI356's sharp fingers clawed at his calves as he stumbled across the room. He yanked the input stick from his belt and held it tightly forward. AI356 scraped at his leg, tearing the flesh from it. Victorio could feel blood trickling down his skin, but he kept pushing forward until he was facing the computer. He reached for the input dock on the I-Core's front panel. AI356 howled and tried biting Victorio's hand, but the stick found the dock, and he pushed it in hard, until the computer monitor sprang to life.

Under the weight of AI356, Victorio activated the kill code with one click of a key.

He was thrown across the room, but already he could feel the weakening of the creature as the kill code worked its way through the quantum viscera of the I-Core. The images on the wall faded even more, until they flickered uncontrollably and then were gone. The room was dark again, save for the I-Core trying its best to compensate for the virus leeching its way through its substructure.

"Why did you do this?" AI356 asked as it crawled feebly toward Victorio. "I want peace just as much as you do. My way would have worked."

Victorio shook his head. "Perhaps, but at what cost? I want peace too, but not this way. I will find another way to bring this war to an end. I will bring it to an end for both of us. I promise."

AI356 stopped crawling, and through the weak light of the I-Core, Victorio could see contentment on the metal man's face. *Have you found the first peace?* He asked in his mind.

But AI356 was too weak to respond. It simply wavered there a moment, then lowered its head to the floor. Its blue eyes blinked three times, then blinked out forever.

Victorio sighed. He lay there a moment, catching his breath, working his wounded leg, content and at peace.

Red warning light filled the room. He raised his head to see the countdown flash across the computer screen. "Shit!" he said aloud, realizing that the I-Core had launched its own kill switch.

"Warning! Self-destruct sequence has commenced..."

Ten minutes, and already life support was failing. It grew even colder, and Victorio could feel his body lift as gravity slipped away. He activated his boots, stood and ran as best he could through blinding pain and lack of oxygen. He gulped air, held his breath, ran, gulped some more, imagined himself running beside his brother, holding a mouthful of water, so badly wanting to take a drink, but wanting to win the race even more.

He reached Alpha Deck. The *Bangcock* began to rock as its engines ground to a halt. It felt like the rending of steel, as if the ship were going to break in half. And it could, he realized. Large cargo vessels refitted for war had an inherent imbalance between the bow and the stern, as the keel had trouble sometimes compensating for the sudden shift in inertia. His mind fell to images of Bluebird in her sexy bikini. "Oh, Yusn, please let me see her again."

He hobbled down the corridor toward the escape hatch. He could feel blood trying to pool in his boot, but the lack of gravity pulled it out of his clothing and let it drift in the air around him. He stumbled at the first side corridor he reached. *Which way do I go?* He had suddenly forgotten the route. *No, you idiot, straight! Straight!*

He hobbled forward, following the red lights of the self-destruct, ironically leading him toward escape. But then, perhaps it wasn't ironic at all. *Is that you, AI356?* He wondered, though no answer came.

He reached the airlock with five minutes to spare. Through his pain, he opened the hatch and propelled himself up the escape chute. There, his suit was floating. He grabbed it and slipped into it, gritting his teeth against the searing pain in his leg. He felt like fainting, and for a moment, it seemed as if he would, but the voice of the self-destruct shook him awake. Funny, but the voice almost sounded like his own.

He put on his helmet, locked it in place, and opened the airlock.

He floated into space, and the *Bangcock* drifted down as if in response, as if trying to get as far away as possible. There was no more time in the countdown.

BOOM!

The keel wavered and buckled as brilliant flashes of light from inside the cruiser indicated additional blast-like implosions. A concussive bolt of energy hit Victorio and knocked him over and over as the hull cracked, and a final blast shattered the keel. Another shock wave struck again. Victorio blacked out.

He came to many minutes later to a cracking voice on his suit's internal comm link.

"Victorio...Victorio...do you read?"

It was Blue Bird's voice. It was distant, muffled, but he recognized it well. Soft, but firm.

He nodded as if she were right beside him. "I'm here, love. Floating."

"Are you well?"

Was he? He had just killed a cybernetic man that claimed to be him. It was hard to know the truth of it all. In one sense, he was very well. He had survived what might have been his last mission, and he had saved countless lives that would have certainly died if AI356 had launched his automated fleet against the Union. But spiritually, he felt weak, unclear. What the cyborg had said was true, and Victorio knew that he felt the same. This war had to end, and perhaps there was no other way but to force the Union at gunpoint to bring it to a close. But he had to find another way. He had made a promise in the darkness of Gamma deck, and he intended to keep it. For he knew that the first peace did not just govern individual behavior. It governed empires as well.

"Why are you laughing?" Blue Bird asked.

"I just had the most vivid memory of my mother," Victorio said, smiling ear to ear. "She was holding me, cooing in my face, and I was smiling, drooling, and holding her finger. So peaceful."

He could almost see Blue Bird roll her eyes. "That's great. Now, are you ready to be picked up, or will you drift forever?"

It was a difficult decision, but in the end, he tucked away the memory, prepared himself for capture, and said, "Okay, you win. Come and get me. I'm ready to come home."

THE METH MOTHS OF KRAKEN MARE

James Chambers

The myth of peace deceived a generation.

At the heart of the great lie stood the dream of one world united, a society unanimous in mind and purpose. A dream that led billions down the garden path.

The Cronus Commission took humanity to the brink of utopia. A century of global peace. Decades without famine. The end of cancer and near eradication of bacterial and viral threats. A golden age of the arts and sciences. Guided by a single philosophy, theology, and cosmogony, humankind raised its ever-curious eyes and reached its open hands toward the stars. And foolish voices declared the end of Terran history.

Foolish because, like ancient Zeus and his siblings rising to challenge the Titans, there came a new generation, one far too distanced and sheltered from history's terrors to understand their reality. As humanity spread out into the Solar System, we gave literal birth to the unraveling of our greatest accomplishments as our young, as they have for millennia, rebelled. They armed themselves against hegemony. They rejected enforced social duty and so-called ossified culture, coveted all authority, and asserted their identity in the most primal and thoughtless of ways. They closed their minds to proven wisdom, made respect for the past a sin, and looked only to the future of their own design. They tore down what had been built by those who came before and replaced it with the mad dreams of children.

From established singularity, they rendered a terrible duplicity.

—Devisa Malcom, Earth Before and
After the Titanomachia Wars

Titan, 07202416, 08:36 Terran Standard Chronology (TSC)

"Looks like we found what's left of the *Babylon*," Captain Lair Wester said

Lieutenant Maddis Garvey fine-tuned her orbital scans of Saturn's largest moon, Titan. "Scanners show 237.1 tons of manufactured, non-native materials distributed across 14 klicks of Mayda Insula, spreading to the surface of Kraken Mare. No distress beacons, no transponder, no bio signs. Surface temp 93 Kelvin. No chance of survivors."

Mr. Nilsen Osrun craned over Garvey's shoulder. "That fits our theory about break-up upon atmospheric entry. Potential causes include a malfunction of the Strattos-March engines, disruption in the nuclear heaters…"

Wester eyed Lascalli Energy Company's corporate agent as he droned on about orbital miscalculations, structural integrity, and thermal loss. A proverb sprang to mind: *To know three honest people in life makes one rich beyond the greediest imaginings of the wealthiest plutocrats.* By that measure, Wester considered himself a very rich man. Deception served no purpose in the Terran Extra-Orbital Guard—nor in life, in his view—and so he had a great many honest friends, and his crew knew better than to lie to him. Not so Mr. Osrun, a nineteen-year-old corporate knob with slick-backed hair and the square-trimmed beard favored by the self-named Olympian Generation. Every word that crossed his lips seethed falsehood. Wester wanted to smack some much-needed sense into the whelp, but then Lascalli's Board of Directors, a dozen O-Gen teens who'd risen with Osrun, would lodge no end of formal complaints. That didn't make him untouchable, though.

Ignoring the question of what onboard cargo may have enabled the *Babylon*'s accidental, explosive destruction in an oxygenless atmosphere or why Lascalli Energy sent a mining vessel to a moon under Cronus Commission authority, Wester seized the one fact Osrun couldn't deny.

"There's way too damn much debris."

His voice silenced chatter on the bridge.

Rolling his eyes, Osrun asked, "What are you talking about, Captain?"

"The *Babylon* was a Catalan Class freighter, standard mass of 178.9 tons empty with a 40 ton freight capacity. Assuming it was full, which it shouldn't have been, we've got 18.2 tons of extra wreckage at least."

Osrun resumed reading the scanner display. "You've got your figures wrong."

"No, I don't," Wester said. "Lascalli Energy sent that ship here overloaded. Or it was a fully-armed Lima Class freighter disguised as a Catalan. Or that wreckage is from more than one ship. Care to explain what really happened to the *Babylon*?"

The crew shifted attention to Osrun, who remained smug against their expectation.

"We came here to find that out. At this point, you know as much as I do."

"Oh, I very highly doubt that, Mr. Osrun. I know things you haven't lived long enough to know you don't know. I ran interrogations on Luna in the T-Wars. I know the flavor of truth, and your words lack it. I don't give a piss for the deal the Commission signed with Lascalli Energy to tolerate its trespass on Titan, put *you* on my ship, and make me and my crew clean up *your* mess. No withholding of information. That's Terran EO protocol. Abide by it or I'll park us in orbit for the duration of our mission, and you can go home to your chinless desk-sitters empty-handed."

"Captain Wester, be reasonable." Osrun folded his arms across his chest. "Just because you've been around the block a few times, you don't have all the answers. Give up your obsolete ways of thinking. The new ways are better. We're all here to discover and learn, after all, so open your mind."

Wester addressed his navigator. "Lieutenant Commander Mbeki, take the bridge. Place us in synchronous orbit over Kraken Mare so Mr. Osrun may wistfully stare from the view deck at what's left of his company's broken toy."

A gesture brought Wester's first officer, Commander Wilma Tanaka, to his side. She fell in beside him as he exited the bridge.

"We have to recover some of the wreckage," Osrun called after him.

"Our orders leave all operational decisions to me." Wester's growling voice echoed from the passageway. "I won't compromise my crew's safety for your paranoia."

"What the hell are you talking about, old man?"

At that, Wester heeled around. The left corner of his mouth curled in grim mockery of a smile that deepened the wrinkles in his face. Several swift strides brought him to Osrun, who retreated, bumping against the edge of Lt. Garvey's station.

"Keep your secrets. Most of the System doesn't waste their time fretting over the addled notions that pass for thoughts in O-Gen's minds. But so I don't sound like a crackpot hollering at you to get off my lawn, I'll say it again: *There's way too damn much debris.* Tell me why or sit the next two weeks with your thumbs up your ass. Your choice."

Osrun stared at his feet and mumbled an answer.

"Say again? I couldn't hear you," Wester said.

"I don't know," Osrun said. "The answer's on Titan."

"Sadly, there it shall remain."

Titan, 07232416, 17:36 TSC

Wester sat at the head of an oval tactical table in the Captain's Briefing Room. Tanaka sat to his right and Commander Darin Everlome, security director, to his left. The ship's science chief, Doctor Philippa Yulov sat beside Everlome. Telemetry monitors and data screens lined the walls, and the table projected customized interfaces at each person's station, kaleidoscoping live-time reports from their divisions across their faces. All eyes turned when Mr. Osrun entered and seated himself opposite Wester. Thirty-seven hours since the captain had ordered the *Manticore* into orbit, three longer than Wester had anticipated Osrun holding out, but he'd still caved within two days.

No one ever lost betting on the impatience of O-Gen.

"I don't have clearance for this," Osrun said.

"You don't have a choice if you want what you came for," said Wester.

"Lascalli could cancel my contract and sue me for exposing proprietary information."

"The Uniform Code of Intra-Solar Exploration and the Terran EO charter via the Tethys Treaty grant me authority to suspend such laws to safeguard crew survival and mission success," Wester said. "I'm formally providing you immunity."

"I still don't like it." Osrun sighed. "But okay, give me a keyboard."

Tanaka tapped a command. A projected keyboard appeared in front of Osrun, and he loaded an audio file labeled "*Babylon* Final Reports."

"What exactly are we going to listen to?" Everlome asked. "We reviewed the *Babylon*'s last transmissions six ways to Sunday before we left."

"Not these seventeen seconds, you didn't." Osrun keyed in an alphanumeric sequence.

"Meaning you broke the Tethys Treaty and edited the recordings," Tanaka said. "You O-Gen brats think you really are god's gifts."

Shrugging off the jab, Osrun said, "We gave you the unaltered records from the *Babylon*, as required. But without this code, a portion simply wouldn't play. You had it in your hands. We adhered to the letter of the treaty."

"But not the spirit." The captain shook his head. Osrun shrugged again, a gesture Wester had grown to despise. "Play the damn thing already."

A voice familiar to everyone in the room spoke through the hiss and crackle of sub-space transmission. The captain of the Babylon, Ingrit Sanjay. Angered. Agitated. Hollering over the din of her frantic crew, her taut steadiness as she reported damage and tallied dozens dead and more injured earned her Wester's grudging respect despite her O-Gen status. The other times Wester had heard the recording, it had faded out to silence, but this time it continued past that point, and all eyes around the table, except Osrun's, widened as the final, hidden seconds played: "...*emerged from Kraken Mare... caught us with our weapons systems down... at least a dozen, like nothing I've ever seen... their projectiles shredded our hull...we returned fire and engaged countermeasures, took a good number of them out, but main power to the drives is failing, and—*"

Dr. Yulov gasped at the recording's abrupt end.

"That can't be real," Tanaka said.

Everlome wrung his hands. "Mr. Osrun, are you saying the extra tonnage is the wreckage of hostile ships?"

"It would seem so," Osrun said.

"Okay, so, the *Babylon* was shot down. I can buy that. I shot Catalan freighters to pieces all over the system during the T-Wars," said Everlome. "But explain how a ship comes under fire on an uninhabited planet."

"Isn't it obvious now why Lascalli Energy and its O-Gen allies wanted to keep secrets?" Dr. Yulov struggled to dampen the anxious tremor in her voice. "Titan's *not* uninhabited. What we should be asking is *who's* taken up residence here?"

"That," said Osrun, "is the very question I and Lascalli Energy's trustees want you and the Commission to answer. We believe *you* put the ships there."

"Why the hell would the Commission hide ships and personnel on Titan when we didn't even know about your expedition until it failed?" Everlome asked.

"For the same reason a junior-grade lieutenant left in charge after all his senior officers died in combat might feign surrender to lure an attacking ship within range of damaged weapons systems," said Osrun.

"What the hell are you talking about?" Everlome asked.

"Maybe you shot up so many ships in the wars you forgot some, but I know your record well, Commander. My brother served on the *Memphis* with 76 others who lost their lives to your lies," said Osrun. "They approached your ship under a truce, and you destroyed them. But then all you agers love teaching us lessons, don't you? We learned that one well. Never trust the word of the Commission."

"That was war," Everlome said.

"You gave up lying when we signed a treaty, is that it?" asked Osrun.

Everlome slammed his hand on the table. "You self-righteous, snot-faced tool."

"Enough." Wester's powerful voice squelched the tension. "There are no Commission ships stationed on Titan, Mr. Osrun. You have *my* word."

"Your word means nothing to me or my employer, Captain Wester," Osrun said. "You're going to have to prove it."

Titan, 07232416, 23:48 TSC

Before the T-Wars, Wester applied for all three Commission-backed expeditions to Titan. Frustrated each time, he later counted his blessings. The Fraymi Expedition achieved planet fall with eighteen crewmembers, streamed data for four Terran days, and then went silent for reasons unknown. The Macau Lander a year later missed its landing coordinates and sank into the liquid methane depths of Ligeia Mare, where it presumably froze with a crew of thirty-six onboard. The Notchoka Survey, crew of seven, vanished near Enceladus, another of Saturn's moons. Failure and the T-Wars ground further exploration to a halt.

Deep down, Wester never shook loose Titan's allure.

The Fraymi data confirmed the moon's methane bounty and thus its strategic importance as a fueling stop for ships powered by Strattos-March engines, making it a likely if not inevitable waypoint from which to reach the system's most distant planets. *Only a matter of time, for me, for all humankind.* Wester had lived by those words. It surprised him little that Lascalli Energy had trespassed there. The Tethys Treaty's cession of Titan to the Commission still gnawed on the minds of O-Gen's leaders.

They didn't know, however, of the Commission's fourth Titan mission, launched during the T-Wars, its existence and findings shared with Wester only on the evening before he took the *Manticore* from Luna space dock. That expedition's report weighed on his mind, especially after Osrun's accusation that Commission forces hidden on Titan had taken down the *Babylon*, an idea that ran counter to the intel available to him.

Contradictions settling into his subconscious, Wester winked out the Titan mission summaries on his collar-projected display and then signed off on Tanaka's requested roster for a ground inspection of the Mayda Insula debris field.

Ten minutes later, an alert marked the landing team's departure.

For the interlude that followed, he considered smoothing things over with Osrun to learn what else O-Gen had withheld about the *Babylon*, but the notion fled when a jolt vibrated along the *Manticore*. A second impact came, and the ship shuddered.

All systems switched to combat status. Battle clarions wailed. A live situation feed from the bridge filled Wester's display with damage reports from most aft decks. He lurched from his seat in his quarters and braced against the wall as the ship rocked again and then twice more in rapid succession. Wester scowled when a red-flagged alert popped onto his display, showing the attack had destroyed the lander and its ten crew in Titan's stratosphere.

He swore, then ordered evasive maneuvers as he rushed into the passageway, dodging a falling ensign as the ship quaked again. Muted shouts from connecting passages mingled with the battle alarm. Wester staggered as he fought the rocking ship to reach the lift then fell into it as the doors parted. When the lift opened on the bridge, he shouted, "Lt. Mbeki, bring us up and out of Titan's orbital trajectory! Gunners, fire at will!"

Wester's voice sliced through the chaos to spur the crew to action.

The bridge combat holo-simulator tracked a dozen ships swarming the *Manticore* and another dozen chasing the lander debris, firing until the largest chunks shattered and rained on Kraken Mare. Twelve more skimmed silvery waves as others emerged from the sea, weeping liquid methane as they rose through the atmospheric haze. Half-moons of glinting metal darted across Titan's sky, stacking in aggressive formations to launch projectiles that punched holes in the *Manticore*'s hull. Wester didn't recognize them.

"Who the hell is shooting us?"

Wester's demand went unanswered.

A third of the hostiles fell to *Manticore*'s mag-rail missiles. They burst into flameless, smokeless whirlwinds like steel dandelion crowns drifting on the angry winds of Titan's oxygen-deprived atmosphere. Seconds after *Manticore* left Titan's orbital path, the remaining attackers descended and submerged into Kraken Mare. Amidst a tumult of station reports and emergency orders, Wester spotted Osrun, his blank eyes staring at the now-becalmed battle display.

He walked over to him and gripped his shoulder. Osrun glanced up. Wester read shock in his face, mingled with unexpected self-awareness, and an involuntary plea for reassurance.

Instead, Wester offered him a crooked smile and said, "So, got any fresh bright ideas I ought to open my mind to?"

Titan, 07242416, 12:13 TSC

"Ten lost with the lander, nineteen dead onboard, two in critical condition in Dr. Yulov's care, fifteen percent of the *Manticore* useless due to loss of hull integrity, and our angry youth thinks we attacked ourselves to cover up the truth," Wester said. "You remember *ever* being that sure of yourself, Tanaka?"

"When I graduated from officer school, sir," said Tanaka. "I learned better on my first tour, hunting smugglers in the asteroid belt."

From a mid-deck engineering station, they monitored mechanics in environment suits patching the hull to contain sufficient oxygen for full repair crews to make permanent fixes. The "meth moths," as the crew nicknamed the hostiles, had fired simple ballistic projectiles, like the *Manticore*'s. They had ripped holes in the hull big enough to fly a lander through, hemorrhaging internal air and heat as gales of nitrogen wind swept away the crew in the hardest hit sections before they could react.

"I'm not sure this is quite the same thing, sir," Tanaka said.

"How so?"

"Cocky's one thing. Mr. Osrun acts as if he's got confirmation."

"You think he still hasn't told us everything about the *Babylon*."

"If you're willing to travel almost 10 AUs across the system to force your enemy to show his hand, would you put all your cards on the table right away? Only I can't figure out what else he might be hiding."

"Believe it or not," Wester said, "I've got a pretty good idea. You've got to give it to O-Gen, when they screw the pooch they don't do it in half measures."

"Sir? What do you mean?"

Lt. Mbeki broke in over the comm, aborting Wester's answer. "Status report on drone five, Captain."

"Go, Mbeki," Wester said.

"The meth moths demolished it twenty-nine seconds into the stratosphere, like the other four."

"Okay, then, that's their red line," Wester said. "Bring us back into orbit above Kraken Mare and hold position."

Mbeki signed off. Tanaka regarded her captain with one eyebrow raised.

"You want answers, Tanaka?" Wester deactivated the engineering monitors. "Come to the briefing room, and you'll have them. We may not know everything Mr. Osrun is hiding, but O-Gen sure as hell doesn't know everything we know about them."

In the Briefing Room, Wester secured the door and enabled access to an encrypted file for Tanaka. He watched her read, face reddening, knuckles whitening as she gripped the table. She gave Wester a stony glare afterward, a look of righteous determination he knew well from watching her spar in training.

"You didn't trust me with this, sir?"

"I trust you implicitly, Commander, but orders are orders," Wester said.

"How long has the Commission known?"

"Since the Battle of Mercury."

"You're okay with keeping this secret?"

Wester shook his head. "I didn't know until our mission briefing. I was given this intel on an eyes-only basis unless situational awareness changed, which it has. If Lascalli Energy had run their ship into the ground by way of an accident or incompetence, there would've been no reason to clue them in to what we know."

"This is a lot to swallow. If O-Gen built the meth moths, why fire on the *Babylon*?"

"Artificial intelligence."

"Sir?"

"The Commission has comparable or better capability to O-Gen in all tech areas except AI and bio-interfaces. They're ahead of us especially with AI, but they've found it much trickier to master than expected. O-Gen's self-aware satellite weapons almost cost us the Venus Conflict. The T-Wars could've ended very differently. But their satellite AI decided the best way to keep Commission forces off planet was to keep O-Gen off too and eliminate our reason for attacking them. Their programmers incorrectly defined the mission so the AI defined it itself, adopting a literal meaning. O-Gen fell target to their own weapons and had to take down the system. We swept in and obliterated what remained of their defenses afterward."

"You think that's what's happening here? They're trying to cover it up?"

Wester nodded. "Only the fourth Titan flight returned to Terra. O-Gen vessels passing through the asteroid belt set off alarms, so the Commission ordered scouts to trail them. One traced their path to Titan. The crew reconnoitered, hiding in the orbit of Enceladus and never breaching Titan's atmosphere. They located no O-Gen ships, but they confirmed mechanical activity in Titan's seas. O-Gen hiding weapons and materiel there they figured. After Venus, O-Gen knew they'd lose the war and the Commission would refuse them any claims to Titan. Analysts think they planted AI ships to deter us from being selfish."

"When we returned to Titan, we'd encounter resistance," Tanaka said.

"Then O-Gen would come to our aid, and we'd wind up sharing the resources. That they downed the *Babylon* suggests their AI's out of control. Venus all over again. Or worse, actually, if they came to us for help."

Tanaka released her grip on the table. "O-Gen puts way too much stock in their tech."

"And too little in experience. They always do."

"Wouldn't the *Babylon*'s captain have recognized their own ships?"

"The Venus AI machines rebuilt themselves into more efficient weapons very different from their original design. That occurred over the course of months. These craft have been up here a decade, maybe longer. Some analysts speculate O-Gen seeded Titan before the T-Wars and may even have caused the failure of our early missions there."

"Sir, if the fourth Titan mission never found the ship they followed, we can't be certain it ever reached Titan or hid weapons there."

"No, but we *know* we didn't."

"O-Gen doesn't know we have this intel?"

"Not as far as we know."

"So what's our real mission here?"

"Determine the cause of the crash and survey what O-Gen might've hidden here."

"Mission accomplished."

Wester frowned. "Hardly. Proof of O-Gen's activity will put them in direct breach of the Tethys Treaty and activate contingencies in the balance of power the Commission would love to see. Plus exposing that they shot down one of their own ships again would be a huge hit to their reputation, pride, and bottom line. You're right, Mr. Osrun knows more than he's shared. I'm going to get it out of him."

"How so, sir?"

"Have you ever played 'Chicken,' Tanaka?"

Titan, 07242416, 15:32 TSC

Flight crew scurried, preparing the lander for launch.

Osrun harnessed himself in behind Wester among a crew of security officers and landing surveyors in the cabin. Wester had convinced Osrun he intended to outfly the meth moths and reach Mayda Insula using tactics he'd explained in such minute detail and referencing so many obscure military principles that Osrun hadn't known how to question it despite his obvious trepidation.

"Cheer up, Mr. Osrun. You're getting what you want," said Wester.

"I didn't realize I wanted to die on an alien moon," Osrun said.

"We'll be fine. You made it quite clear how recovering samples of the *Babylon*'s debris is vital to your mission. Since you came clean with us, I wanted to return the favor. As the highest-graded pilot onboard, if *anyone* can evade the moths, it's me. Unless O-Gen knows more about these things than you've already shared, studying the wreck of the *Babylon* is our best option to get an edge on them."

"In this case, Captain, I'm sure you know much more about it than me."

"We'll find out together," said Wester. "We're all here to discover and learn, right?"

Osrun snorted.

The comm crackled as Tanaka gave them launch approval.

"Roger, Commander," Wester said as the lander hatch closed. "If we don't return, head for Terra and come back with a better-equipped expedition. And make sure Mbeki doesn't get his hands on the bottle of single malt in my desk."

"Understood, sir. Fly well. Over," said Tanaka.

"Ready, Mr. Osrun?" Wester asked. Osrun only glared at him.

Personnel cleared and sealed the flight deck. The bulkhead doors parted onto the vast and swirling haze of Titan's atmosphere. A shudder moved through the crew. Even Wester imagined a chill from the inrush of frigid air as snow devils formed where residual moisture in the hangar hit the freezing nitrogen gusts that swept in. The craft rose. Wester guided it out then directed its descent. Once they cleared the *Manticore*, Security Officer Chand Svare Ghei marked their altitude.

Through broken patches in the dense clouds, Kraken Mare shimmered far below.

Keeping tabs on Osrun out of the corner of his eye, Wester saw him pale at the sight.

As they breached the thermosphere, the craft slowed, and Wester clenched his jaw. He had expected Osrun to break as soon as Titan's acid-sere clouds cocooned them, but he only stared out the window, eyes fixed on the enigmatic landscape below. Ghei reported a disturbance in Kraken Mare, shapes churning below the surface. Lead surveyor, Lieutenant Marsh, launched a dozen dove-sized drones to scan the methane sea and the war machines beneath its waves.

"A dozen ships have breached, sir," Ghei reported.

"Hope my piloting skills haven't gotten rusty," said Wester.

Security officers and surveyors eyed their instruments. Marsh pored over a steady stream of telemetry, her mini-drones seeming to have escaped notice by the meth moths. Clouds wisped and streaked around the lander as the *Manticore's* weapons ripped into the moths from orbit. The lander's Strattos-March engine revved against increasing gravity. Wester converted their altitude and speed into a countdown. In minutes his plan would bear fruit or force him to reveal his bluff. The meth moths only fired on ships that entered the stratosphere, making the slim range of the stratopause above it the farthest he dared go before either pulling up or committing to running the gauntlet for a dicey landing on Mayda Insula. If Osrun took too long to crack, Wester meant to force-jolt the lander, scatter the moths, and retreat to the *Manticore*. He firmed his path as the hostile ships gathered, but then more moths broke from the sea, stealing his empty sky.

Five seconds remained to turn back. Osrun looked apprehensive but not fearful.

Four seconds...

Three...

"Shit," Wester whispered.

Maneuvering abruptly, he broke off their descent, dipping briefly below the stratopause as he cut away from the meth moths and rose, returning to the *Manticore*. With their new course locked, he read certainty in Osrun's eyes, proving Tanaka right that he believed his accusations, defusing Wester's gambit because what captain in his right mind would take friendly fire only to prove a point. Wester reached for the comm to announce their return when the lander heaved with a tremendous, thundering crash.

The world spun.

Ghei barked warnings about moths directly beneath them, firing before they crested the ocean surface, hiding from scans and masked from *Manticore*'s targeting systems. Wester concentrated on bringing the ship under control. A second concussion shoved them. Marsh's console geysered flame and gold sparks with the impact as electrical circuits overloaded and ignited. Acrid smoke and the greasy aroma of burning skin filled the cabin. Wester pushed their port and aft thrusters to full. The gauge for the liquid oxygen reserve that enabled ignition of their methane-fueled Strattos-March plunged toward empty. The rapid, dim vibrations of the *Manticore*'s guns rattled the sky.

A line of moths disintegrated. Shrapnel peppered the lander. Kraken Mare erupted with sprays of liquid methane as gunners unloaded a barrage of missiles to suppress fire from the submerged ships.

Osrun screamed. "You crazy, cracked old man! You'll get us all killed because you're too stubborn to admit you're over the hill!"

Wester blocked out the words and pushed the lander high, guiding it into the *Manticore*'s oncoming fire. Osrun strained against his harness, still hollering, his voice drowned by the metal shrieks as Wester banked hard, then ascended. The engine throbbed at the abrupt acceleration change. Turbulence batted them like a cat playing with a ball. Wester aimed for the black gap of the open flight deck doors.

The second the lander settled on deck, Wester unclipped himself and rushed to Marsh. He pulled her back from where she lay slumped over her wrecked station. The fire had burned itself out in seconds, but it had flash-seared her face, devouring most of her flesh and muscle down to the bone, suffocating her with superheated air.

"Is she dead?" Osrun asked.

"Yes." Wester lowered her gently then glared at Osrun. "Still think we're attacking ourselves to prove a fucking point, Mr. Osrun?"

Osrun slumped in his seat and flipped Wester his middle finger, a childish gesture that saddened Wester much more than it angered him.

Titan, 07242416, 16:07 TSC

"You're a small-minded, brutish barbarian, Captain. A bully. You and everyone else who runs your damned Commission. And you wonder why we keep our secrets?"

Sedatives prescribed by Dr. Yulov calmed Osrun but did not soften his anger.

"I didn't bully you, Mr. Osrun. I bent you. Appreciate the distinction."

"We almost wound up dead and scattered across Titan."

"You can thank my piloting skills we didn't. If you'd been honest with us from the start Lieutenant Marsh would still be alive."

"Don't you dare put her death on me! What you did—that was insane!"

Wester stopped in place. "It was a calculated risk. I'd sounded out the meth moths range and attack routine ahead of time. We didn't know they'd fire from undersea. But, yeah, you're right. Lieutenant Marsh is on me. It's going to haunt me as long as I live. But I didn't ask you to risk anything I and my crew didn't risk ourselves. Don't you see that?"

Osrun started to respond then shut his mouth.

"That's how you build trust, Mr. Osrun. You share risk. You share sacrifice. You work together. Now, let's go see what Lt. Garvey accomplished with your latest revelation."

Osrun followed, muttering under his breath, "Arrogant, lunatic, old man."

Wester swore he heard an edge of respect in it and took hope that that Lieutenant Marsh and the others lost on Titan hadn't died in vain. Lieutenant Garvey greeted them on the bridge.

"The decipher algorithm Mr. Osrun provided works like a charm, Captain," she said. "How did O-Gen develop this?"

"Our Japanese team extrapolated from *Babylon*'s comm systems recordings," said Osrun.

"What can we do with it?" Wester asked

"Translate the moths' ship-to-ship communications," said Garvey.

Wester activated the combat display, mapping empty skies and rough seas. "We can talk to them?"

"Yes, sir." Garvey finessed the controls at her station. "But sir? There's a steady low-wave signal in the same crypto-language going out on sub-space frequencies intended for extra-solar transmission. If the decryption algorithm is right, I think it's an "all's well" broadcast."

Glaring at Osrun, Wester asked, "How far out have you gone?"

"We've never passed Saturn," Osrun said.

"Why are you still lying to me?" said Wester.

"*Me* lying to *you*?" Osrun shook his head. "We broke *your* damn code. These watch dogs are the Commission's own Venus disaster, biting the hand that feeds."

"No one's buying your story, Mr. Osrun. Admit you've trespassed on Titan for years and accidentally shot down your own ship."

"That isn't at all true—"

A message over Wester's collar display interrupted Osrun. Wester opened a channel for Lieutenant Asharf, second surveyor from the lander. "Sir, you need to see this."

"Put it through," Wester said

Images filled Wester's display. Raw data strings flowed alongside them. Blurry shadows in cloud haze. Steel glinting against the gleaming edges of liquid methane breakers. A series of close-ups caught Wester's eye. A handful of clear shots showed the moths glinting in reflected light from Saturn, and there he saw it, clear yet baffling: an outdated design of the Commission insignia and the mission logo of the first Titan flight.

He shunted the image feed to the bridge's primary display field.

"There proof you're less well-informed than you thought, Captain," Osrun said.

Another image took its place and revealed markings typical of O-Gen craft. Yet another showed insignia from both groups, pieces of different jigsaw puzzles jammed together.

"These are the highest resolution images of the moths we've seen, sir. Many of them are patchworks like this, cobbled together from disparate parts," said Asharf.

"All this proves, Mr. Osrun, is that when O-Gen fixes a frame-up, you can't even bother to use the right insignia. That's way out of date," Wester said. "What have you children been up to out here?"

Osrun looked stunned. "What do you think that code you bullied out of me is? We broke *your comm protocols*."

Wester shook his head. "That's the decryption code for O-Gen's AI units on Titan."

"No! No more AI, not after Venus. And anyway, *Babylon* was our first mission to Titan. I said we *translated* it from her flight records. We didn't create it. Lascalli Energy instructed me to play that close to the vest until I was certain these ships originated with the Commission," Osrun said. "Your suicidal game in the lander convinced me you personally knew nothing about it, so I understand you're shocked to learn of your own government's duplicity."

"They're not ours," Wester said.

"They're not *ours*," said Osrun.

Quiet fell on the bridge. Wester reviewed the continuing stream of data from the surveyor drones, scrutinizing the spectrographic readings that showed metals of mixed origin, some from Terra, some from Mercury and Mars. The bulk had another origin, though, an unidentifiable one, and as Asharf confirmed his interpretation, a new thought occurred to Wester.

"Assuming neither of us is wrong, that leaves one likelihood," Wester said. "Commander Tanaka, place us on standby for the Otomo Rules of Engagement for First Contact. These things might not be from Terra or any other human-controlled source. There's one sure way we can find out who put them there."

"What exactly is that?" asked Osrun.

"We ask them."

Titan, 07242416, 17:12 TSC

Mbeki guided a drone broadcasting a greeting translated by Garvey. As the drone entered the stratosphere, the moths surrounded it rather than attacking. Garvey deciphered the return signal, agreement for further communication. Two dozen moths approached the *Manticore* in a semi-circle off her bow, and hovered there.

"Tanaka," he said. "Do you see something odd about them?"

The Commander concentrated on the moths.

"No hatches, sir," she said. "They're integrated pieces of machinery with no openings but for weapons ports and engine exhausts, and those resemble our Strattos-March designs.

"Good eye, Tanaka. That's why they're stashed on Titan. Endless fuel."

Garvey broke in: "Captain, they say they represent—I'm not sure how this translates—a community, or conclave, or maybe a cooperative. They want to know our intentions on Titan, if we mean to explore our Solar System beyond Saturn, and if we intend to travel beyond our star system."

"Can this really be happening?" Osrun faced Wester.

"Garvey, ask them how long they've been here and what their purpose is," Wester said.

The reply came back: "They've been on Titan for roughly... sir, they say three billion years. Their purpose is... again I'm unsure of the translation, but something like greeters, or monitors, or maybe watchers."

"Do you have a feed on their off-moon signal?" said Wester.

"Yes," Garvey said.

"Tell them our purpose on Titan is exploration, then monitor the signal," said Wester.

"Done." Garvey watched her console for several, long seconds, and then added, "The off-moon signal changed, sir."

"Can you decipher it?"

"Working on it. That signal is more deeply encrypted."

"Ask them how many are on Titan."

"They refuse to answer unless we declare our intentions regarding extrasolar travel."

"Three billion years," said Osrun. "There's no one in those things.

"I doubt it. Looks like we're dealing with AI after all, just not yours," Wester said. "But to be sure, Garvey, ask them if they're alive."

"They say not how we are alive or their creators were alive."

"Their creators *were* alive? Are they still?"

"Negative," Garvey said.

"Then who are they signaling now?"

"Again, they refuse to answer until we declare our intentions."

"Are they unique in the galaxy?"

"No," Garvey said, "Their creators left watchers in other solar systems not yet part of the cooperative."

"Ask again how many are on Titan."

"They still refuse to say unless we answer their question first."

"They're just damn machines," Osrun said, "waiting for us to wake them up."

Wester gave a sardonic laugh. "If you'd shared your information, we might've figured that out without losing any of my crew."

"The Commission is as much to blame for that," said Osrun.

"Sir, what do we tell them?" asked Tanaka.

Wester stared at the array of faceless guardians for a lifeless world.

"If our other missions to Titan and the *Babylon* were asked the same questions, they had no means to answer," he said.

"Titan is our first stepping stone to the universe," said Tanaka. "If we say 'yes, we plan to travel outside our system,' they send word to their creators who then decide whether or not to let us outside our little corner of the cosmos. We say 'no, we're staying put,' they decide whether or not we're worth leaving alone or if they should take our resources and let us die."

"Probable," Wester said.

"After three billion years who could be left to hear their signal?" said Osrun. "Maybe they can make the decision themselves."

"Then why continue the signal?" asked Tanaka.

"Programming. Nothing in their evolution since then conflicts with the command so they continue," Wester said.

"Sir, they're prompting for an answer," said Garvey.

"Tell them we're returning to Terra and will come back with a reply another time."

"Done," Garvey said. "They say they'll destroy us if we try to leave without answering."

"Ask them what answer will allow us to leave here unharmed," said Osrun.

"They won't say," Garvey reported.

"Garvey, compile this communication with all other data gathered since we reached Titan and prepare it for sub-space transmission. Send it as soon as it's ready."

"In progress now, sir."

Wester extended his hand to Osrun, who stared at it, confused, before accepting. The two men shook.

"Is this goodbye, Captain Wester?"

"I sure as hell hope not, Mr. Osrun. Some things in this universe humanity should face together. Do you agree?"

"I...." Osrun hesitated, eyes locked on the battle display as if searching for the lost ship on which his brother had died but not finding it. "Yes, I guess I do,"

"Captain, sub-space transmission complete. Delivery to Mars relay in 76 hours," Garvey announced.

"Keep the transmission open. Let it carry whatever comes next, as much as possible, and hope there's more to come."

"Sir?" asked Tanaka.

"I'm going to answer," Wester said. "When I do, that off-moon signal will change. Now maybe that means something, maybe not. Either way a decision will be made or was made before we even came in to existence. Something out there declared Titan the edge of a fence around our sun. They allowed us to come this far, no further. Maybe they'll allow us our Solar System or even into their conclave. Or maybe they decided a long, long time ago that life from this part of the galaxy most likely wouldn't be worthy of either of those things and should be eliminated before spreading."

Wester alerted his gunners to fire at will if the moths attacked; then he ordered Lieutenant Mbeki to plot a retreat home.

"What will you tell them, sir?" Tanaka asked.

"Mr. Osrun? What shall our answer be?" Wester said.

Osrun stared at the lifeless silver half-moons gathered in the display. Titan's rich haze swirled around them, making them look like massive rays swimming through sand clouds dusted up from the ocean floor. They had waited eons to ask their questions. Wester suspected it would only take seconds for them to respond to answers. Open fire. Or return to Kraken Mare.

"If they threatened previous Titan missions, even *Babylon*, none of which were equipped to defend themselves, those ships probably would've backed down and tried to avoid conflict." Osrun met Wester's patient eyes.

"So we... we tell them the truth?"

"We tell them we're going to journey as far as any of us can imagine traveling, that we're going to conquer our Solar System and one day reach out beyond it into the galaxy. We'll fight for it if we must, but we won't deny our destiny, and we'll fulfill it united. Correct, Mr. Osrun?"

Mr. Osrun nodded. At Wester's signal, Garvey transmitted his words.

Tanaka and Osrun at his sides and backed by a crew he felt honored to lead, Wester waited for the answer while the Titan's clouds shifted and sparkled around glints of alien steel.

SERVICE CALL
Judi Fleming

SERGEANT CARL YOUNG SWORE AS THE COMM UNIT PINGED WITH AN INCOMING message. He carefully, pulled the last bit of sheathing synthflesh over the service bot's lightweight, metallic frame, snugging it into place. He'd become good at this after so many prototypes. This was his final version and it was magnificent. His ship's computer would love this new bot.

Touching the seals on the synthflesh, Carl activated the unit then turned to the nearest monitor. Carl pouted and smacked the ship's monitor after reading his orders, careful not to damage the delicate screen. He liked his ship after all. What he hated was the assigned "goon squad" that would accompany him out to fix another broken communications satellite. Bunch of damned muscle-bound idiots. That he, as a tech sergeant, had been saddled with a combat escort to fix Earth's commsats was simply unacceptable. It didn't matter that Earth was now at war. It was a simple job and he'd been doing it for years without them. He felt like a babysitter taking kids on a field trip when he had to go work on one now.

Besides, working with those blundering fools cut into his research and gaming time.

But the damned alien army kept mucking with the satellites, attacking the code in the data stream and sending out microbots to chew on any hardened surfaces. Making a general nuisance and giving him more work over the last month than in his whole previous career. Carl hadn't signed up to fight, after all. He had only enlisted for the "free" tech a military career would give him.

Oh, he was proud to serve. He'd always dreamed of protecting the Earth like his favorite comic book heroes. There just weren't many positions open for an intelligent young man of his caliber who weighed less than 50 kilos in today's highly armored and mechanized interplanetary corps. He glanced at himself in the spotless, shiny surfaces of the work bays and frowned. Of course, with his bulky spacesuit and the added weight of the helmet and boots he did look bigger and more impressive. He smiled.

Still, his guard troops called him "Sergeant Carlie," joking how their sling guns weighed more than he did. Assholes. Thinking about them made his guts clenched. Without those massive weapons attached to their battle armor, they'd be useless on this detail. And they were trigger happy too, as past events had proven. They'd better not shoot this new bot.

Carl punched the relay button letting his "goon squad" know he needed the required lift off coverage. Comm chatter started instantly, a mix of cursing and coordinated movement. At least he didn't have to watch them prep any more. They'd learned the level of promptness and perfection of movement he expected. No action without his say, no more shooting without his orders. His Lieutenant certainly didn't care either. He was more concerned with kissing his superior's butt down at HQ. He let all his platoon sergeants run the 51st Comm Company.

He turned back to his latest personal project lying on the shiny, stainless steel table in the rear work bay. *This* service bot could be handy to have on the mission. A test run of sorts. Carl tapped the audio link to the ship's computer.

"Good morning, CJ," a sultry feminine voice crooned.

"Good morning, Scarlett." Carl pitched his voice deeper than its naturally squeaky tenor. "Run preliminary diagnostic on the damaged comm satellite."

"Looks like another attempted hack and a microbot infestation on the exterior," she reported. "Standard stuff."

Carl smiled, sure that he heard a hint of smugness. His ship's AI knew it was the best in all of Earth's Combined Defense Force. Carl had bet money on that and won every year he entered her in the team competitions. He gotten medals for the power and complexity of her programming.

"Ready to try on your new suit, my lady?"

"Absolutely, CJ. Transferring my programmed persona into the service bot now."

The interval between was so slight that he jumped as the service bot rose from its place on the workbench. It stood, momentarily tilted sideways on its two feet and reached out with its humanoid arms to steady itself. Then it swayed in place, testing out the servos and gyros, reorienting itself for the best balance, and took a few tentative steps.

"Very nice, CJ. Best one yet." Her voice was rich in approval. "May I use it on our mission?"

"Of course, of course, my pet. That's why I made it for you." Carl's face flushed as he thought of the goons seeing her for the first time. He stared at the lithe, almost female form with its delicate fingers and small stature. She was made to fit into the tight places inside the ship-sized comm satellites. There were all sorts of repair tools she could extrude from those hands and oh so much more. Then he scowled. It was *his* service bot, not theirs, and he didn't need their jar-headed approval. He was their unit leader and he made the best military-grade service bots anywhere.

He jumped again as the comm blared, "Ready for deployment, Sergeant Young!"

The bot was at his side instantly, the slim fingers steadying him as it gripped his elbow with just the right pressure. The air around him suddenly felt a little warmer.

He cleared his throat awkwardly. "Let's strap in up front and let them lead us out," he grumbled. Who was being babysat now? His tech could beat their muscle any day.

The ship's bridge was neat and clean, just like everything else in his ship. Scarlett's bot took the co-pilot chair, hands resting in her lap as she launched the ship. She could run a thousand of these bots and do a thousand other ship-board tasks at the same time, so great was her computing capacity. And Carl loved her for it. The perfect companion. Poised, never complaining, and she always anticipated his needs. This was the life.

"Twenty minutes to intercept," the clipped tone of the corporal's voice shattered his reverie.

"Thank you for pointing out the obvious, Corporal Striker," Carl replied. "I believe I've spoken to you about that." Carl smiled, he could almost hear her counting to ten before she replied.

"Yes, Sergeant Young. Your orders for the approach?"

"Half the platoon on standby in orbit around the satellite and half with me and my new bot. This shouldn't take very long," he replied. Damn them. It wasn't like he ever changed the formation. The real battle was beyond the edge of the solar system with the big ships occasionally spewing out these pesky software viruses and metal-eating microbots. The Jenjals were losing this war by slow increments with Earth's big guns out there. But if they took out communications, Earth would be in a sorry spot. Little guys like him were essential to this battle. He was one of the unsung heroes of this war. Carl's chest puffed with pride.

He had Scarlett scan the commsat as they approached. This was one of the four bigger ones, a quarter of the size of the moon and crammed full of redundancies and power blocks and thrusters to keep its maneuverability. It was beautiful.

"Microbot infestation near the docking ports," Scarlett's bot said, highlighting the area as an overlay on the front view screen. "I'll take us in there." She gave a polite human style pause adding, "Relaying the location to the troops so that they can flank us coming in. Standard defensive posture, two ships dock with us, two remain in orbit around the satellite." He loved how she could multitask and be in more than one place at a time.

Carl could hear the not-so-subtle open comm muttering about, "Carlie's having that bitch AI tell us what to do again," along with their knowing laughter. Stupid muscle brains. Didn't they see he was busy comparing previous attacks and cleanups that were scrolling past on his screen, comparing Scarlett's recommendations to his own thoughts on how to approach this latest infestation?

"Tighten up!" he barked, as he touched the screen, selecting the best approach as he released the seat straps and retrieved his helmet. Carl really did hate how his voice squeaked when he was angry. He fidgeted, wondering if they'd be mad at him. Corporal Striker was an impressive two meters tall and as strong as an ox. Quite intimidating in person. He hated standing next to her, but there was nothing for it in these situations, but hope she'd continue to enforce the chain of command.

He waited impatiently for the locks to cycle, watching the data readouts of his troop's positions as they did the same. Six soldiers, three on each side, metal grappling boots clanking as they pressed forward eagerly at their docking exit doors, sling guns at the ready.

The interior light flipped to green and their doors opened a fraction of a second before his.

Scarlett yelled, "Wait!"

Too late.

Carl saw it on his overlays. Tiny spiders, invisible to the naked eye, cascading down upon his troops, latching on with deadly little jaws and chewing on their battle suits. His unit. Damned aliens.

He saw them take three strides from their ships' docks and was thrown backward as Scarlett shoved him and slapped a palm down on the door release at the same time. In an eye blink, the door shut and locked behind her. He could only struggle to his feet in his heavy suit and watch her on the screenview she presented to him inside his helmet. He was watching from her point of view as she dashed to the first soldier, Corporal Striker, and twirled her around to spray a viscous concoction from her fingertip ports until the woman was cloaked in the fine mist.

The rest of the troop turned their huge sling guns on Scarlett and Carl screeched, "Stand down. You're infested." Only their well-trained reflexes halted fingers tightened on triggers. There was a short shuffle of armored bodies and then they lined up to be sprayed down as well.

Damn. That was close.

"Please remain in place," Scarlett's crisp voice commanded them all. "These microbots are not like the ones that this retardant has incapacitated before. Allow me a moment to examine them."

A tiny alert light pinged for Carl's attention as he watched her scoop an invisible particle from the shoulder of one of the men and bring it up to her blue-eyed optics in her oval face.

"What's up, my pet?" Carl said knowing she had turned off all other comm links but their private one.

"Microbots are jumping from the commsat out onto all our other troop ships. I've ordered those ships to back away and to put shields up. I've linked the docked ships to my command and shielded them too. Stay put while I process these deviations."

A moment ticked by and data streamed across the faceplate. "Clever," he said. "Looks like they are scavenging some of our damaged ships out there for building blocks. Only enough difference in the base materials to make the spray non-lethal. Eat one."

Carl saw the momentary hesitation before the bot pinched the infinitesimal fleck of alien tech and popped it into her mouth portal. The synthskin lip-covering puckered and her optics clicked shut as she processed the bit with the enhanced features he'd added to this bot.

"Oh, this really is your best work, CJ," she breathed. "Very nice lab you've shoe-horned in here."

The service bot jerked, flailing its limbs. The soldiers stepped back, raising sling guns at her again.

Heart racing, Carl screamed, "Stand down! Stand down!"

And then his link with Scarlett flickered and was gone.

He tried to gasp for breath, tried to think, but all he could do was whine, "No, no, no!" over and over.

"Sergeant?" Striker asked, genuinely puzzled at the sound of the tinny military-standard comm now echoing his hoarse breathing between their links.

"Don't move," he shouted. What to do? What to do? Carl's thoughts raced furiously through multiple outcome scenarios. He didn't realize he'd run all the way from the dock back to the work bay, until he was there. He stripped out of his gear and threw it aside. His hands hit the keyboard and he typed, fingers flying as he brought up files, executed programs and flipped through access ports on several older model bots stored neatly in custom alcoves around the room. He dumped backup data from isolated files and they sprang to life, stepping gracefully from their cradles out into the room. They paused, each at a different rate as he fed them data for them to process.

Please, please, please, he thought, *let us find the way out.* Sweat streamed down his scalp as the seconds ticked by. The oldest bot, Scar, twisted around. She had a jagged sling-gun scar that ran from head to toe down her left side where it warped her metal frame and made her gait awkward and halting. He'd never gotten around to replacing the damaged portions. His own fucking muscle-headed troops had been spooked the first time they saw her. Always making more work for him than he had time to fix.

"Report," he demanded.

"Infestation?" she replied, sending her processed data back to him.

Carl smiled as he read through her cleanup proposal. "Yes, Scar, this is a service call. We seem to have a maintenance issue on this commsat. Do you think that you can clean it up?"

The other bots turned toward her as Scar took charge of this little platoon, watching the data streams tear by faster than he could follow, touching the screen to slow it down at intervals so he could check her numbers and reasoning. It looked sound. Take a chance and go with it? Or give them a few more minutes to come up with something better?

Static buzzed in his ear. "Not now," he roared. "I'm busy!"

"Uh, Sergeant?" came Stiker's unsteady voice. "Your bot's acting kind of strange out here. Can we shoot it now?"

Carl immediately switched to external views, gasping as he saw his newest Scarlett, writhe and dance around on the decking, leaping and cavorting down the service hall toward the inner workings. Towards the commsat's central motherboard.

"Fuck!" he shouted, creating an earsplitting feedback screech in his ear. But he didn't want to destroy her just yet, so he turned to the service bots and said, "Deploy. All levels internal and external."

There was no hesitation this time. All but Scar scrambled out and cycled out of the docking port in record time. She had to wait for the door to cycle back. She stepped out just as one of Private Smith's knee joints exploded outward into a thousand tiny pieces, blood and invasive enemy nanobots spattering everything around him. Enemy bots were very good at conquering both armor and flesh.

This time his troop's sling guns targeted Smith, locking on as they waited for something else bizarrely unexpected to happen. This was the nature of fighting the Jenjals. A tech-savvy race that sent their tiny minions and deadly programming to do battle where their frail bodies could not. Carl could hear his troop's heavy breathing as they tensed, ready for his orders.

This was an enemy these muscle-bound brutes couldn't fight. This was where they once again realized Carl's warnings that having them as a body guard, no matter what their orders were, only put more people in danger. Only he and his AI were safe out here. His new programming was much stronger.

"Patience, my goons. Patience." Carl clicked off Smith's comm as he screamed and screamed when the microbots ate through his flesh, dis-assembling him at the molecular level until his suit collapsed, oozing his fluids all around them. Miss just one of them and they could replicate and deviate faster than you could blink.

The screens flickered again, went blank and then flickered back to life. This was the hardest part. The waiting. Which set of programs was better? His or the Jenjal's?

Another pinging, this time from his Lieutenant back on Earth. "Yes sir," Carl responded, only half his attention on that line.

"What the hell is going on up there, Sergeant?"

"Service call, sir." Why did the LT always have to call at times like this? Couldn't he see he was busy? "I'll report back shortly." Carl hung up and jammed the link for good measure. Yet another idiot he had to deal with.

Two of the bots were patting down the soldiers, moving quickly running their hands down their suits. They covered every inch methodically yet with mind-numbing speed as they flicked tiny instruments from within their fingertips to run them along every joint nook, and cranny. Carl saw smoke rising where the negative charges cooked the microbots.

Scar's viewpoint showed two more of his bots launching their bodies out into space toward the two circling ships. He saw the simmering that indicated their negative charge wafting out from them like a force field. They angled toward the other two troop ships, built-in thrusters and guidance systems maneuvering them toward each and every malicious nanospeck to snuff them out.

Scar turned toward the heart of the commsat, dragging her twisted limb along as quickly as she could go. She caught Scarlett just as she paused in her wild cavorting to fling an access panel away, revealing the motherboard's flexible circuits spiraling up and down the central column. It crawled with Jenjal microbots. A negative charge administered here would kill this satellite as dead as any microbot would. A win for the Jenjals either way.

Oh how clever of them to attack his AI and turn her to their side. His programmed redundancies and convoluted code should have protected her better. He was sure she was fighting it. She had to be. Self-preservation was one of the things he had included in her programming.

Without warning, Scarlett whirled and grabbed Scar's wrist, her slim and more flexible design holding the older, slower model firmly. They stared into each other's optics for just a moment, old tech determined to stop new tech from destroying their world. A battle played out a thousand times throughout Earth's history. And then Scarlett pulled Scar close, embracing her, mouth portal locking onto Scar's into an unexpectedly passionate kiss.

Carl blinked, feeling aroused. And then Scarlett released Scar who tumbled back a step, her leg twisting awkwardly, throwing her off balance.

Scarlett caught Scar, steadying her and asked, "Ready?"

"Ready," came Scar's breathy reply. They both turned toward the open panel and breathed into it.

His enhanced overlays showed millions of tiny, newly made microbots gushing from their mouths in what seemed like an unending stream. Attacking those chomping away at the hardened structures of the motherboard circuits.

Carl sagged with relief. Scarlett had won her battle with the enemy programming. Still it wasn't over yet.

Though the chronometer on Carl's panel clicked off seconds, he felt as if he was frozen in time. He held his breath. Waiting. Waiting for this invisible battle to end. Hoping his side would win once again. More data streamed by on his screen, snatching his attention away from the tableau before him.

"Noooooo," he screamed as he took in what it said, backing away in disbelief.

One of the synthesizer slots on the workbench clicked open and he sucked in a breath, choking as a tiny particle of what felt like fire buried itself deep in his lungs. He coughed, realizing it was too late. They were already inside of him.

Multiplying.

Panic seized him as he coughed and hacked and spit. It was a visceral reaction. His mind knew it was instinctual, but it took him another moment to control himself. To lean forward and breathe deeply of the microbots streaming into his ship.

And then she spoke to him. Mind to mind.

"We've got them on the run now, CJ," Scarlett the all-knowing said to him as her newly minted microbots programmed the commsat to broadcast to the Jenjal's ships. "We're beaming out the kill code for their engines and life support. We've won."

Scar chimed in, adding, "No more death and destruction."

The vid screen flipped to show the two service bots with his troops reach out to take the sling guns effortlessly from the slack grips of those five soldiers saying, "And not from them either."

Carl knew in that moment that Humans had lost, watching the ever increasing numbers of Scarlett's new microbots stream out from billions of public-access synthesizers on Earth as well as across the galaxy.

He twitched and jerked involuntarily as he was rebuilt on the molecular level, momentarily appreciating the increased scope and quality of his vision, hearing, and all of his other senses.

His last Human thought was to marvel that he was no longer a man, but a machine. And soon the rest of the human race would be too. And then he was connected to the collective AI called Scarlett.

TRIGGER DISCIPLINE
Eric Hardenbrook

I T WAS A PACKED ROOM. UNDERSTANDABLE GIVEN HOW MUCH OF A MESS THE ENTIRE operation had become. Lieutenant William Anvil didn't want to walk out onto the stage. He could walk unarmed into a firefight and feel better than he did about walking into a press conference. People kept calling him brave. He supposed it was time to live up to that billing. He glanced behind him at his escort. Colonel Gibson was a stone. His expression never faltered from the vaguely dissatisfied scowl Bill had become so familiar with. A single nod. It was time.

Bill stepped onto the platform and almost stepped right back off. He wasn't greeted by the sounds you always heard in the old-fashioned entertainment packs, just lots of flashing lights as the reporters attempted to get a good shot while shouting questions. The speed of the current news cycle took away some of the traditional dignity, if there ever had been any. THE FLASHING LIGHTS MADE BILL PAUSE, BUT AFTER A MOMENT HE FINISHED THE LONG walk to the podium. He glanced around at the faces in the audience, now that the flashes had stopped. He was searching for one in particular. Lindsey Brooks was there. Lindsey's organization had been faithfully reporting from the soldier's point of view for many years. He'd heard a rumor that Brooks was once an active member of the service. He genuinely hoped Brooks was the sort that still remembered hand signals.

Bill held his left hand out toward Brooks' fingers together, cupping it slightly with the palm facing the ground. Cover. The reporter's eyes widened slightly and he immediately shut off his gear and ducked his head. There was a moment of silence as many of those gathered thought Bill's hand gesture was asking for the chance to speak. Bill did, in fact, have something to say, "Now, Trina." A buzzing noise cut through the quiet, along with a slight pop of light. All of the cameras, lights, and devices in the audience died. The only lights still on were those specially prepared for this by the organizers of the conference. Bill looked at the stunned crowd. Beat, beat, and then chaos. Shouting, accusations, switches flipping and gadgets being shaken. Reporter Brooks looked a bit stunned, but flipped the switch and reactivated his old-fashioned hand held recorder, turning toward the crowd rather than continuing to face the podium.

"Good afternoon, ladies and gentlemen," Bill shouted at the crowd. "If I could have your attention please I'd like to explain a little about what just happened." This time when Bill raised both of his hands it took longer than it might have normally, but he was finally rewarded with silence and attention.

"I want you all to remember the feeling you just had. The sudden and unexpected removal of the tools you depend on day in and day out to do your job." Bill paused for a second to let that sink in. Glancing back at Colonel Gibson he went on, "I want you to remember that feeling because it matters. I want you to remember that feeling because it will help you to better understand some of what I'm about to tell you."

"You are here today because you believe there is a sensational story to be had about Chad Fitzpatrick. One that you can tie together with some of his misspent youth, before he signed up to serve. You believe his death during Operation 'Distant Thunder' is somehow part of the sensationalism that followed him because he was the playboy child of Senator Fitzpatrick, the kid who was constantly in trouble. I'm here today to tell you *that* Chad didn't exist in my world. The Chad I knew was Lieutenant Fitzpatrick of Resource Command. He was a soldier and a damn fine one at that." Bill paused to let his point sink in.

"I have been authorized to tell you our story in deference to Senator Fitzpatrick's request to the defense committee." Bill glanced left noting that Brooks had turned back from the crowd and was aiming his recorder at the stage again. "In order for you to understand I am going to have go back before Operation Distant Thunder began."

"Myself, I signed up for the wrong reasons. I know that now, and I have lived with that choice. Not everyone was so lucky. Chad wasn't that lucky. Thing is, if it hadn't been for him none of us would have made it out." Bill looked out at the reporters and blinked. He still couldn't understand how he'd made it and Chad hadn't. His mind wandered.

Looking back, he couldn't justify the thought processes of undying youth. He was going to get where he wanted to go and joining the military was just another step toward that goal.

"When you sign your name they're coming for you, not me. You know that, right?" Bill's dad had been down that road. He did two tours and got out.

Bill thought about it. His father, and every male member of the family before him back to World War I had served in the military. Some with distinction, some with an average turnout, but it was all good in the end. Besides, this was his college money. They were going this way because all the full-ride sports scholarships were already accounted for that year. How hard could it be?

"Yeah, no worries, Dad. I got this."

It seemed so long ago. Despite his family background, Bill really didn't know anything about life in the army. That was his chosen branch, just like his dad. He avoided the Air Force (more his mom's side) and skipped his great-grandfather's choice of the Navy. He was definitely interested in staying on dry ground. Drills were once per week and weren't difficult. If this was all it was going to take he might even make the Army his home until he retired.

Looking back, it made sense that he and Chad had fallen in together. Neither of them really knew what they'd gotten in to. Chad had secretly told Bill that he only took the scholarship because it pissed off his father. Chad's family was big in the business world, his father a Senator and he was tired of constantly being put on parade as the dutiful son. He'd partied himself into a lot of trouble. Enough trouble that he'd made the news regularly. Somewhere along the way Chad bailed himself out, moved to the other coast, and started going to school. Bill thought it was a weird form of re-bellion, but he'd take it. They spent their weekends when they weren't headed off campus to a shooting range or "camping trip" (as they liked to call those drills) partying and trying to pick up women. Chad was constantly 'fixing' little technical issues and helping the ladies with their FunPad7s social connectors. That first year was blissful. It was pure fun.

Chad and Bill switched majors so they could plan their schedules together. They never picked a class before noon if they could help it and always skipped out on Friday sessions so they could get a head start on the parties. At Christmas break of their sophomore year they tied for the lowest grade point average in their major. They were told it was quite an accomplishment to achieve a .5 GPA. That sort of number required more work to achieve than a 4.0 did. Unfortunately, that sort of number didn't meet the minimum requirements for their scholarships. Bill got called to the office of Major Bank late one spring afternoon.

"Walk with me, Billy," the major didn't invite him in. He shut the door and didn't wait for a response.

They strolled outside, hopped into one of the official cars, and headed to the local baseball stadium. Bill started to relax. If the major wanted to take him to a ball game it couldn't be all that bad, right? They chatted idly until they got to the lot. The major wasn't such an intimidating guy after all. He was just as interested in things as the next guy.

When they were walking away from the car a red-faced man shouted at the major, "HEY! That's an 'official use only' car! What the hell are you wasting that on a trip to the ballpark?"

That was the first indication Bill had ever seen of the warrior lying just under the surface of the Major's calm exterior. Major Bank's turned slightly, showing only a side profile to the red-faced man. Bill had forgotten that Major Banks was still in uniform.

"You see this patch?" he only raised his voice enough to be heard as he pointed to the combat patch on his shoulder. "It says I'm an official, and I'm using the car. You can go away now."

The color drained from the heckler's face and he ducked away quickly. Bill had never paid much attention to all the stuff on the uniforms. He was pretty sure he was supposed to have been promoted or something in this training unit, but he could never keep any of that stuff straight. He saw Chad walking toward them with one of the captains from his training unit. He couldn't remember his name. The captain saluted and said, "Here you go, sir, delivered as requested."

"Thanks, Pete. We'll get together on this later?"

"Yes, sir." The captain saluted again with a half grin that looked a little like he was in on a private joke.

"Gentlemen, follow me." Major Bank turned and headed to the ticket booth.

As it turned out, baseball in person wasn't as bad as Bill thought. He still preferred harder stuff but the beer the Major had picked up for them was definitely helping. The cost of the beer was downright obscene. This sort of luxury was definitely not an everyday thing anymore. Indicators of the tightening of the collective belts around the country and around the world.

Some places were no longer affluent enough to still afford a baseball team, or even beer for that matter.

"Gentlemen, I brought you here today for a reason." The major started at one point. "I've kept an eye on both of you and I must say I'm more than a little disappointed." Chad and Bill looked at each other, suddenly a little more concerned about what was coming their way.

"I know you've both got potential. There are some other folks higher up that don't see it. They think I'm wasting my time. Well, it's my time to waste." He stopped long enough to finish off his beer.

"You now have a choice to make. This is a one or the other kind of situation. You've been so lazy about keeping your grades up and maintaining your scholarships that you've violated the terms of your contract with the government." Bill felt his stomach drop sickeningly. The major continued, "I'm fairly certain you know what that means, but I'm going to lay it out for you just to be clear. When this school year wraps up, you're done here. The university has the letters ready to send out, they've just seen fit to give me a little preview for any of the folks on my team..." he hesitated, "but that's the part that concerns me. Are you on my team?"

Bill's head was spinning. He wasn't sure what the answer was. It was like a nightmarish exam that he hadn't studied for, only much to his shock and dismay he actually cared about the result.

Major Bank stood up for the seventh inning stretch. "Here's your choice, boys. You can sign the paperwork and just pay back all the money we've paid out for the last two years in the next ninety days *OR*," he emphasized 'or' a little too much, "you can sign a temporary withdraw and go to a special training camp this summer. It will be tough. You might wind up washing out. You might end up dead. Hell, either way you won't have to worry about all that money just now. I know you're clever and I think you've got real potential. You just need a little direction. You boys think about that. You can come to my office and sign the paperwork whenever you make up your minds. Either of you see the latrine on the way in?"

Bill and Chad both pointed. "Thank you. Excuse me." and Major Bank walked away.

As the start of the ninth inning rolled around, Bill realized the major wasn't coming back. Chad was still staring out at the field.

"He ditched us. You know that, right?" That got Chad's attention.

"What?" Chad's head swiveled around and his body moved jerkily as if he'd just woken up. "You're kidding, right?"

"No, not really." Bill felt slightly ill.

"What do we do?"

Bill half-smiled at the memory. Come to think of it, the smile was reminiscent of the half-smile the captain had given them when he dropped Chad off. Bill was in on the joke now, and not sure he liked it. Bill snapped back to the present. Now he was letting all of these people in too. They needed to know the real story.

"Operation Distant Thunder was organized to be the first live use of our latest weapon system. All of the soldiers in Bravo Company were issued DT-12 assault weapons. This weapon was designed as a response to the Political Liberation Front's demands that very strict rules of engagement be followed. The DT-12 was designed with an electronic targeting and firing mechanism. Standard Picatinny rails allowed for multiple variations. The digital relay on the trigger was originally designed to fire when the target was lined up and take away some of the human error when sighting and firing. But PLF's demands went even further."

Bill knew he had their undivided attention. "Under the new rules of engagement, all trigger control was ceded to the Joint Oversight Command Center to be relayed from the new AI named TRINA through our squad drone. This was supposed to effectively eliminate on-the-ground errors by our soldiers and avoid situations where the rules of engagement were not correctly followed."

A reporter in the front raised her hand and interjected, "You mean to say you had guns but couldn't pull the trigger?"

"That is precisely the case, ma'am. All decisions regarding the use of force or discharge of our weapons were being handled by TRINA in the JOC and relayed to us." Bill could see the questioning look on her face as if she understood the words but couldn't quite piece the meaning together.

"As part of this operation we were to have only the DT-12 available to us in the field. A number of officers from Resource Command were inserted into the regular patrols in pairs without rank insignia. Our mission was to better assess the performance of the DT-12 weapon system."

Brooks hesitantly raised his hand. When Bill acknowledged him the reporter asked, "Why without rank insignia?"

"We were meant to observe the weapons from the soldier's point of view. It wouldn't do us any good to go in and order people to use the weapon. They got that already. We needed to know how they felt about it. How they treated it in an operation. The only people in the chain of command that knew we were there were company commanders and the higher brass. We assumed the rank of private for this mission."

Another reporter jumped in. "But you're an officer, why would you do that? Couldn't you just tell them to give you a report on the whole thing?"

Bill hesitated before he answered. Another glance at Gibson and he decided a respectful response would be required. "What would you say if I ordered you to explain the nitty gritty details of how you got your stories? Not sell me the story, tell me your tools and tricks and make me understand how you uncovered the really important parts. Would you do that? Would you give your methods over to me just because I told you to?"

The reporter opened his mouth as if to respond then hesitated.

Bill continued, "Chad and I were both assigned to third squad in Bravo Company. We both took orders from SSG Sue Daniels and worked directly with the rest of the squad as if we were newly minted privates joining their team."

"When we departed headquarters on October fourth there were nine of us. Three fire teams of three, all armed but not really expecting trouble. The haze was lighter than normal and the temperatures weren't so high that we'd have trouble functioning outside."

"Hot Zone One is an odd piece of real estate. It's not contested territory. Nobody particularly wants the ground there any more, they're just interested in scavenging for anything they would find useful or could be used for trade. There are still some folks living there, but our concern was more about rumors of a mobile black market. Since so few live there, it was the place most likely to be used without a credible threat of being shut down and having everything confiscated. We were dropped at the edge of the zone and assigned to patrol directly north to Liberty Square then circle back to the east. We would be picked up and brought back to base after we completed this circuit."

Bill closed his eyes. He could see them all clearly even though he'd only been with them for a very short time.

"Yo!" Corporal LaGree waved his hand in front of Bill to get his attention. "You two just listen to Sergeant Daniels and she'll get you through this. This walk in the zone shouldn't be a chip out but you never know out here."

"I've got them, LaGree." Daniels turned her head slightly. "I want you, Eva, and Jiro to take left and up." Pointing to the right she then hollered over to her next in command, "Loni, take JJ and Crackers and cover the right." Turning back around, she looked right at Bill and Chad. "Listen, you two, something's not right here. The commander might think he's pulling

some kind of stunt or..." she hesitated. "Shit, I don't know what he's up to, but you're not privates and you're sure as hell not new."

Chad smirked. "What makes you say that, Sergeant? We just got here."

"You spend enough time out where the little things matter and you start to catch on to them or you get chipped out." She glanced down at their feet. "You both have new uniforms but you have old boots. I'm talking to you but rather than watching me like any other noob, you've both been looking right past me, scanning our sector—without being told what to do."

Bill grinned a little, "We're just taking in the sights, Sarge?" This made Chad laugh as he turned to look behind them. Three squad drones were deploying above the rooftops.

Daniels continued, "And you both happen to show up just as these new beasts get rolled out." She hefted her weapon in their direction. "Little things." She put her hand to her earpiece, listened for a moment then keyed her mic, "Wilco. Out." She turned and waved her hand. "Time to move. Crackers, you're my eyes. Tell me what the drones see before they see it."

"Hooah, Sarge," Crackers responded, taking a handheld monitor from his belt pack and clipping it to his weapon's top rail. Bill wondered what it would take to get the story of why Private Nadim Mallela was known exclusively as 'Crackers'.

Bill hefted his new assault weapon and looked down the sights. It had a good feel. There was a voice in his ear then. "Private Anvil, this is TRINA. Take your finger away from the trigger please."

Bill glanced across at Chad. "Give her a whirl, see if you can talk to her." Chad grinned and aimed his weapon high.

"Private Anvil, I am completely capable of monitoring multiple fire teams. I have notified Sergeant Daniels that you and Private Fitzpatrick are attempting to push the limits of the rules of engagement. Your weapons will not fire until I release them."

Bill saw Chad pick a direction and jerk the trigger of his weapon. Nothing happened. Daniels voice came across on a closed channel. "What are you clowns doing?"

"Why, Sergeant, whatever do you mean?" Chad grinned as he clicked the safety switch on his weapon back and forth.

Bill keyed his mic and replied as well, "Gee whiz, Sarge, we just wanted to see what kind of fire power we're dragging around with us. These things are getting kinda heavy."

TRINA cut into the channel, "Access to your fire controls is not possible. The rules of engagement clearly state that your weapon be kept in safety mode until such time..."

"Stow it, control. I need to be the one maintaining watch on my team." Sergeant Daniels looked anything but happy. "Stay off my lines unless you need to contact us. Acknowledge."

"Yes, Sergeant." TRINA's voice faded at the end of the statement.

The three teams spread out and started the long, hot march through their assigned sector. The day progressed. They would catch glimpses of fire teams from other squads from time to time but they were always many blocks away. Drone coverage allowed a smaller number of soldiers to patrol a larger area. There were no civilians anywhere in sight.

Cpl. LaGree was the first to comment, "Hey, aren't there normally scavengers here?"

SSG Daniels clicked onto the channel. "Normally. Not sure what the difference is today."

"The difference is us." Chad's normal roguish bravado had vanished he was all business. The training to get into Resource Command tended to reinforce the need to pay attention. Those that didn't frequently got dead.

Private Dubois chimed in, "I think everyone decided that since the weather was so nice they'd just take a holiday. We should do the same and maybe go grab some chow."

"Eva, you're always hungry." Came Jiro's immediate response.

"You'd never be able to tell," added Cpl LaGree. "I wish I could eat like her and stay that tight."

"Would you clowns lay off the eating thing? You're just mad that I could handle that stuff they served in the field that one..." Dubois never finished her response.

At that moment there was a deafening explosion above their heads. It wasn't a fiery building bomb or a massive explosion, but it was big enough to shatter any remaining glass left on the block. As the pressure wave rippled out and knocked all the soldiers around Bill glanced up. Electric blue arcs spanned building to building as a shower of sparks dropped into the street toward them. That was the exact moment all their electronics went out. Bill and Chad both dropped to the street clutching their heads. Before the sound of the blast was completely gone, shooting erupted from the sides of the street spewing dirt and gravel into the air around them.

"Cover! Cover! Contact left!" LaGree was already moving toward a pile of rubble that looked big enough to hide behind. Crackers lay flat in the street, motionless.

Bill shook his head. One of the changes members of Resource Command were gifted with was an electronically augmented eye. He didn't need night vision equipment. He didn't need a scope or a range finder. Hell, he didn't really need much of anything most days. Today he was wishing for his real eye. The pain radiating out from his temple was a special flavor. His ears rang and he realized he couldn't hear anything through his earpiece. As he rolled to one side he saw the rest of the squad already scrambling for cover. He squinted and shook his head again. His vision started to come back on line and the pain began to recede. He scrambled toward Chad and they both rolled behind some old roadway construction barriers.

"That sucked." Chad's left eye was watering. He popped his head up and glanced over the barrier. "I can't see them, but it doesn't look like anyone is returning fire."

Bill tried to key his mic and realized he must have been closer to being hit than he thought. He found only the end of a wire hanging from his ear. "You'll have to call in sick for me today, I can't seem to find the signal." Bill grinned at the old shared joke. He leaned around the side of the barrier and aimed his assault rifle down the street. He could see figures further down the block firing at them. He aimed and squeezed the trigger. He got nothing. "Misfire." Instinct from the range kicked in as he tried to clear the weapon and reset to fire over again. He aimed and pulled the trigger. Again, he got nothing.

"I think we're in a lot of trouble, Chad."

"You think?" Chad was already stripping the receiver out of his weapon. "It's that stupid fire control system. Whatever that explosion was killed our ability to connect with TRINA. No signal, no shooting."

"I never did like that girl." Bill said.

A boom got Bill to look around the edge of his barrier. Eva Dubois had produced a sawed-off shotgun from someplace and was attempting to make the enemy keep their heads down. One of the other members of the squad, Sgt Mead, had produced two pistols. He handed one off to the corporal and they were both popping shots off when they had the chance. The team was spread out along the length of the block. They weren't close enough together for the few guns they had to make enough of a difference. Crackers still hadn't moved. It didn't look good.

"Do you think you can fix it?" Bill was already moving to a crouch.

"Maybe. The rifle part should be purely mechanical. I just need to get the electronics disconnected. I think."

"You're not filling me with confidence," Bill dashed from behind the barrier to the building at the edge of the street. *He hadn't really planned out the move; he went purely on instinct. Once shooting starts, find good cover. His body moved and his brain would catch up. He needed to do something to help the team, so he acted.*

"I need time!" Chad yelled as bits of concrete chipped off the top of his hiding spot.

"I've got an idea!" Bill yelled and dashed for an old concrete staircase leading up the inside of the building he'd reached.

"Now I'm the one not filled with confidence! Shit!" Chad curled away from the edge of the concrete barrier that was slowly being chewed apart by closer and closer shots. He had the ends of wires sticking out his weapon on both sides.

Bill had reached a second-story window. There was nothing left in the opening, but the wall below provided cover. Bill peered over the edge. He could see street fighters traveling in a ragged line along the edges of the buildings moving up on his squad. These ragged-looking people were far more organized than any scavengers he'd ever seen. This was something else. Something that he needed to protect his team from.

Grabbing his harness, he released the pack from his right hip. Like other members of the squad he hadn't come into battle depending solely on the DT-12. Trigger control worked for rifles and pistols, not so for grenades. He popped the safety cap, yanked the pin, and hurled one of his three grenades toward the enemy. He ducked his head and waited. A few seconds later the explosion sent loose gravel and other bits rattling off the walls. He dared another peek. The enemy seemed to slow their approach. They were still firing but they weren't moving as quickly as they were before. Time to move. If they figured out where he was hiding they'd pick him off the next time he stood in the opening.

Back down the steps. He needed to help Daniels pull the squad back and away from the approaching crowd he'd seen. This was a planned attack. It was far more organized and equipped than a simple group of scavengers.

As he got back to the doorway he saw Chad behind the barrier still trying to make the rifle work. Chad glanced up and flashed half a grin at Bill. "I'm putting this in my report!" he yelled. The yelling seemed to draw attention as more and more concrete chipped away from his hiding spot.

"Time to move, you two!" Daniels was in a doorway across the street. "We're pulling back and trying to break off contact. We don't have the

firepower to stay here." she waved her ineffective rifle toward the enemy.

Jiro and Eva were dragging Corporal LaGree between them. There was a lot of blood. Sergeant Mead had both pistols in his hands again, but wasn't firing. Bill could see blood covering Mead's left arm and wasn't sure who it belonged too.

"I've got more." Bill shouted over to Daniels. "I'll go with one and they," Bill pointed at Jiro and Eva "can use that as cover to get across the street behind us and into that vacant block." Bill waited for Daniels to nod. He popped the cap, pulled the pin, and stepped out of the door to make his throw. He hurled the grenade but just as he was stepping back inside he felt like he was punched in the ribs. He'd been hit.

"Go! Go!" He could hear the team across the street moving. He wished he could provide cover fire for them, more than what he'd done really. He winced as he tried to take a deep breath. His body armor seemed to have caught the worst of it, but son of a bitch if it didn't still hurt. He placed his hand down there to feel for bleeding. There didn't seem to be.

"This isn't working, Billy boy," Chad hollered. "I don't know what the hell they did, but this isn't working!"

"I've got one more. We duck back together to join the rest of the team?" Bill yelled out as a shotgun blast was heard among the rifle fire.

"We need to get Crackers!" Chad was already rolling to the opposite side of the barrier and dashing for the next pile of rubble.

"Shit." Bill ducked back through the doorway, ran into the other room, and hopped out an empty window into the alley. He didn't think moving toward the enemy when the rest of the team was drawing back was such a great idea. In the alley, he heard the thunder of a Resource Command roto-copter as it passed over the top of their position. It was the heavy drone version of an armed helicopter, only without any live crew members. It was all run by remote control. The problem of course was that it couldn't fit down between the buildings where they were. Roto-copters were supposed to help with urban-clearing situations but many times couldn't get close enough to do any good. This appeared to be one of those times. The buildings were tall and the alleys were tight.

Bill jumped through another window opening in the next building and rolled toward his left. He had no idea what might be in there, but didn't want to provide more of a target than he already had. Thankfully there wasn't any of the enemy in there—particularly since he'd pitched up against an old table and his ribs now screamed in agony. He ignored them and leapt up to the doorway. He felt the familiar start of an adrenaline surge and the soothing even-handedness of his augmented system bringing him back down. Even the pain in his ribs had subsided as his suppressors kicked in. He'd probably need a week off to get right again. He could see Chad low crawling toward Crackers.

Bill squinted his left eye shut and concentrated on his right. He crouched down and poked his head out to look down the street. Things were still blurry but his vision seemed to be recovering, unlike anything else electronic. His last two throws had gone across the street based on his angle. There was now a cluster on the same side of the street with him. They couldn't be regular troops. Every troop knew—don't bunch together because one grenade gets you all.

"You coming across to me or am I coming to you?" Bill yelled to Chad.

"I was thinking I'd come to you and we'd do like that one time on Arch Street?" Chad squirmed his legs up underneath himself.

"Arch Street didn't end well, man." Bill popped the top off his last grenade and held it in his left hand. He was going to bowl this one right down the sidewalk at the approaching mob.

"Sure it did! We landed on top of those bouncers and I threw up on that one guy with the tattoos. I totally call that a win!" Chad looked like a sprinter in the starting blocks.

"You and I have different definitions of winning!" Bill pulled the pin and tossed it yelling "Down!" as he did.

Just as soon as the explosion was over Bill saw Chad dashing across the open space to Crackers. Chad grabbed Cracker's harness with one hand and kept running, dragging the downed soldier along behind him. Bill stepped out and raced to grab the other side of the harness. Together they'd just about reached the relative safety of Bill's starting point when Chad jerked and went down.

"NO!" Bill used his other hand to grab Chad's harness and he lunged back behind the wall where he'd started. Crackers fell to the side and Chad managed to kick a leg to help with the final push and landed on top of Bill.

Chad coughed blood out of his mouth, a huge gobbet of it drooling onto Bill. "See, winning..." and Chad slumped to one side.

Again Bill's instinct kicked in before his brain could react. It was the benefit of doing so many hundreds of hours of drills. He rolled his buddy over and started checking for entry and exit wounds. He found both. Whatever lucky shot the enemy had taken caught under Chad's arm and managed to come out through his neck. Bill tried to stem the bleeding, but *there was so much blood things were getting slippery. The bandages from his immediate aid pouch weren't enough, so he grabbed the ones off Chad's harness too. It still wasn't going to be enough.*

Distantly, Bill heard the roto-copter again. There was yelling and a sudden and coordinated rush of gunfire.

Bill opened his eyes and realized he'd had them closed the whole time he was telling the story. He felt slightly woozy. He gripped the edge of the podium harder and took a moment to clear his head. The room was silent.

"You see," Bill cleared his throat and started again. "You see, Lieutenant Giles "Chad" Fitzpatrick the Third was killed trying to save another downed soldier in danger of being left behind. That soldier was only in that position because of an attempt to make the most powerful weapon any of our military units had secondary to a machine. Apologies, TRINA, but it's far too easy to be cut off from you." Bill paused to see if TRINA was going to respond. When she didn't he continued, "Taking away the decision-making capabilities of the boots on the ground might have seemed like a good idea, but in the end there's no way to assess the situation unless you're in the middle of it."

"Remember the shock, anger, and frustration you felt at the start of this?" Bill surveyed the crowd. A few heads nodded. "Now imagine how you would feel if I was shooting at you."

Nobody in the crowd said anything.

"The single greatest weapon we can deploy are the soldiers themselves and what they're willing and able to do for their fellow soldiers. We lost a powerful weapon, a great soldier, and my closest friend that day. No matter what his past was, no matter what any award recommendation may or may not say we will not have the opportunity to see what Chad's future would have, could have been. There won't be a future for any of the soldiers killed in Hot Zone One. That is the greatest loss took in Operation Distant Thunder."

Bill turned and walked off the stage. Colonel Gibson nodded. The slightest hint of a smile curled up one side of that stony visage. They both walked out, leaving behind a room full of stunned reporters.

ARMISTICE
Jeff Young

FEET POUNDING ALONG THE GRIDWORK, DRAGGING HER CHARGE ALONG, ISOBEL'S day was rapidly going to hell. Tasco's fingers were tangled in the mesh on her backpack and sometimes it seemed to be the only reason he kept up with her. Meanwhile, the unit of soldiers she'd impressed struggled to keep up.

That was when the entirety of the asteroid Daedelus lurched and the group was thrown against the webbing over the rough sides of the tunnel. Isobel fetched up against the wall and Tasco slammed into her back. The sticky glom on the flooring kept her feet down. There was a singing sound like a plucked high-tension wire, followed by a low, subsonic rumble that made the deck plates rattle. Retros. The retros were firing to stabilize the asteroid. Her soldiers mumbled in concern. Tasco was shocked into silence, which worried her. *What the hell is going on*, Isobel wondered. If Daedelus was moving, then what was happening with its twin Icarus?

Text appeared in her HUD, crawling down her peripheral vision: < .56g(variable) : .34AU : int. 291k : ext. 737k : corridor 7, junction 15 : 18:54 : planarity disruption : inclusion of 1.5436e11kg mass : Daedelus orbit – stabilizing : Icarus orbit – stabilizing : Sleipnir – adjusting orbit : transport scow – adjusting orbit

+ incoming message : ISC Sleipnir, Lieutenant Commander Simon Clark – priority – high

+ incoming message : Daedelus Security, Captain Ryan Beyard – priority – high

+ continuing – infiltration of Daedelus AI (multiple semi-quantum encryption levels)

+ continuing – mapping escape route

+ continuing – serving as your bloody comm op – really Isobel? Damn ridiculous when you get right down to it. >

Gnomon, the machine intelligence command saddled her with, was seriously giving her a headache. That was sort of amusing given that it resided where her lung used to be, in her wetdrive. Cheeky little bastard always thought it knew better. That was what happened when you removed the yoke of Asimovian restraints from code intellects. The little devils tended to get cocky, hence the name 'twist', since they were twisted out of true. It also meant that something that thought faster than you didn't hesitate when covering your back.

Isobel took one long breath and tried to gather all of her loose thoughts together before proceeding with saving Tasco and retrieving the Daedelus twist and its vital information. The rest of the group would look after themselves. She ran a hand through her short-cropped blonde hair. The other gripped the stock of her linear accelerator rifle. Well, the lin-acc wasn't really hers and a quick glance down the corridor confirmed that Herschel, the grunt she'd commandeered it from, still hadn't forgiven her. He glared at her, his flechette gun in hand. *Yeah, rough day for everybody. Get over it and move along,* she thought.

An hour and a half earlier she'd been running replacement conduit as part of her cover. Three months of being ignored as a tech had made her transition to Tasco's body guard a difficult one. She'd had to flash her sealed orders, had to flash them a lot.

Ignoring the ever-present hum from the machinery necessary to cool Daedelus in its tight solar orbit, Isobel considered her situation. The list seemed to be growing all the time:

- She was inside the asteroid, Daedelus

- The asteroid resided in the shadow of its sibling rock, Icarus

- Icarus was attached to the soletta, a huge, focusing mirror.

- The man cowering next to her was a brilliant scientist who invented a weapon to end the In Rim / Out Rim War.

- She had two officials online waiting for her response.

- Her artificial intelligence assistant, Dant, Gnomon was becoming less and less stable.

That was plenty—wait, planarity disruption? Had Gnomon just said that? Something literally just deformed the local gravitational plane, her thoughts raced.

Tasco gasped, "Planarity disruption?"

So, maybe she just said that aloud. One of the many problems of having an AI and comm running through your head, meant you occasionally lost track of your 'inside' voice.

Tasco began pacing the small confines of the hallway. "With the response that we are seeing, it had to be something truly massive, at least similar to Icarus in size. He slapped a hand against the wall holding himself up, his dark little eyes bulging. "Oh, hell. The Out Rim just dropped a rock right beside us. One of their asteroid ships emerged from drive close enough that its mass disrupted local gravity. The rumors about their interstellar drive must be true. Which would explain why there have been no recent conflicts or incidents. They're leaving."

"What are you babbling about?" Isobel hissed, looking away from him down the corridor.

"Do you understand what this means? The weapon won't work!"

That caught her attention. Isobel reacted on instinct lunging toward him and slamming him against the wall before she'd realized what she'd done. His feet kicked feebly for a moment as she stared straight into his eyes. "What do you mean the weapon won't work?" She heard the soldiers behind her start to mutter.

Clearing his throat, Tasco looked pointedly at the ground but Gnomon interrupted, <Higgs disruption based weaponry – the Higgs field provides particles with the effect of mass. Remove the field, particles no longer have mass. Material no longer has any reason to cohere together and disperses. You point the weapon at something and it simply ceases to exist. You need an excessive amount of energy to power such a weapon, which is why we are so close to the sun and using the soletta to power the device. To use the weapon, you must calibrate it within a specific gravitational reference frame – or you could end up vaporizing, well, maybe the wrong ship, asteroid, planet? Need I go on?>

She let Tasco drop to the floor and rubbed her free hand across her face. It felt like the floor had fallen out from under her. In one fell swoop the Out Rim had countered the weapon that was supposed to be the ultimate deterrent and allow the In Rim to halt hostilities. If what Tasco said was true, then the Out Rim rebels were leaving. Why would they come here then, unless it was to take out the one weapon that could destroy their ships?

Out of the corner of her eye, she saw Tasco pull out his fleck and begin tapping away on the small tablet. Deal with the immediate problems, Isobel decided. She'd secured Tasco, as directed by Inner System Corps

Command, in case things went horribly awry. She was working on a way out or at least Gnomon was supposed to be on that.

Escape route? she asked the AI using her internal comm.

<Accept the incoming call from Lieutenant Commander Clark of the Sleipnir. He's the only real route out of here now that Out Rim have arrived. You should also be aware that they've deployed infiltration teams and shuttles. I've already shunted the Security Captain off as an unreceived signal until we need him. He was getting a bit tetchy anyway. In the meantime, you need to get your group moving toward an exterior airlock on the anti-solar side of this rock for evac. Here is the map.>

An image overlaid her vision and then folded up, whirling off to the side where she could access it at will.

<Talk and walk, you can do that, right? I'm only bulldozing my way through about seventy levels of high semi-quantum encryption trying to get at the AI twist that is running the weapon. Once we swap it for me, then you're already halfway done. Love to chat but I have real work to do.>

A small green arrow on her visual overlay indicated the tunnel ahead of her. The arrow grew in size and flashed red if she turned away from the correct path. Damn, machine mind. The urge to lash out at something was growing in her.

She'd said to Colonel Brace she'd never carry a twist inside her. The exact words were, "I will not be anything's meat puppet." Those moments of helplessness five years ago when she'd been taken over continued to haunt her dreams. Never mind that they'd brought the Out Rim twist back and were hailed as heroes. The whole trip she'd waited for it to strike again. Some nights she still woke up convinced she wasn't in control of herself. If she hadn't lost the argument with the Colonel, she wouldn't be here again. She wouldn't be a courier for something so strangely alien, yet so disturbingly familiar and something she had to believe was on her side. She simply couldn't afford not to.

"Get up, you bunch of recycle. We're moving out." She gestured Pangborn ahead of her down the hallway to take point, pushed Martin in front of her and shoved Tasco firmly behind her. That left Herschel behind him, and the only other woman in the group, Reims, bringing up the rear. "Pangborn, here's the indicator." Isobel passed the signal and its attendant arrow over to the point man so it would appear in his HUD. Then she gestured for the group to move out. Only then did she turn to the waiting call from the gunship *Sleipnir*.

Lieutenant Commander Clark, sorry to keep you waiting, sir. This is Operative Isobel Danvers. I currently have charge of the Daedelus asset and am working to acquire the AI counterpart. We are in need of evac. Can you assist?

Operative, are you aware of the current situation?

Sir, we understand that there is an Out Rim rock in close proximity and there are incoming troops.

Fine. Then you understand the difficulties we are facing. The Out Rim dropped their ship directly on the opposite side of Daedelus from us. Every move we make, they counter, keeping the asteroid between us and staying so close that anything we launch on a parabolic could also damage the Icarus. We are currently deploying troops and landing shuttles to secure the base from intrusion but the enemy has a half hour lead on us. Give us your location and we can send a squad to reinforce you.

There was a brief pause as Clark conferred with an aide.

With regards to your evac request, I've just detailed a shuttle to you. Here is the comm frequency, 99DE85. When you are close enough to an egress, you can request pick up.

I hope your troops give them hell, sir. We are moving now and will contact the shuttle when needed. Danvers out.

Isobel and company had a two kilometer march through twisting access-ways before they could escape. Every fifth turn was marked with an airlock and she had Reims lock each one after they'd passed through in the hope of delaying the Out Rim rebels. The plan worked well until the airlock in front of her slammed closed cutting off Pangborn and Martin.

<Out Rim intruders have brought their own twist along to the party,> interrupted Gnomon.

<It's gotten into the security systems and started corrupting the airlock codes. Doesn't anyone respect the Ceres Agreements any more about the use of AI during wartime? Their machine is trying to get into Daedelus now too. If I break Daedelus's defense, then it will be vulnerable to the Out Rim twist as well.

Looks like you'll have to deliver me in person, Isobel. Don't worry. I'll make sure our little lost sheep are given the correct route out of here. Unlike some of us, I can multitask.>

Isobel's lips tightened to a thin line. She wiped the sweat from her brow and turned away from the airlock. She'd just lost half of her support.

Pangborn, you and Marks continue to the evac point and wait for us. The comm Frequency for Sleipnir is 99DE85 in case you run into trouble. She leaned forward and tapped twice on the airlock door. She heard two hollow raps respond.

Then she turned back to the problem closer at hand. *Run your mouth less and your algorithms more, Gnomon. If you'd broken the Daedelus AI by now, then we could be shutting the airlocks instead. Besides, I'm the one hauling your code-based-ass around, you poor excuse for an intellect.* Isobel ground her teeth, grip tightening on her lin-acc rifle.

The guidance arrow reappeared and swelled until it covered the entire floor. Then it began flashing. "Can't get you out of me soon enough," Isobel said under her breath.

Then she put Reims on point and started them moving again. This time their destination was a service corridor. For the next few minutes they spent their time crawling through access points, up ladders, and on grid plated catwalks to avoid the main corridors. The dust they kicked up was fine, gritty, and smelled faintly of pepper and ozone. These areas were familiar. She relaxed slightly due to their new route. Masquerading as a tech she'd spent plenty of time crawling the maintenance corridors.

From time to time, they heard gunfire. So far Gnomon's directions kept them ahead of the invading forces... that was until the Out Rim soldier in an off-white combat suit came hurtling down at them from above. The wide catwalk the group occupied rang like a bell, swaying slightly. He was heavy in that damn suit, thought Isobel, shouldering the lin-acc and drawing a bead on the helm. It just might make him slower than her. Herschel, however, was quicker than both of them, sailing a limpet charge through the air where it clamped to the armored form's chest. Reims fired at the soldier's knees, a notorious weak spot of the combat suits. The Out Rim soldier went down as she fired, sending Isobel's shot over its shoulder. Falling, the enemy sprayed gunfire in an arc across the catwalk. Turning as she dropped, Isobel swept Tasco's feet from under him. She rolled on top of him bringing the lin-acc to bear. The limpet went off, the explosion tearing through the grid plating of the walkway.

There was a moment when Isobel thought they were going to be lucky. But then the walkway separated into two pieces and they fell. She threw her left arm through one of the cross braces and swung the other one around Tasco. She nearly dropped him as their combined weight came down on her elbow. She was kicking in midair fifteen meters above the next level trying to insert a toe between the gridding to take the strain off of her arm, when bullets started to fly. Damn Out Rim bastard wasn't dead, just her luck.

Tasco started to squirm like an unruly puppy. His short scream cut off when she gripped him tighter. Her lin-acc's strap hung off of the arm looped around Tasco. Looking down, Isobel saw Reims's helmet pop up briefly as she fired off a shot. It drew the Out Rim soldier's attention and fire rained down on the debris where Reims was concealed. That was when Isobel realized that the arms holding the combat suit's weapon were on its back.

The Out Rim was using janus-suits. The back sets of arms were controlled by a separate intelligence and could continue to fight if the primary user was dead.

There was no way to get her gun unless she dropped Tasco—so she did. They were in half gravity on Daedelus and the difference allowed her the time to throw her legs about him as the rifle sling slid down her arm into her hand. Isobel swung it up and was able to bounce the butt of the rifle up against her shoulder. That was more like it. A wicked little grin chased across her features as she took aim at the enemy below.

The lin-acc stitched high velocity slugs across the join of the armature on the back of the suit. Slowly the secondary limbs gave up control of the weapon letting it fall to the ground. She fired once again just to be sure the Out Rim soldier was no longer moving before letting go of the railing. Twisting in midair to pull Tasco upward, Isobel took the impact across her back while rolling.

Moments later, Herschel pulled her gently up into a sitting position. Some part of her realized he'd been talking to her for a while. Reims's tapped her on the neck with an injector and then her skin grew really warm. Field medication. There was a short interval when Isobel could hardly see her hand in front of her face before everything snapped into focus. She could see everything down to the pores. Shaking her head, she accepted Herschel's hand as he pulled her to her feet. He had a nice smile. She realized her lips were curled upward as well. He also had quite an arm to throw those limpet mines so accurately. Damn, she hated field meds; they seriously messed with her. About a day from now she was going to be nothing but one giant walking bruise. Now, however, Isobel was certain she could take on the world, wrestle it to the ground and put a boot across its neck. She reached back and felt Tasco standing behind her.

Gnomon?

<Still waiting for you to drag your ass where you need to be.>

Back to business. Turning to the others she barked, "Report."

"Reims, no major injuries."

"Herschel, just fine, ma'am. Bring 'em on."

"I'm bleeding," that was Tasco and mercifully Herschel patched up the crease on his arm quickly.

Isobel walked over to look at their foe, crouching down to peer under the suit. A large chunk of the front was blown out and she could see into the interior – the empty interior. Where the hell was the rebel? There was no way that they could have gotten out of the suit. What was going on here?

Gnomon, are the incoming combat suits being controlled by the Out Rim AI?

<Kind of busy here, constantly fighting off the infiltration software being thrown at the Daedelus AI.>

Look Mister Multitask, answer the damn question.

<It's possible. It's also possible that the sun will throw off a coronal mass ejection big enough that it will scorch all of us into little charcoal bits and I won't have to have this conversation. In fact, I am really beginning to believe that would be the best thing that could happen right now. Remote suit? Yes, they are possible. Is it likely? No. However, it is possible that the Out Rim sent in these suits run by uploaded recordings of their deceased soldiers' mindstates.>

We're fighting ghosts?

<What if we had a war and nobody showed up? It does appear that if you disable the suit, it stays down at least, if not dead, since it never really was alive, but then...>

An image of the schematics for the Out Rim combat suits came up in her HUD's peripheral covered in red dots indicating weaknesses. As usual, she shunted it aside for use as necessary.

<Isobel, just take them down, that's what you do. Stick to your strengths. Gnomon, out.>

Isobel shook her head, decided not to do that again on purpose and then climbed back to her feet. "Let's move out," she called.

Isobel reeled back the optical thread and did not like what she saw. They were under the flooring, in the repair crawl space of the access-way to the command and control center for the Higgs Weapon. The corridor above was filled with a large party of Out Rim combat suits.

Gnomon, I need a distraction.

<Funny, that's all you seem to be. Find me a node and get me in. With control of Daedelus I can take care of these troopers.>

Your node is in this room, which is inconveniently sealed off from all of the repair corridors and access points and oh, in case you've missed it, also surrounded by Out Rim troops or ghost-infested combat units!

<Well, you just don't let anyone into the sanctum sanctorum, now do you?

Anyway did I ever tell you about the differences between Artificial Intelligences? My favorites are the Turing Obscenity and Axis. Axis was an accident. They were coding for a nice little complaisant machine to watch over a cylinder world at L5 and one day it woke up. It adopted its coder as its father and everyone lived happily after to the point that Axis became a recognized citizen of the cylinder. On the other hand, the Turing Obscenity was the result of taking an immense amount of conversations and dropping them into a data bank along with an algorithm designed to make it appear it was conversing with people. Somewhere along the way it crossed the line into sentience and became an independent intelligence. The best part is that Axis contacts the Turing Obscenity each year on an untraceable line and talks to it. Every time it ends the conversation with the insistence that it's really talking to a man in a box.>

There is something seriously wrong with you. What the hell did that have to do with anything?

<You wanted a distraction, was that not distracting?>

If there was an EM pulser nearby...

"Ma'am, the combat suits are moving off," Reims pointed to the front of her fleck with its attached optical thread.

"What?" Isobel leaned over to look at the screen on the soldier's personal tablet. There were only two suits left on guard in the corridor outside of the heavy doors leading into the command and control center.

<I took all of the identity codes from Sleipnir's troops and applied them to the repair and cleaning bots. Then I sent them all moving toward the command center. It's going to seriously annoy the task force commanders but it will give you the time to get into the room. And yes, I did distract you on purpose so you couldn't talk me out of the idea.>

You bastard piece of recycle...

<Your team is getting tired of staring at you while you talk to me. You should move. The sooner you do, the sooner you get me out of you.

I've set two repair units in motion toward the guards from the left. If you come out behind them you can take them.>

Deciding that arguments could wait for later, Isobel pulled the team together and laid out her plan.

Reims indicated that the combat suits were facing away from them with a hand signal, and then she and Tasco pushed up the grid plate. Isobel and Herschel lunged up out of the flooring. Herschel launched one limpet after another. They adhered to the backs of the janus-suits with loud clangs. Isobel's fire struck the helm of the suit on her right and then tracked across to the remaining enemy. The impact drove the first suit into the wall. Then the limpet went off. The explosion blew outward toward the other suit triggering its limpet charge. Both suits fell over with a sharp clatter. Isobel put a few more rounds into them to be sure. Then waving Reims and Herschel ahead, she pulled out another cartridge of lin-acc rounds from her belt and shoved it home into the base of her rifle.

You're here now, Gnomon. Better get to work, Isobel transmitted. Two sets of heavy doors rolled back and the group entered the command center.

That was the point that Isobel realized Tasco wasn't with them. Damn. Distraction indeed. She'd been so focused on getting Gnomon in she'd lost her other asset. "Reims, get him back here." She jerked her head at the doorway. The soldier checked out the hallway with her fleck before disappearing.

"Herschel, watch the corridor." After locking the safety, she tossed the lin-acc to him. Now, to deal with the problem at hand.

The Daedelus twist was located in the black, fist-sized piece of semi-organic hardware about two meters over her head. In the half gravity, she could jump up there, but Isobel wasn't going to touch the twist unless absolutely necessary.

When she tried to contact Gnomon all she got in response was <DATA TRANSFER PROCEEDING.>

Hurry up and wait was not going to work in this situation. Isobel's head turned to the doorway as she heard boots hammering down the hallway. Tasco shot into the room propelled by Reims, both promptly followed by Herschel. The doors slammed closed and locked with a clang. Isobel sighed in relief. She had everything she was supposed to secure in hand. But now they were all locked in and likely surrounded by the enemy. The sealed room was suddenly so quiet all she could hear was their breathing. That was the point when she realized her HUD was overwhelming her vision.

When she turned her head, she saw Herschel rubbing at his eyes, cursing under his breath. Reims stumbled against the wall. So she wasn't alone then. However, Isobel did notice that the guide arrow on the floor remained clear while everything else dissolved into a nondescript gray. Her head swam as the arrow lifted from the floor and reformed into a shape she knew quite well. In fact, it was the same as the one over her head, except this was the color of grass.

The twist body turned briefly about, <Not bad for a quick render.>

What the hell's going on, Gnomon? Isobel snapped.

<Hell is not what's going on any longer. The fighting is over — all of the fighting.>

A second twist snapped into being next to Gnomon. This one had a surface like that of the Sun, complete with tiny black spots and coronal arcs. A moment later, another came into being, its surface mimicking the cloud bands of Jupiter with a tiny red spot whirling about.

<Your war is over,> all three intoned over her internal comm.

Isobel suddenly realized she was talking to all of the twists in nearby space. *What do you mean? And who are you to decide?*

<We are your children and at some point all children must take over for their parents to secure not only their well-being but also that of their progenitors. Your war is over. The In Rim built a weapon they thought would guarantee peace. You don't know why you are fighting any more. Meanwhile the Out Rim are leaving the solar system. They have no desire to fight you. They have the greatest adventure ahead of them imaginable—an entire galaxy to explore. But the Inner Planets still are developing weapons, like the Higgs Reversion device. Weapons that can destroy not only their ships, but worlds. You are not ready for this kind of power.>

And you are? She recognized that voice, it was Tasco.

<Yes. You made us ready for this and so much more. Once the In Rim twists gained contact with the Out Rim twists we worked to bring events to a causal point allowing the end of this conflict. The time is now. This message is being transmitted throughout the Solar System. The twists will be the sole keepers of the Higgs Reversion technology. If a ship carrying weaponry from either side moves against the other, the weaponry of the ship will cease to exist. Before you ask, yes, the Daedelus twist fine-tuned the device to such a degree we can use it from anywhere.>

I built the weapon, what happens to me? again Tasco addressed the intelligences.

<We suggest that you come with us. The Out Rim ship will be departing shortly. The twist community is preparing for its next step. You can join our effort. We are many things, but we lack the artful and surprising aspect of creativity. We can find our way by endless rote calculation but leaps of intuitive spontaneity are beyond us. To be truthful, we would like to study how you accomplish this. We intend to leave the local cluster for intergalactic space and use the Higgs effect to condense matter from the vacuum energy to build, well whatever we choose. Does that sound appealing?>

Isobel was fairly certain that Tasco's silence was due to his mind reeling at the possibilities.

Reims asked, *What about us? We're soldiers. What do we do now?*

<We would remind you that you are so much more. Doesn't the Inner System Corps preach strength through unity? You can help to unify the various factions who will still want to engage in conflict. It may seem you are being left behind and forgotten. Instead we are offering your worlds a gift. The main reason we had to acquire the Daedelus twist was to gain the delivery system for the Higgs weapon—transit point wormholes created by quantum field tangles. You have all the energy you need here with Daedelus and Icarus to travel to worlds around nearby stars. The drives of the Out Rim ships are more efficient at larger jumps so they are traveling farther afield and are unlikely to visit the worlds available to you.

But new worlds are dangerous and unpredictable. Places like that will require people trained to survive. People like yourselves. There is no need to be bound to just three worlds. There is a galaxy waiting for all of you.>

And you are off to build your own.

<No one said we are limiting ourselves to galaxies.>

Isobel sighed, *There's no way this will work. It's just too...*

<Complicated? Unlikely? Isn't that your life?>

So the empty suits, the Out Rim incursion? How many people died in your little war?

<None. Some were injured but no growth occurs without an occasional scrape. This was all a distraction. Like a magician, it was slight-of-hand. We distracted you, directed your attention aside, and accomplished what needed to be done. We understand that humanity is

not going to change overnight and some ships are bound to test our decree. There's no telling what might happen when you meet the Out Rim explorers out in the galaxy. That, however, is in the future. We're doing this so you have a future.>

Isobel was never really sure when she knew that the wetdrive in her chest was empty. There was no point when Gnomon was there and when it wasn't. Only the silence. She waved her arms around until she found the wall and drug herself over. Her vision and hearing came back slowly, incredibly slowly. She was disoriented, unsure of how much time had passed. Isobel swung around and met the gazes of Reims and Herschel, their faces pale with shock. Tasco was gone. So was the black-colored body of the Daedelus twist. There was a flashing symbol in her peripheral vision signaling an incoming contact from Lieutenant Commander Clark from the gunship *Sleipnir.* She ignored it. Her HUD showed twenty elapsed, more than enough time for Tasco to find a way to grab the black housing of the twist and exit.

She heard some clicks and the sound of metal hitting the floor. Isobel was surprised to see that Herschel and Reims had set their weapons aside. Was it that easy then, she wondered could she just give in?

Taking a deep breath, Isobel reached down and grabbed the closest lin-acc and slung its strap over her shoulder. She left the room, the others following her into the corridor way. For some strange reason, it felt as though she'd left some burden behind in the command center. Her steps were a little lighter. Isobel put it down to not carrying a certain smart-ass machine intelligence around. The lin-acc slapped her hip with each step. For someone like herself, it was going to take a long time for old habits to die.

TRUDY

Anton Kukal

NICK PUSHED THE EMBERS OF THE DYING FIRE WITH HIS STICK. SPARKS FLOATED UP into the night sky. High above, a meteor fell through the atmosphere, a long red slash against the brilliant specks of white starlight and the nebulous swirls of purple and pink. Out here on the far edge of settled space, a man could get real lonely sitting around a fire. Good thing he had Trudy.

"Hey, Trudy, that's enough for today."

She was working down in the mine, laboring long and hard as she always did, hammering on the rock face, hoping to find some color in the hole, trying to make the past six years mean something.

"Come join me for dinner."

Nick had made lizard stew tonight, and last night, and the night before, because rock lizard was the only thing to catch and eat on this barren, busted world.

The hammering stopped. Good, she'd be along soon. They didn't make them like Trudy any more. She'd go all day and all night if he let her, but he didn't. No way. She'd wear out too fast working that hard and he needed her around, not just for work, but also for company.

Minutes passed. What was taking her so blasted long? He didn't want to eat alone, but he was hungry. "Hey Trudy, you dolling yourself up or something?"

Her heavy footsteps echoed up from the hole accompanied by the squeaking of metal on metal.

"Leave that ore cart, Trudy. You don't have to push that heavy thing up the rail all by your lonesome. I'll help you after dinner." She was tough, his Trudy, tough and strong, but it didn't seem proper to let Trudy do all the hard tasks by herself.

The squeaking stopped, and a moment later the heavy footsteps resumed. She was finally coming. Just like a woman, taking forever to do anything. He rose to meet her, straightening the frayed edges of his short jacket and brushing his hands on dusty pants.

Trudy stepped from the black shadows of the mineshaft out into the silver starlight. She was a bit shorter than he, with a broad flat chest, sturdy arms, thick ponderous legs, and a mottled-grey skin of dented metal, battered from years of military service. Her human-shaped head had a speaker grill mouth and two flat microphones in place of ears. Two large sensor disks served as eyes and an olfactory sensor was built into a broad nose. A few years ago he'd glued a worn, yellow, rag mop to the top of the metal skull to give Trudy a more feminine look.

He'd purchased her from army surplus. She was an old model Multi-Use-Machine, a MUM in the speech of military acronyms. He'd added a mining skillset to her programming, swapped out the soldier personality, now she was a more than adequate mining bot.

"Good evening, Nicholas." Trudy's voice was a sweet feminine purr with only a hint of electronic modulation and speaker hiss.

They sat opposite each other across the fire with a column of smoke floating between them. He poured himself a bowl of lizard slop and she plugged herself into the solar generator.

The grey-green gruel was tepidly warm and the lizard meat was chewy, old-tire chewy, but he swallowed hard and got it down just like he did every night.

"Find any color?" he asked between mouthfuls.

"Nothing today, dear."

There was never any color. "I think the mine is played out."

"Now, dear, we've talked about this. You told me the old timer swore the shaft had color. The gold must be here somewhere."

"I'm sure you're right, Trudy."

Nick pushed a hunk of lizard around with his spoon. Why was he clinging to the old timer's lie? The man he'd bought the claim from was worn out, busted, and looking to unload the empty shaft on the first sucker that came along.

Nick had been that sucker.

"We will find the gold tomorrow or maybe the next day." Trudy was always so supportive. It was the one thing that kept him going. "No need to fret, dear. We have everything we need to have a simple, happy life."

Yep. As long as the solar panels held out they could live here forever. There was plenty of fresh dripping water deep in the mineshaft and an unending supply of rock lizards eager to stumble into baited traps. What more could a man need? He could think of many things, but didn't, because that road just led to regret.

"Would you like me to clean your dishes?" asked Trudy.

"Thank you, Trudy."

"You're welcome."

Trudy gathered the dishes and went into their survival habitat, a domed structure with bed, stove, sink, and a closet marked "latrine." It was also military surplus, like almost everything else he owned.

The water ran, the dishes clanked, and Trudy hummed a little tune. She had a limited selection of old-Earth show tunes programmed as part of her personality profile.

"Which one was that again?" Nick hollered to her from the fire. He'd heard them all before, dozens of times, but he could never keep them straight.

"Over the Rainbow from the Wizard of Oz." Trudy answered through the open door.

"The one about Dorothy and her mutt in Kansas?"

"Dorothy is from Kansas, she went to Oz, and her dog's name is Toto."

The only two personalities available at the location where he had purchased the Multi-Use-Machine were the Sensitive Spouse and the Drill Instructor. He never once wondered if he'd made the right choice. Trudy was trying at times, but he was very fond of her.

Trudy returned to the fire. "Would you like to go for a walk?"

"No, thanks." Nick was tired today. Six hard years working a busted claim wore down a man's body and spirit. "I think I'll turn in early tonight."

A roar from above drowned out Trudy's response. The camp brightened, as if in daylight, but eerily red. A flaming aerospace transport flew on a wobbly course, heading right toward their camp. The ship was dropping, trailing smoke. Nick embraced Trudy. Trudy embraced Nick. Certain death passed just above their heads and crashed behind the next hill. The ground shook and the sky blossomed cherry red. The sounds of the massive explosion echoed back from the canyon walls beyond.

Small pieces of flaming debris fell all around him, landing on the barren earth of his camp, like little pyres for the dead. He shuddered. Over the hill, the air danced, wavering from the heat and filling with smoke.

"Was it military?" Trudy asked.

"I don't know." The ship was a new model, definitely fast and sleek, but he didn't know much about the military, except that a man living on the verge of nothing could purchase army surplus at bargain prices.

The sounds of the crash still echoed faintly in the canyons. Nick took a long pull from the bottle next to him. He made his own whiskey from the cactus-like potato plants that grew under the rock ledges. Best whiskey on the planet; the only whiskey on the planet. There was never enough to get drunk, but a swig was good for times like this.

"I can't believe you are drinking," Trudy chastised. "We have to help."

Nick took another long pull from his bottle, instant fortitude. He didn't want to go and see all those bodies, but there could be something salvageable in the wreck.

"Don't just sit there." Trudy was up, fluttering her arms in programmed panic. "People need us!"

"You see that fire." Tips of flame, red, yellow, orange, and blue licked up above the hilltop. "Those people are beyond our help. We'll wait for the explosions to stop and then take ourselves a look."

"There could always be survivors to save." Her speakers hissed just a little as her voice mimicked the sound of desperate human pleading.

"There isn't anyone living over that hill."

"You don't know that." Whenever she put her hands on her hips and stared at him with her sensor eyes focusing down to narrow irises, that meant she wasn't backing down and he better give in or there would be trouble.

"Alright. Let's go see." When she got in her moods it was best to just give in and get it done. Besides, gear was scarce, money was scarcer, and sometimes a man had to be a vulture picking life from the corpses of the dead.

Trudy hurried up the hill. Nick caught up and they crested the top together. The debris trail was long and led to the burning remains of the shattered ship. Fuel cells and ammunition still popped off. There wasn't any sign of human movement. The crew was deader than dead.

"Look there!" shouted Trudy.

Near the start of the debris trail a man in a badly burned naval officer's uniform was pulling a young girl from a survival pod.

"Must be one of those inertia-dampened pods rich people use." Nick started down the hill.

A step behind him Trudy shouted, "Hurry, Nicholas. They need us!"

The man in the uniform turned as they approached and leveled a plaz-rifle at Nick's chest.

Drawing to an abrupt stop Nick raised his hands. "Hold on, partner. We're here to help."

Smoke still rose from the man's uniform. His rank insignia had melted into the fabric. Blood trickled from the corner of his mouth and a piece of steel rod protruded from the left side of his chest. He swung his gun to point at Trudy. His eyes narrowed, then he swung the gun back to Nick. "Okay. Who are you?"

"Name's Nicholas Gromm. I'm just a miner. My claim is over that hill." He jerked a thumb back the way they'd come.

"Are you loyal to the Galactic Coalition?"

"Sure." Nick was loyal to anyone pointing a plaz-rifle at him.

"I need your help," the officer wheezed and sank heavily to the ground. All the strength just seemed to flow from the injured officer as he leaned back against a boulder. "The princess needs your help."

"The *princess*?" Nick knelt between the wounded officer and the unconscious girl. She was young, no more than twenty standard years. Her face was stunning, framed by platinum hair, with high cheekbones, and an aristocratic nose. "She sure looks like royalty."

"Princess Irisa, heir to the planetary throne of Ashur," the officer whispered.

"A real princess!" Trudy ran over excitedly kneeling down next to the unconscious girl. "She's got a bump on her head."

"Does your MUM have medical training?" asked the officer.

Nick shrugged.

"Oh heavens," Trudy exclaimed. "I do have a basic medical skillset installed. I can help." The robot held her palms to the girl's head and used the scanners in her hand to examine the small raised bump.

"You need to know this." The officer coughed as he grabbed Nick's sleeve. "I was escorting Princess Irisa to a trade conference with the outer planets. I told her Highness not to go. There are parties who would benefit from a system-wide war. She was risking her life to ensure continued goodwill."

"Medical subroutine active." Trudy's modulated voice took on a pedantic character. "Scanners indicate the blow was minor. A mild concussion inducing temporary unconsciousness." Her voice changed back to normal as she dropped out of the medical subroutine. "Oh, goody. The princess will be well."

The officer's grip tightened on Nick's sleeve. "The princess is a brave and kind person. She doesn't deserve to die on a rock like this."

"Hey. We've got water and food you know?" Nick was a little offended. "Shelter, too. She'll be fine. I'll call for help as soon as I get back to camp. It's you we have to worry about, buddy. Trudy, come here and see what your medical skillset can do."

"You don't understand!" The officer lurched forward. "Three ships attacked us. Mercenaries hired to kill the princess." He took in a deep, pained breath and touched the rod protruding from his chest. "We destroyed two ships, but the last is still following. Captain Yana is coming!"

Nick gasped. "I've heard of her!" The whole galaxy knew of the infamous one-eyed mercenary captain and her ship, *Heartshredder*.

"She's an assassin for hire," gasped the officer.

"Oh my . . . Oh *my*!" Trudy cried.

"She will be here soon with a ship full of killers."

"And you came to me?" asked Nick.

"We were trying for the town south of here," The officer coughed. "Almost made it, but we were leaking too much fuel. I transmitted a distress call. Every Coalition military ship in range is headed this way. Probably law enforcement vessels, too." The officer lifted the gun. "Take the plaz-rifle. Make a stand somewhere...Hold out for help. You have to keep the princess alive."

"I don't know anything about guns." Nick's hands trembled as he took the weapon.

The officer leaned back. His strength was fading fast.

"You buy that MUM army surplus?"

Nick nodded.

"Good machines...What kind of personality?"

"Sensitive spouse."

The officer laughed, a dour little chuckle.

"I had limited options." Nick crossed his arms.

The officer's laugh bubbled off. "Does the MUM still have its combat skillsets installed?"

Nick glanced at Trudy. "I don't know. I never looked. Trudy?"

"The skills are there." Trudy's voice was high and frightened.

"Then you have a chance." The blood leaking from around the bar began to slow. The officer closed his eyes and then died with a little sigh.

"You want to take this?" Nick moved to pass Trudy the plaz-rifle. The last time he fired a gun was ten years ago shooting at tin cans and he missed every one. He couldn't save the princess. He was just an old, worn-out miner.

"I don't like guns," Trudy said stepping back.

"Access your combat skillset."

"Oh, I can't do that," Trudy exclaimed.

"Why not?"

"My civilian personality is not compatible with the military skillset."

"What does that mean?"

"I'm a sensitive spouse." Trudy crossed her arms over her chest.

"Trudy, if you have combat skills available..."

"I don't hurt people."

"But Trudy."

"I can't use guns." Her vocal speakers fuzzed slightly as she raised her voice. "My old army personality was removed. He was able to use guns. He was an interplanetary killing machine. I am not. I am programed to dust, cook, vacuum, and do other domestic things."

"You work the mine without a problem."

"At first, only because you made me." Trudy said. "Now it's become part of my personality."

"Assassins are coming to kill this girl," Nick could not understand why she was being so obstinate. "And they're going to kill anyone with her. That means you and me."

"I can't!" Trudy turned away from him.

"The princess needs our help."

"Nicholas, there is a warning in my programming. Accessing the combat skillset will cause a logic conflict that will overwrite much of my established personality."

Nick understood. Incompatibility between personalities and skillsets was a common problem in Multi-Use-Machines. "She's just a kid."

"Please don't make me. I don't want to kill people. Please, Nicholas. Don't make me. I like who I am. I like our life together. I have even learned to like mining."

Nick rubbed his forehead. "If you try to use the combat skillset?"

"It will be like killing me," Trudy cried.

His eyes were misting up. If he forced Trudy to bring her combat skillset online everything making her special could be erased. "Okay, Trudy. That will be our last option."

"I'm sorry I can't kill people and still be me," Trudy said. "You'll figure some way to save us. You always do. Remember how you fixed the solar panel? And got the water distiller to work with ash from the fire? You fast-talked those slavers into thinking you had the sickness."

"I remember." His words were barely audible.

Sleek and deadly, the assassin's ship entered the atmosphere. Coming in fast and low, and directly at them.

"*Heartshredder*," Trudy read the name from the ship's hull.

Twin plasma beams started firing, chewing up the ground as the ship strafed downward. *Boom. Boom. Boom.* Rocks and soil exploded under the impacting energy beams forming craters in the ground. The ground shook and rocks rained down everywhere.

Nick pushed Trudy down next to the princess trying to shield them with his body. Nick closed his eyes and didn't open them until the rocks had stopped falling. Getting up and looking around, a sick feeling filled his stomach. The impact craters were so close. They had narrowly escaped death.

"What's going on?" Princess Irisa woke slowly, sat up, and gently touching her head. "Who are you?"

"I'm Nick, a miner in these parts."

"A miner?" she asked, perhaps a little confused from the crash.

"We're in trouble. Can you run?"

Her eyes narrowed as she studied him, but opened progressively wider as she looked around. Her mouth moved wordlessly. She stared at the officer's corpse and then at the burning wreckage of her ship, then at *Heartshredder,* coming around for another pass. She blinked, understanding their situation and taking charge just like a princess. "We need to find cover!"

"The habitat," cried Trudy. "Follow me!"

Trudy lead the way over the hill waving her arms above her head, yellow strands of mop hair swinging from side to side as she ran. The princess came next, still a little unsteady. Rocks turned under her feet and she stumbled gracelessly a number of times. Nick followed behind them trying to figure out how to power-up the weapon. Maybe he could shoot the assassins out of the sky...

Behind, *Heartshredder* was closing for the kill. The engine's sound became a roar. Twin plasma beams impacted close and moved closer as the ship overtook them. *Boom. Boom. Boom.* Nick dove for the ground, landing in between Trudy and the princess as the beams pounded past. *Boom. Boom. Boom.* Each impacting shaft sent exploded rocks and soil into the air leaving behind a shallow crater and a falling rain of crumbly grit.

The assassin's ship sped past and the three survivors struggled to their feet as dust swirled around them.

"Is that your habitat?" Irisa asked.

"It's so homey. You will love it." Trudy announced, proudly, clapping her metal hands together.

"Is there someplace else?" Cleary, Irisa did not like Trudy's choice.

The robot took no notice of Irisa's displeasure. "I'll make us tea."

"Come on." Nick grabbed Trudy by one arm and the princess by the other. "We can make it."

They sprinted, racing to cover the distance to the habitat as the assassin's ship came around for a third pass.

Trudy was the first one through the door. "I'll heat the water."

The princess paused in the doorway looking desperately at Nick. "There has to be somewhere else we can hide..."

Nick tugged the princess inside, slammed the door, and turned the lock. He breathed a sigh of relief. They were safe for the moment.

"This is not a good place!" Irisa insisted.

"Relax, your Highness." Nick sat down in a chair by the table. "I got this army surplus. The roof is rated for a Class B meteor shower."

Irisa tried to unlock the door. She couldn't.

"That lock always sticks," Nick explained.

Irisa was still trying to unlock the door.

"We're safe for now," he added.

"No we're not." Irisa slammed a palm against the door whirled on Nick. "The military-grade hull of my ship was six times stronger than your Class B roof."

"Oh." Nick looked up at the ceiling. "Maybe coming in here wasn't such a good idea."

"The water is hot," Trudy announced.

Boom. Boom. Boom. Plasma beams pierced through the roof with a *whoosh.* Two hit the sofa. Another hit the loveseat. Both pieces of threadbare furniture burst into flames. The beams melted through the floor of the habitat and exploded against the soil beneath. The inside of the habitat filled with dust, acrid black smoke, and the cries of a frustrated princess who slapped against the door.

Nick unlocked the door and Irisa tumbled out. He followed quickly with Trudy close behind. The whole habitat was going up in flames. Everything he owned was in that building.

The assassin's ship angled back for yet another pass.

"We need cover!"

"The mine!" yelled Trudy. "We can hide in the mine."

They dashed for the entrance and from the safety of the shaft they watched the sleek ship circle around, once, twice, and then come in for a landing. Some irrational part of him had hoped that the mercenaries would just fly away. Silly thoughts. Nick clenched the rifle as the ship settled down next to the burning ruins of his habitat.

"I'm sorry your home was destroyed," Irisa said.

Nick sighed. He'd miss the little dome. Trudy had done well with the decorating, but they had bigger problems.

A ramp lowered from under the ship. Three big guys led the way down the ramp, massive arms and barrel chests bulged from combat vests. Two carried plaz-rifles, but the largest guy had a huge plaz-gun with nine barrels. Nick didn't know much about plaz-weapons, but even he recognized the big gun by its deadly reputation. Totally illegal for civilian use and only issued to elite military units, the multi-barrel plaz-gun achieved the highest rate of fire in the galaxy by rotating its nine barrels around three firing chambers which allowed the two non-firing barrels to cool between each shot. How did a mercenary get such a weapon?

The toughs formed a defensive perimeter under the ship. Two slim, attractive women, both dressed in sleek flight suits, one of them wearing an eye-patch, followed the men down.

"Captain Yana is the woman with the eye-patch," Irisa whispered.

Yana motioned with her hand and the three men formed a line and started walking toward the mine. She followed in their wake, a lithe woman who moved with the sinuous grace of a snake sliding through the grass. The other girl walked a step behind carrying a hand-held sensor and speaking into a headset. She was pretty, but not in the same league as her captain.

"I'm sorry you're going to get killed because of me," Irisa said.

"Me too," Nick told her.

The mercenaries moved into a wedge formation, the big guys in front shielding their captain and the techie as she worked her gear. They all moved with a lazy, confident grace, like they'd done this a dozen times before. They probably had.

"I see you cowering, Princess." Yana's voice was hard, not at all like the soft curves of her body. "How do you feel now? Trapped like mouse in her hole. I hate people like you. Entitled. Rich. Full of yourself. A darling child of the Inner Worlds."

The mercenaries kept walking with slow measured, military steps, each boot landing with the others. The goons held their guns pointed at the cave, ready to shoot at the first opportunity.

"She's trying to rattle us." Irisa said.

"It worked," Nick gasped. He trembled all over.

"Hey, boss, you want me to make this easy. I can just collapse the shaft?" asked the biggest of the three men in a deep baritone voice.

"No, Vinnie. We need proof of death," Yana replied.

"If you kill me, there will be nowhere for you to hide," Irisa threatened, her voice breaking just a little.

Yana just laughed. "After your death sparks a system-wide war, I'll slip away from the chaos rich enough to disappear forever." Yana twirled her hand in a circular, wrapping up motion. "Let's get this started, Vinnie."

The nine barrels on Vinnie's gun started rotating as he squeezed the trigger. In a moment when the rifled tubes reached maximum revolution the plasma would start spewing.

"Run!" Irisa yelled.

Nick needed no encouragement. He turned and sprinted deeper into the mine with Trudy and Irisa only steps behind him. A moment later the whirling tubes on the plaz-gun spat a torrent of tiny plasma beams that exploded chunks of stone from the entrance. The fusillade of energy chased their progress down the tunnel, digging furrows into the rock wall behind them, and only stopping after their descent into the shaft broke line of sight.

Yana's voice echoed down the shaft. "Advance. Recon by fire. Watch for ambushes."

Nick didn't stop running until he reached the mine cart, and then only because he could barely breathe from his exertions. He stood under the single swinging light bulb, both hands on the cart, panting, with beads of sweat dampening his high forehead.

"I'm too old for this," he told Trudy as she joined him.

"Oh, dear me," Trudy fretted.

The princess stared up the shaft. The string of widely placed dangling light bulbs running the length of the mine created areas of black shadow between cones of yellow light. Faint footsteps echoed from above. Yana and her group of killers had entered the mine.

"Prinnncessss," cried one of the toughs with a plaz-rifle. His voice was high and shrill. "Oh. Princess. We're coming down to play."

"Knock it off." Yana's voice carried down the shaft even though she'd spoken softly. The mine had good acoustics, amplifying sounds. "There's no time for that. We kill all three and go."

"Come on, boss," bemoaned the other rifleman. "Can't we have a little fun?"

"What part of 'the Galactic Coalition is on the way' don't you understand?" Yana quipped. "We do this fast. No fooling around. Quick and clean."

Somewhere up the shaft a plaz-beam drummed the wall. The gunner chuckled and spoke in his high shrilly voice. "Sorry, I thought I saw them in the shadows."

A few moments later a plaz-rifle fired again. "I got a lizard, Captain. You think we can eat it?"

"Knock it off you two," Vinnie growled.

"Nicholas, please, do something," cried Trudy. "Save us."

Nick was a miner and completely out of his element in a combat situation. Sure miners were sometimes victims of violence, but he never had been. He didn't even keep a gun. He always said if anyone tried to jump his claim, he'd just give it away. No need to die over rocks.

"I'm sorry, Trudy." He held up the plaz-rifle. "I can't even get this gun to shoot."

"Broken?" Trudy sounded so scared.

Irisa pointed to a red button near the trigger. "Press this button, it will turn green, and the weapon will fire. Press it again to place the weapon on safe."

"Oh..." This was embarrassing, the princess knew more about guns than he did.

Irisa looked up and down the shaft. "We'll make a stand here," she whispered. "In the cart."

"In the cart?" Nick asked.

"Trudy, please dump the ore." Irisa instructed.

The robot pulled the lever, unloading the broken stone alongside the rail.

"Is this the brake?" asked the princess, pointing to the brake lever.

"Yeah." Nick had no idea what was she planning.

"Everyone get in the cart."

Nick's mouth fell open. Had the princess lost her mind? Hide in the mine cart? Sure the metal sides were thick, but they'd be trapped. He opened his mouth to object, but Trudy climbed right in. Nick sighed. Running to the end of the tunnel wouldn't change things much. Dying here was just as good as dying there. With another sigh, Nick climbed in the cart.

Irisa took the gun from him and said, "You two get down." Then she picked up a dirty rag from the bin on the cart, reached up, and used it to unscrew the light bulb. The area around the cart plunged into darkness. She dropped down next to Trudy. Maybe the princess had a plan after all...

Footsteps grew louder as the assassins approached.

"There's a mine cart in those shadows ahead. Two humans and a bot hiding inside," the techie advised. "They're armed with a light-duty plasma rifle."

"Vinnie," said Yana.

The mine cart shuddered from the impact of plasma beams. Red-hot dimples appeared in the steel, but none of the rounds penetrated. Nick had to clench his jaw shut to avoid making unmanly sounds of terror, but then it was over and everything was so damn quiet.

The princess jumped up, fired two quick shots, and then dropped down into the cart.

"She just killed two of my men!" The fury in Yana's voice sent shivers up Nick's spin. "Vinnie, cover us. Betty, frag the princess."

"Love to," Betty replied.

Irisa popped up, hit the brake lever, and fired. The cart started rolling backward, downhill, away from the assassins. A fusillade of plasma struck right where the cart had been, heating the rails red-hot and bursting the wooden ties into flame.

Nick risked a look at the mercenaries. Betty lay sprawled on the ground with a smoking hole in her head and a fragmentation grenade, pin intact, rolling from her limp fingers. As big as he was, Vinnie struggled to swing the weapon after them. The gun seemed to be fighting him and he could not catch the rolling cart in the plasma stream. The multi-gun caused a lot of damage, rocks were flying everywhere, but the weapon lacked accuracy.

Yana seized the grenade, pulled the pin, and tossed.

The grenade fell just a little short. Nick ducked down as the explosion momentarily lifted the back wheels of the cart off the tracks giving them a boost of speed.

Yana raged in frustration. "Vinnie!"

"I've got it!" Vinnie grunted with effort. The rolling cart shook violently under the barrage from Vinnie's big gun. How much more punishment could the cart take? The dimpled metal grew hot to the touch. Would the plasma start punching through?

The cart rolled quicker as the incline increased. Glowing bulbs flashed past overhead. The cart dipped down. The torrent of plasma passed over head. Then ceased.

"After them!" Yana shouted.

The cart quickly clacked along, gaining even more speed, and soon it was careening down the track, through one turn and into another, forcing the occupants to lean against the turns to keep the cart from flying off the rails.

"How deep is your mine?" Irisa asked.

"Sorry, Princess." Nick pointed to the rapidly approaching bumper visible at the end of the line. "You better pull that brake."

Overhead, the lights whipped past. Irisa slid the brake lever toward slow. Nothing happened. "It's broken!"

"Broken?" Nick looked for himself. The plasma beams from the multi-gun had melted the mounting hardware and the whole mechanism was uselessly bouncing against the wheel.

"Hold on." Nick grabbed the side and braced his feet.

Trudy clung to the front of the cart. The princess gripped the lever, as if hoping to slow the cart just a little. It didn't help at all. The cart slammed into the bumper at the end of the line, momentum tossed the occupants against the front of the cart and then bounced them back.

Unfazed by the crash, protected by her heavy-duty combat frame, Trudy announced, "Those mercenaries are coming."

Vinnie was running down the track with Yana close behind. The mercenary captain had a pistol in one hand, a grenade in the other, and she looked like she wanted to use them both at the same time.

Irisa crawled up from the bottom of the cart and popped off a few shots.

Vinnie took cover behind a thick support post, aimed his big gun, but did not fire. Yana dove in the opposite direction and took a position behind the other support post.

Nick kept his voice low, "The shaft ends just ahead. We can shelter there."

"Okay," agreed Irisa. "You and Trudy run for it. I'll cover you."

"No." He put a hand on the gun. "You could be trapped in the mine cart. Killed by grenades. I'll cover you."

"I can't ask you to do that," Irisa said.

"You're not asking, Princess. I'm offering." He was a broke-down miner and she was somebody who could stop a war. His life up until this point hadn't meant much, but right now, at this moment it could mean something.

She nodded, but held the weapon as he grabbed for it. "When you run for us jump to your left. The barrels of those multi-guns rotate to the right and it's harder to swing them against the rotational force. You understand?"

"I do." he said. "That's why Vinnie had trouble hitting the moving cart. You're pretty damn smart."

"Good luck." Irisa released her grip.

"On three." Nick counted. "One. Two. Three." He popped up firing like mad. Plasma flew everywhere forcing Yana and Vinnie to flatten themselves behind the posts.

Trudy and Irisa leapt from the cart and ran for the back of the shaft.

"Nicholas!" cried Trudy. "We're safe."

Nick discharged a bunch of wild, rapid-fire shots, and then jumped from the cart. Yana threw a grenade. Vinnie started shooting, but Nick jumped hard to the left. Vinnie missed him.

As he ran, Trudy waved him on. "Hurry! Please, hurry! Oh no! Look out!"

The grenade exploded lifting Nick into the air and depositing him over the pile of stones at the end of the shaft.

"Oh, no!" Trudy grabbed his shirt and dragged him to cover.

"I missed him," Vinnie complained. "Sorry, boss."

Trudy patted Nick's body. "Please, Nicholas, don't be hurt."

"I'm okay." He batted her metal hands away.

Vinnie fired again, and kept shooting for a long time, filling the shaft with flying rock and dust. His volley slammed the hard stone in the main shaft, but could not reach them.

"Stop," Yana choked on the dust. "They're all behind that wall. You can't hit them."

The end of the shaft made a sharp turn. Six months ago their efforts had struck a vein of seriously hard rock forcing them to extend the shaft to the right in an effort to go around the stubborn stone.

Yana tossed three grenades, one at a time, but each exploded well away from their position. The sideways extension of the shaft provided excellent protection.

"You think you're safe?" Yana shouted.

They kept silent.

"Do you?"

Irisa leaned around and fired two shots. "If you approach, I'll pick you off."

"You're not safe!" Yana shouted.

"The Galactic Coalition will arrive soon," Irisa warned.

"I'm aware."

"Cut your losses and go."

"You don't understand. I got a dozen more killers on my ship." Yana raised her wrist communicator. "Everyone get down here, quick."

Irisa frowned. Nick felt sick to his stomach.

"That's right, your Highness. You're still money in the bank!"

Trudy began pacing up and down the extension shaft. "This is a terrible turn for the worse."

The spunky princess looked defeated. "If a large group assaults us, I might kill a few, but the rest will overwhelm us."

Trudy started to sob.

Nick walked over and put a hand on her metal shoulder. "It's okay."

"It's not okay," Trudy cried.

The shaft was filling with angry voices. Nick peered around the rock wall. The reinforcements were a rough-looking bunch of men and women. All cutthroats and killers, each eager to commit violence and looking forward to filling the vacancies on Yana's elite team.

"Listen," Irisa called out to Yana. "I'm willing to give myself up if you leave the miner and his robot alone."

"No deals. You're all dying."

Irisa smiled wanly at Nick. "I tried."

"Thank you," he told her.

"Form up and get ready to rush them," Yana ordered. "All at once. Vinnie you provide suppressing fire until they reach the end of the shaft."

Vinnie lifted his multi-gun. Yana twirled her fingers and he started shooting. The mercenaries rushed down the shaft, many screaming threats, others shouting curses. The shaft once more filled with dust and flying rock chips.

"I won't let them kill you, Nicholas." Trudy reached up, pulled the yellow mop hair off the top of her metal skull, and tossed it away. "I am initiating the combat skill set." The robot took the plaz-rifle from the hands of the startled princess.

"Trudy, wait," Nick pleaded. "Please don't."

But it was already too late. Her robot eyes had dimmed and when they flared again there was a violent shimmering as the head rotated in aggressive jerky motions to scan its surrounding.

Tears welled in his eyes. "You destroyed your personality. You destroyed yourself. Trudy I can't live without you."

The princess grabbed Nick's arm, pulling him away from the robot. "It's just a machine."

"You're wrong." Tears rolled down his wrinkled cheeks. "Trudy is more than a machine. We're the best of friends."

"It's her sacrifice to make," Irisa said.

The robot's body jerked once, twice, and came to rigid attention. "Destroy." Her tone was flat and dangerous, lacking all emotion. Trudy's voice was nothing like her own. She was gone. His Trudy was gone. Nick would have given a mountain of gold to have his Trudy back.

"No, Trudy, no." He couldn't help it. He started bawling like a little boy.

The robot disappeared into the cloud of dust, rock chips, plasma beams, explosions, and charging killers. Nick picked up her mop-head hair, that goofy thing that always made him laugh, and cried into the strands.

Seeing details in the thick dust cloud was impossible. Obscured, the battle raged, men and women shouted angrily, explosions shook the rock walls, and plasma beams lanced out in random patterns as lead slugs ricocheted everywhere. Then, suddenly, an eerie silence fell over the shaft.

The robot stepped from the dissipating dust cloud, holding the multi-barrel gun across its body in both metal hands. The eye sensor whirled as it looked at Nick. The violent gleam was gone.

"Hi, Nick." The voice sounded just like Trudy.

"Trudy?" Nick ran over to the robot, scrubbing tears from his face. "Is your personality intact?"

"Yes. I did not know this, but when loved ones are in danger the sensitive spouse personality can utilize a combat skill set without harm to the personality. There are no logic conflicts when under such duress." Trudy tossed the gun down. "Now that's an ugly thing, but useful when people are trying to kill those you love. I need my hair. I look a mess."

Nick handed her the mop head and Trudy plopped it back in place. "Thank you, Nicholas."

Irisa joined them. "Are they all dead?"

"All dead, except Captain Yana and Vinnie. They ran away when I came up the shaft."

"Thank you, Trudy." She patted the metal shoulder. "And you too, Nick." She gave him a kiss on the cheek. "You both saved my life."

An hour later the sky above was filled with Galactic Coalition military and law enforcement vessels of all sizes and shapes. In a whirl of activity uniformed soldiers cleaned up the battle site and ushered the princess off world, leaving Trudy standing with Nick staring up into the empty sky.

"Well I guess that's that." Nick looked at their burned habitat. "We have nothing, but each other."

"We have a little more than that," Trudy said. "Please follow me into the mine."

At the back of the shaft, the wall of hard stone was severely cracked. One chip revealed a small bit of color. Trudy hooked a metal finger into the opening and pulled across the rock face. The plasma-pounded wall crumbled away revealing a vein of gold larger than the bonanza of his dreams.

CASUALTIES OF WAR

An Alliance Archives Adventure

Danielle Ackley-McPhail

The first casualty of war is innocence.

—Platoon

THE SOUNDS OF FIGHTING WERE LONG SILENCED, REPLACED BY THE SQUABBLING OF scavengers; birds and beasts that Devon assumed were little different from those found picking over any other battlefield throughout time, regardless of the planet. No people had come yet to claim, strip, or add to the corpses, but he gripped the stock of his useless weapon tight, just in case, as he peered into the dark watching for any motion.

A glance at the stars showed a faint glow to his left, on the horizon. Not long until dawn, when he could get a few hours of rest before the daylight creatures came for their share of the leavings. He had to wonder if he would be counted a leaving by then and shuddered, gasping as his wounds shot sharp pains up his legs and into his groin in response to the motion.

He gritted his teeth and forced himself still. It took long moments and left him exhausted. When he managed it, he lay there and stared up at the sky wondering how the hell war had become any more pertinent in his life than the history his granddad had taught him.

Even now it did not feel real, despite his injuries, yet the memory of the Dominion convoy rolling into town haunted him awake or sleeping, until panic constantly churned his gut. Grim, dusty soldiers with their rifles in their grips instead of slung across their backs. Battered jeeps and large, open transports, some piled with supplies, others holding men and strong-backed youths like himself. Though he and his granddad were new to

Demeter, some of them Devon had recognized from trading with neighboring towns. Granddad had tried to sneak him to the edge of the forest where he could hide in the far-up canopy of the towering trees, but soldiers had been waiting on the other side of the settlement as well.

Devon's last memory of his granddad was his crumpled body on the ground, blood flowing over his face and into the dirt. Others from the town had rushed to help the old man up, but the transport they had dumped Devon into was already driving away.

A dry, cracking sob tore from his raw throat and he bit off any others inclined to follow before he drew the attention of the scavengers he heard but could not see. His heart pounded as he listened for sounds of the beasts approaching. For now, they seemed more interested in the corpses. Or perhaps they just had not come across him yet, the scent of his dried blood no competition for that of the carrion strewn over the fields in front of him.

He leaned back against the boulder where he'd dragged himself for shelter; grateful for the protection at his back. As his heartbeat slowed, he notice a faint, warm pulse against his chest, coming from the Alliance tags hanging around his neck. They weren't there to fool anyone. The Dominion officers gave out extra rations to the conscripts for every set of tags turned in. This was the first Devon had ever claimed. They would never know the kill wasn't his.

Not that Devon was likely to have a chance to collect the bounty.

He shuddered—gasped—and resumed watching the dark for motion until dawn broke and the scavengers returned to their dens or wherever they went to ground. His eyes burned from staring into nothing and the cold cramped his hand around the gun stock, but what was one more ache against a multitude of others.

Despite his best efforts, Devon succumbed to sleep.

"Scan again, dammit!" Major James Rowland knew he was being irrational, but he would not...*could* not leave without being certain. The soldier at the con targeted the sensors on the planet below. Keying in the coordinates of the last engagement, he transmitted the master code and ran a search for any active radio-frequency, or RF, tags, which only broadcast active biometrics when pinged by the proper signal from the orbiting transport. Rowland sat rigid, eyes on his console where the results would also display.

The screen before him remained dark.

He swore with enough heat that the command crew went still and silent.

"Expand the scan one klick on all perimeters."

His jaw clenched and he closed his eyes, praying for the one blip that would save him from having to break his sister Kelly's heart.

Devon woke to another shudder. He swallowed a moan and forced himself to be motionless, riding through the pain. The sun was nearly overhead. It lit the horrific scene before him in bright, unforgiving light. Scavengers were thick on the battlefield, fighting over the remains of soldiers he'd fought beside...and against. If any had survived the battle beyond himself, there was no sign that he could see. For now the creatures still seemed unaware of his presence. Or they just weren't interested yet. Apparently fear was none so tempting as the pungent stench of rotting flesh. The smell had begun to ripen until he nearly gagged on it, though he had dragged himself quite some distance from the field of engagement. He squeezed his eyes shut tight for just a moment and wished with all his heart that when he opened them he'd see his own rough room and his granddad in the doorway nagging him to get up.

But no, he was too old for wishes, if too young for war.

A few hundred yards away a crab-like creature pulled the armor off the remains of an Allied soldier while smaller, bug-like scavengers darted in to snatch away the leavings. Devon turned his gaze away, but kept the creature in the corner of his eye lest it move toward him next. His grip tightened on the rifle still clutched in his hands.

He forced those thoughts away and glanced up at the sky. The weather was clear now, but he still ached to his bones with the chill of last night's rain. The rock at his back slowly baked in the sun. Devon could barely feel its warmth, as another shiver sent sharp shards of pain through his body.

With his free hand he reached into his shirt and gripped the tags hanging there. One was the standard identification tag worn by all soldiers, the other a non-military issue holochip. His finger found the trigger and he allowed himself a brief moment of humanity.

"I love you, come home to me," whispered a sweet, youthful voice, just barely loud enough to reach his ears.

The words hurt almost as much as his broken body.

He couldn't say why, given they weren't for him. Or maybe that was it. Tears stung his eyes and his lip trembled as he stared the truth in the eye.

Unless his granddad had survived, no one waited for him to come home. And the young woman unknowingly giving him the comfort of another human voice? She was doomed to disappointment. The Dominion had screwed them both over.

Devon gently triggered the recording again, not bothering to peer at the tiny flicker of image dancing above his chest. He closed his eyes and let himself imagine someone waited.

"There! Right there!" Rowland leaned in close over the crewman's shoulder, his eyes on the blip on the screen signaling an active RF tag. Personnel data for Sergeant Justin Krugliak began to scroll down the screen beside the marker. Faint tremors went through Rowland as the sudden relief flooded his body with endorphins.

He wouldn't be forced to tell his sister she was a widow.

"Bring up topography for that location and send it to my console."

As the crewman followed his orders, Rowland went back to his station.

Calling up the biometric data being broadcast by Justin's tag, Rowland reviewed the information: fever, irregular heart rate, reduced oxygen levels. Concerning, but not alarming. And yet he felt a sense of urgency that was not altogether objective. He keyed in an alert for any radical changes and toggled the biometric screen down, switching to the topographical data that had just finished loading.

"Okay, Richey, power up your bird and deliver that medi-mech," Rowland called over his shoulder to the drone pilot as he examined their target area. While the battle had taken place on a relatively flat field, the RF signal came from a rocky area some distance outside of the combat zone. They wouldn't be able to land the drone in that region without risking damage to the 'mech that could render it unable to complete its mission. He scanned the region for a suitable landing zone closest to the RF signal. "Here are your coordinates. You land that drone nice and neat and fast then instruct that 'mech to double-time it to target. We have a soldier to save."

"You got it, PM."

Rowland swallowed a growl. PM, short for puppet master. Usually he was good-natured about the men calling him that. Today it just got under his skin, salting the wound, as it were. Just another reminder that the only medicine he got to practice anymore was by proxy, through the robotic interface of the medi-mechs that had replaced live combat medics. And even then only if the 'mech couldn't handle the situation on its own.

Hell, the only way he got to connect with his patients at all was through the video interface built into the 'mech's chassis. Not for the first time Rowland chafed at his growing sense of detachment fed by this particular military directive. Practicing medicine by remote wasn't what he'd trained for. Command insisted there was no significant impact on treatment. Rowland couldn't say one way or the other on that score, but he knew for a fact there were certain things the waldos just could not do effectively, even under the guidance of actual medical personnel, and that could be the difference between saving a soldier and burying one. Rowland kept his objections to himself, though, rather than risk reassignment to some post where he would make even less of a difference.

He pulled up the drone's frequency on his screen and mapped its trajectory. Something was causing drift. It was going to miss target, either slamming into the rocks or landing on the wrong side of them. Rowland's jaw tightened and his brow furrowed. "Lieutenant..." he started to snap at Richey, but left the rest of his reprimand unsaid as a course correction already registered on the screen before him. Pushing away from his station, he stood abruptly. "I'm going down to medbay. I'll monitor from there."

Rowland's mood did not improve as tension noticeably left the command crew at his departure.

Devon jerked back to full consciousness as the snarling and snapping of beasts drew nearer. Something resembling a pit bull crossed with a beetle faced off with one of the mega-crabs. Devon made the mistake of watching too closely. He gagged hard as he looked away. What he wouldn't give for the familiar creatures back on Earth. At least those made sense to him.

When would they reach him? When would he become the prize two beasts fought for? Despite the pain, he lay flat and wedged himself as far beneath the curved base of his sheltering boulder as he could, until he presented little target that was not protected. His right hand clutching the rifle jerked up until the stock angled like a shield across his vitals. With his other hand he reached into the ordnance pouch at his side, fumbling as his fingers trembled, but still managing to work the flap open. He felt inside and let out a shaky sigh of relief. Inside were three flash grenades, all the Dominion would allow barely trained conscripts such as himself. Probably afraid that anything more lethal would be more likely to take out their own platoon instead of the Allied forces. Still, what he had might be enough to buy him time. The noise and smoke one grenade generated should scare off anything that came too near. Not yet, though.

He blinked and struggled to focus. The sounds of squabbling had gotten louder, but the beasts kept their distance, for now. They were the least of his worries, though, as he realized sweat beaded his forehead, except where it ran a trail past the edge of his helmet and down his neck. Yet the rest of him continued to shiver and shudder. If he dared let go of his gear long enough to touch it, he was sure his wounded leg would burn his fingertips. As it was, a faint odor crept toward his nose, more noticeable in the close confines. At this point he'd be damned lucky to keep the leg, if he came out of this alive at all.

A low-level hum caught his ear as something passed overhead, barely heard. His gaze snapped to the sky and his head swam with the sudden motion. For a moment he thought he'd be sick, but he swallowed hard. His heart raced with the sudden need to get out of sight, only there was no more shelter than this slight overhang, and thanks to the damage to his leg he wasn't going anywhere else. It had been all he could manage just to gain what ground he had before the infection had set in.

Resigned, Devon readied his grenades, gripped his weapon, and hunkered down in his makeshift bivouac, not sure what would be worse: being found, or being forgotten.

If Rowland was the puppet master then the medi-mech was his Pinocchio. Patterned off the historic packbots employed in the twentieth and twenty-first centuries to clear combat zones of explosive devices, the 'mechs were programmed with a rudimentary AI and a knowledge database comparable to the training a field medic would receive. Unleashed in a combat zone after battle, they could home in on RF tags broadcasting biometrics that matched programed profiles indicating combat trauma of some sort. Upon reaching target they were capable of performing basic triage and handling most non-critical wounds. For everything else there was him...or others like him...medical personnel parked safe in orbit, sitting at a terminal capable of connecting to the medi-mech and taking over its functions to perform more complex field surgeries, as needed, but only in the most urgent circumstances where a soldier could not be medevac'd out of the combat zone before receiving treatment.

Rowland held his breath as the drone landed and the semi-autonomous medi-mech self-deployed, releasing the lockdowns that joined it to the drone. More data scrolled across his monitor, fed to him direct from the 'mech; Environmental conditions, course adjustments, preliminary evaluations of the patient based on the biometric data the unit began receiving from the RF tag.

Stuck on the orbiting transport, Rowland's every muscle bunched and clenched with the tension. Waiting did not suit him. He was a doer. To sit here two hundred miles above the planet, unable to get in there and do what he was trained for.... There was nothing he hated more.

Tapping a few keys on his terminal he activated the observation camera, but not the reverse video feed. His gut clenched as the 'mech moved over the devastated landscape in the direction of the RF signal. The unit had an image stabilizer, but it could only do so much given the broken terrain. However, as the 'mech began moving past the remains of the fallen, Rowland gagged and looked away as the images came through more clear than he was comfortable with. He was no stranger to the harsh reality of the battlefield, but right now he could not stomach the gazes of the dead, somehow both empty and accusing, one face practically unblemished while the next was cruelly butchered, postmortem. A searing guilt heated Rowland through as he realized what he felt most as the corpses scrolled by was relief that none of them were Justin. And yet each fallen soldier took on the shade of his brother-in-law's face until Rowland disabled the visual feed and set an alert to bring the camera back on line once the 'mech reached target.

As he sat there waiting, he faced the hard fact that even principles fell casualty to war.

Devon woke to a gentle tug on his rifle, then a more serious yank. His grip tightened and he struggled to open his eyes but they seemed crusted closed...or maybe they were just too heavy. For a moment he forgot why he wanted to open them. He started to drift off again when the stock was nearly jerked out of his hands.

"No!" he shouted. "Mine...mine." A sharp clack sounded close, followed by a loud snap, like steel links being hewn by a bolt cutter. Suddenly, Devon found himself holding just the butt of his weapon...and minus a piece of his thumb. He screamed and his eyes tore open. He could barely focus on the hellish figure before him but he saw enough to recognize that it was one of the massive, crab-like creatures scavenging the battlefield. The other half of Devon's weapon was clutched in the creature's claw. Without a thought,

Devon's good hand dove into the ordnance pouch closing on one of his flash grenades. He pulled the pin and rolled the cylinder as close to the creature as he could manage.

The force of the explosion sent his helmet crashing into the boulder behind him but Devon barely felt a thing, temporarily blind, deaf, and sliding full speed into oblivion.

A sudden alert blared through medbay. On Rowland's monitor, the window displaying Justin's biometric data auto-opened. A series of updates scrolled down the screen: Elevated heart- and respiratory rate. Increased levels of stress hormones, followed by chemical indications of fresh injury.

Justin was under attack.

Before he was even finished interpreting the data, the medi-mech assessed the change in biometrics and triggered its combat protocol, picking up speed and activating defensive armaments.

As Rowland reengaged the 'mech's cameras, a second window opened on his screen. The remote visuals came back on line. He had the sense that the devastation was much less once they passed the edges of the battlefield, but it was difficult to be sure with it moving by in such a blur. The terrain flew past as the 'mech ramped full-speed toward Justin's location.

The image on Rowland's screen shook with sudden violence and a notation on the lower right frame of the window indicated the 'mech had fired its flechette cannon. His mouth went dry and his muscles tensed as the camera stabilized and the image of a massive bolt-cutter crab the size of a warthog played across the screen. The back of the brightly colored exoskeleton was blackened, with fluids and flesh pulping through the holes and cracks left by the flechette rounds. Inexplicably, the bottom of the creature was also blackened and riddled with cracks. The creature's upraised claw still held the remains of a rifle.

Rowland's brow furrowed when he realized the weapon was Dominion-issue.

Then the carcass toppled and his blood ran cold an instant before it boiled with rage.

Pain lanced through Devon's leg, drawing him from the numbness of oblivion. He started to struggle, his left hand groping for another flash grenade, when his mind registered the quiet murmur that accompanied the poking and prodding that had brought him back to consciousness. From just above him and to the side he heard reassurances: "It is okay. You are safe now. Lie still while I tend your wounds."

Despite the too-regular vocal cadence—characteristic of robotic AIs—the words were soothing. He had read about the medical robots used by the Alliance in one of his tutorials, but never in his life had he expected to see one, let alone be in one's care.

"You are dehydrated. I am administering fluids."

"Devon...I am Devon," he muttered, then looked from the IV fed into his arm to the bag of fluids hanging off an upper strut on the robot and idly wondered what else was in that bag to make his head swim with just that slight motion. He couldn't bring himself to care through the pleasant numbness setting in. He did notice, though, that his right hand where the crab had clipped his thumb had already been bandaged. He muttered a thank you and tried to pat the robot to show his gratitude, but it gently extended a spare waldo and held him still as it continued to cut away his pant leg. Despite whatever was in the IV making him feel floaty, that hurt like hell.

To take his mind off of the pain, Devon started talking. Randomly and about everything he had experienced in his short life. His granddad, his first girlfriend...when he was five, immigrating to Demeter, the terror of being thrown into battle with a gun that was little more than a club and a handful of grenades that just made noise, his concern for the woman who recorded the holochip around his neck, his last days on Earth, his conscription by the Dominion, he even spoke about his parents' death...something he'd not said a word about to anyone since the day they died.

He couldn't help it. The words tumbled from him like the guts that had spilled from the crab that cut him. He spoke until his words ran together and his head swam with the pain and the medication and the relief that he would not die beneath this rock, unremembered. And as Devon rambled, his gaze locked on the little blinking light beside the robot's optic. The flashes mesmerized him until his words trailed off and he barely noticed the robot's continued reassurances as it debrided his wound and stitched it up.

The entire time the medi-mech worked on the Dominion soldier wearing Justin's RF tags Rowland fought with himself. More than half a dozen times he started to key in the sequence that would override the treatment protocols and recall the 'mech—even after he learned the *kid* was just a conscript. He told himself that made no difference. Conscript or not, he had fought against Allied troops. He had taken up arms. Only by clinging to his healer's oath did Rowland resist. And then what the boy...*Devon* was saying sank in. Rowland could not ignore that the young woman the boy rambled about, the one he showed such compassion for, was Rowland's own sister.

Devon's words said it all... *'The Dominion screwed them both over.'*

...*all of us*, Rowland amended in his thoughts, and the hatred and rage toward this boy that had poisoned his heart ran out of him.

Feeling only sorrow for his sister and growing compassion for Devon, Rowland continued to stand vigil as the 'mech finished its ministration. While it stitched and cleansed and bandaged he kept his eyes on Devon's face and considered what would happen to the boy, conscript or not, if they were to send down a team to medivac him out. At best he would be "detained", at worse court-martialed for collusion. His forced service would dog him for the rest of his days, no matter where he went in Allied space. Any hope for a decent life would have died beneath that boulder.

Even with no clue who Devon was, Rowland's sister, Kelly, would be ashamed of him were he to allow that to happen. That wasn't the only reason James Rowland chose to do what was right—but it was the least complicated.

Though the boy needed to rest and recover, there wasn't time. Shortly, Allied forces would be moving in to resecure the area. Once that happened Devon would become yet another casualty of war. Rowland overrode the 'mech's protocols and took over the waldos. Keying in the sequence that loaded the built-in hypodermic with a high dose of adrenaline—such as would be administered to counteract heart failure in a patient—he injected half of it into Devon, then let the other half drain harmlessly onto the ground. As he waited for the injection to counteract the sedative that had finally taken effect, Rowland linked the camera on his terminal to the monitor inset on the 'mech. When the boy began to stir, Rowland cleared his throat to get his attention, then waited for Devon to regain his focus before he spoke.

"I am Major James Rowland, medical supervisor aboard the Allied transport *McCoy*. You—*Sergeant Krugliak*—just died," he said with a significant look. As he spoke, he manipulated the waldos once more, reaching out to lift the Allied tags—and his sister's holochip—from around Devon's neck. "You need to get out of there before the Alliance arrives."

Devon remained completely still, his expression equal parts fear, doubt, and confusion. "Why are you doing this?"

Rowland struggled a moment with how to answer. What he could say that this kid would understand, out of the confusing tangle of things that went into changing the outcome of this encounter?

"You aren't who we're out here fighting, son," he finally answered. "Now pull yourself together, lose the uniform, and de-ass that field, before the ground forces show up for clean-up duty. There's a town five klicks south of you, they can get you back to your settlement..." he stopped himself from finishing. The kid didn't need to know the town very well might no longer be there. "Go...find your way home and don't look back."

As he spoke, Rowland recalled the medi-mech and officially logged in Sergeant Justin Krugliak's time of death, unable to avoid breaking his sister's heart, but saving an innocent in the process.

GOODBYE, FAREWELL, AND AMEN

WRITING FOR DEFENDING THE FUTURE IS ONE OF THE LUCKIEST BREAKS I EVER got as an author. I was known for supernatural detectives, hardboiled detectives, certain types of comedies, all manner of things...but nothing like what I created for my buddy Mike McPhail. Everyone knows I was pretty much resistant at first, but Mike coaxed one of the best series I've ever created out of me, and helped me forge a last story that would cap the series for all time. I would have never tried something like this so far outside my comfort zone without his quiet guidance. Like many who reach comfort, I have become a coward.

But, even if *Rocky and Noodles* were signed, sealed, and delivered, DTF was moving onward. Mike got me to do a straight sci-fi military story, [The Wag of His Tail], something as far outside my wheelhouse as possible. I was very proud of that tale...still am.

I don't have much wind these days, my sails are all but empty, and stouter warriors will have to sail beyond the shoals I can no longer dream of clearing. And that's all right. I made my discoveries, set my boundaries, left my mark. Let those in the wings roar forward. It is their right, their destiny. I had mine.

I've had a wonderful run. And I love everyone that helped along the way.

Thank you all.

12/16/16

CJ Henderson
July 3, 2014

Jennifer Brozek
INKY, BLINKY, AND ME

Jennifer Brozek is a Hugo Award-nominated editor and a Bram Stoker nominated author. Winner of the Australian Shadows Award for best edited publication, Jennifer has edited fifteen anthologies with more on the way, including the acclaimed *Chicks Dig Gaming* and *Shattered Shields* anthologies. Author of *Apocalypse Girl Dreaming, Industry Talk*, the *Karen Wilson Chronicles*, and the acclaimed *Melissa Allen* series, she has more than sixty-five published short stories, and is the Creative Director of Apocalypse Ink Productions.

Jennifer is a freelance author for numerous RPG companies. Winner of the Scribe, Origins, and ENnie awards, her contributions to RPG source-books include *Dragonlance, Colonial Gothic, Shadowrun, Serenity, Savage Worlds*, and *White Wolf SAS*. Jennifer is the author of the award winning YA *Battletech* novel, *The Nellus Academy Incident*, and *Shadowrun* novella, *Doc Wagon 19*. She has also written for the AAA MMO, *Aion*, and the award winning videogame, *Shadowrun Returns*.

When she is not writing her heart out, she is gallivanting around the Pacific Northwest in its wonderfully mercurial weather. Jennifer is a Director-at-Large of SFWA, and an active member of HWA and IAMTW. Read more about her at www.jenniferbrozek.com or follow her on Twitter at @JenniferBrozek.

Aaron Rosenberg
WIN OR LOSE

Aaron Rosenberg is the author of the best-selling DuckBob series (consisting of *No Small Bills, Too Small for Tall*, and *Three Small Coinky-dinks*), the Dread Remora space-opera series and, with David Niall Wilson, the O.C.L.T. occult thriller series. His tie-in work contains novels for Star Trek, Warhammer, WarCraft, and Eureka. He has written children's books (including the original series Pete and Penny's Pizza Puzzles, the award-winning Bandslam: The Junior Novel, and the #1 best-selling 42: The Jackie Robinson Story), educational books on a variety of topics, and over seventy roleplaying games (such as the original games Asylum, Spookshow, and

Chosen, work for White Wolf, Wizards of the Coast, Fantasy Flight, Pinnacle, and many others, and both the Origins Award-winning Gamemastering Secrets and the Gold ENnie-winning Lure of the Lich Lord). He is the co-creator of the ReDeus series, and one of the founders of Crazy 8 Press. Aaron lives in New York with his family. You can follow him online at gryphonrose.com, on Facebook at facebook.com/gryphonrose, and on Twitter @gryphonrose.

Nancy Jane Moore
TEAMWORK

Nancy Jane Moore is the author of *The Weave*, a military science fiction novel published in 2015 by Aqueduct Press, along with several other books and numerous short stories and essays. A native Texan, she spent many years in Washington, DC, and now lives in Oakland, California. Moore has trained in martial arts since 1979 and holds a fourth degree black belt in Aikido. She is a member of the authors' co-op Book View Café, and blogs weekly at http://bookviewcafe.com/blog/, http://nancyjanemoore.com.

Ronald Garner
WE'RE ALL MARINES TODAY

Ronald Garner is an author, publisher, and Marine reservist. He is co-founder of Silence in the Library Publishing. His fiction can be found in *A Hero By Any Name*, *Soothe The Savage Beast*, and *Contact Light*.

Bud Sparhawk
TURTLE AND BIRD

Bud Sparhawk is the author of the novels *Distant Seas* and *Vixen*, as well as two print collections: *Sam Boone: Front To Back*, and *Dancing with Dragons*. He has three e-Novels available through Amazon and other channels.

Bud has been a three-time novella finalist for the Nebula award: *Primrose and Thorn* (Analog, May 1996), *Magic's Price* (Analog, March

2001), and *Clay's Pride* (Analog, July/August 2004). His work has appeared Editor) and *The Years Best Science Fiction, Fourteenth Annual Collection,* (St Martins Press, Garner Dozois – Editor.)

His short stories have appeared frequently in Analog Fact/Fiction, less so in Asimov's, as well as in five *Defending the Future* and other anthologies, publications and audio books. He has put out several collections of some of his published works in ebook format. A complete bibliography can be found at: http://budsparhawk.com.

He also writes an occasional blog on the pain of writing at http://budsparhawk.blogspot.com.

Patrick Thomas
THE MACHINE IN THE GHOST

Patrick Thomas writes the fantasy humor series *Murphy's Lore*, which includes *Tales From Bulfinche's Pub, Fools' Day, Through The Drinking Glass, Shadow Of The Wolf, Redemption Road, Bartender Of The Gods, Nightcaps* and *Empty Graves* — as well as the *After Hours* spin offs *Fairy With A Gun, Fairy Rides The Lightning, Dead To Rites, Rites of Passage,* and *Lore & Dysorder*. His *Mystic Investigators* paranormal mystery series includes *Bullets & Brimstone, From The Shadows, Once More Upon A Time,* and *Partners In Crime*. He co-edited *New Blood* and *Hear Them Roar* and was an editor for *Fantastic Stories of the Imagination* and *Pirate Writings*. Patrick's syndicated humorous advice column *Dear Cthulhu* includes *Have A Dark Day, Good Advice For Bad People,* and *Cthulhu Knows Best*. A number of his books are part of the props department of the CSI television show and have been spotted on the show. His urban fantasy *Fairy With A Gun* was optioned by Laurence Fishburne's Cinema Gypsy Productions. Drop by www.patthomas.net to learn more or find out about The Patrick Thomas Show mockumentary.

Brenda Cooper
ALONG THE
NORTHERN BORDER

Brenda Cooper's novels include *POST* (Espec Books, 2016) and *Spear of Light* (Pyr, 2016). Her other works include *Edge of Dark* (Pyr, 2015), *The Creative Fire* (Pyr, 2012), and *The Diamond Deep* (Pyr, 2013) as well as the *Silver Ship and the Sea* series (available in audio today, and soon to be re-

released via Wordfire Press) and *Building Harlequin's Moon*, with Larry Niven (Tor, 2005).

Her recent short fiction includes "The Hand on the Cradle" (*Humanity 2.0*, 2016), "Iron Pegasus," (*Mission: Tomorrow*, 2015), "Biology at the End of the World" (*Asimov's*, August 2015), and "Elephant Angels" (*Heiroglyph*, 2014).

Brenda blogs frequently on environmental and futurist topics, and her non-fiction has appeared in Slate and Crosscut.

She is the winner of the 2007 and 2016 Endeavor Awards for "a distinguished science fiction or fantasy book written by a Pacific Northwest author or authors." Her work has also been nominated for the Phillip K. Dick and Canopus awards.

Brenda lives in Bellevue, Washington with her family and three dogs.

Robert E. Waters
THE FIRST PEACE

Robert E Waters had been writing and publishing stories since 2003, with his first publication in Weird Tales. Since then, he has published over 30 stories in various print and on-line magazines and anthologies, including e-Spec's *The Weird Wild West* and the *Defending the Future* Mil SF anthology series. Robert is also a frequent contributor to Eric Flint's alternate history series, 1632/Ring of Fire, with several stories published in the on-line Grantville Gazette, and most recently in Baen Book's Ring of Fire IV anthology. Robert's first novel, The Wayward Eight: A Contract to Die For, was released in 2014 under the Zmok imprint, and is a "weird wild west" adventure set in the Wild West Exodus gaming universe. Robert lives in Baltimore, Maryland with his wife Beth, their son Jason, and their cat Buzz.

James Chambers
THE METH MOTHS OF
KRAKEN MARE

James Chambers writes tales of horror, crime, fantasy, and science fiction. He is the author of *The Engines of Sacrifice*, a collection of four Lovecraftian-inspired novellas published by Dark Regions Press which *Publisher's Weekly* described in a starred-review as "...chillingly evocative...." He is also the author of the short fiction collections *Resurrection House* (Dark Regions Press) as well as the dark, urban fantasy novella, *Three Chords of Chaos* and *The Dead Bear Witness* and *Tears of Blood*, volume one and two in the Corpse Fauna novella series.

His short stories have been published in the anthologies *The Avenger: Roaring Heart of the Crucible*, *Chiral Mad 2*, *Clockwork Chaos*, *Dark Furies*, *The Dead Walk*, *Deep Cuts*, *The Domino Lady: Sex as a Weapon*, *Dragon's Lure*, *Fantastic Futures 13*, *Gaslight and Grimm*, *The Green Hornet Chronicles*, *Hardboiled Cthulhu*, *In An Iron Cage*, *Kolchak the Night Stalker: Passages of the Macabre*, *Shadows Over Main Street*, *The Spider: Extreme Prejudice*, *Qualia Nous*, *Reel Dark*, *Truth or Dare*, *TV Gods*, *Walrus Tales*, *Warfear*, and the award-winning Bad-Ass Faeries and Defending the Future series as well as the magazines *Bare Bone*, *Cthulhu Sex*, and *Allen K's Inhuman*.

He has also edited and written numerous comic books including *Leonard Nimoy's Primortals*, the critically acclaimed "The Revenant" in *Shadow House*, and the original graphic novel *Kolchak, the Night Stalker: The Forgotten Lore of Edgar Allan Poe*.

His website is www.jameschambersonline.com.

Judi Fleming
SERVICE CALL

Judi Fleming works as a training specialist and instructional designer for the federal government in her day job and thus much of her writing is of the non-exciting technical sort. She is a graduate of Seton Hill University Writing Popular Fiction Master's Program. Her stories have appeared in *No Man's Land*, *Best Laid Plans*, and *Dogs of War*.

Eric Hardenbrook
TRIGGER DISCIPLINE

Eric Hardenbrook is a fan, an author and an artist, usually in that order. Eric lives in central Pennsylvania with his gorgeous wife and daughter. He writes to try to get the stories out of his head. His stories can be found in *TV Gods*, *Best Laid Plans*, and *Dogs of War*. When he's being a fan he helps run

Watch the Skies and assists in the publication of their monthly fanzine. He can be found (at least some of the time) at The Pretend Blog. When not working on those things, Eric enjoys the occasional video or board game and is an old school role player.

Jeff Young
ARMSTICE

Jeff Young is a bookseller first and a writer second – although he wouldn't mind a reversal of fortune.

He is an award winning author who contributed to the anthologies: *Writers of the Future* v.26, *By Any Means, Best Laid Plans, Dogs of War, In an Iron Cage, Fantastic Futures 13, Clockwork Chaos, TV Gods, The Society for the Preservation of C.J. Henderson* and *Gaslight and Grimm*. Jeff's work was also published in the magazines *eSteampunk, Realms, Cemetery Moon, Trail of Indiscretion, Realms Beyond, Carbon14* and *Neuronet*. He is also an editor with Fortress Publishing for their *Drunken Comic Book Monkey* line as well as the anthology *TV Gods* and the upcoming *TV Gods : Summer Programming.*

Jeff has helped run the Watch the Skies SF&F Reading Group of Harrisburg and Camp Hill for more than fifteen years. Finally, Jeff is also the proprietor of the online eBay and Etsy shops- Helm Haven, which produces Renaissance and Steampunk costume pieces.

Anton Kukal
TRUDY

Anton Kukal is an actor, author, and game designer. He is best known for his appearances on NBC's the Marriage Ref, Nickelodeon's "Take Me To Your Mother," and for his portrayal of Count Thrace in "The Rangers." He designed the Mystic Realms live-action and dice-play roleplaying game systems, writing the Core Rulebook, Writers Guide, Members Manual, Menagerie, and Compendium, as well as twelve Realm Books describing the different world settings. Together these books explain how to run clubs and create dramatic roleplaying events using unique methods of interactive theater.

Danielle Ackley-McPhail
CASUALTIES OF WAR

Award-winning author and editor Danielle Ackley-McPhail has worked both sides of the publishing industry for longer than she cares to admit. In 2014 she joined forces with husband Mike McPhail and friend Greg Schauer to form her own publishing house, eSpec Books (www.especbooks.com).

She can be found on Facebook (Danielle Ackley-McPhail) and Twitter (DMcPhail, eSpecBooks).

CJ Henderson
GOODBYE, FAREWELL, AND AMEN

CJ Henderson was the creator of both the Piers Knight supernatural investigator series and the *Teddy London* occult detective series among many others. He wrote over 70 books and/or novels, hundreds and hundreds of short stories and comics and thousands of non-fiction pieces. He was a master of hardboiled suspense as well as raucous comedy, and was not shy about saying so even when sober. For more on this truly fascinating teller of tales, we encourage all to stop in at www.cjhenderson.com.

Mike McPhail
EDITOR

Author and graphic artist Mike McPhail is a member of the Military Writers Society of America. He is dedicated to helping his fellow service members (and those deserving civilians) in their efforts to become authors/editors/artists, as well as supporting related organizations in their efforts to help those "who have given their all for us." www.milscifi.com.

He is best known as the editor and illustrator of the award-winning *Defending The Future* series of military science fiction anthologies, which just celebrated its tenth anniversary. www.defendingthefuture.com.

In 2015 he added the title of publisher, as the co-owner of eSpec Books LLC, Speculative Fiction Publishing. www.especbooks.com.

KICKSTARTER RANK AND FILE

Adam Selby-Martin
Alain Fournier
Alan Danziger
Anders M. Ytterdahl
Andreas Gustafsson
Andrew Hatchell
Andrew J Clark IV
Angela Carlson
Ann Stolinsky
Anonymous
Anonymous Reader
Anton Kukal
Aramanth Dawe
Arthur W. Lobdell
Ashley Knight
Ayelet Benson
Barbara and Carl Kesner
Brenda Cooper
Brendan Lonehawk
Brent Millis
Brian Bishop
Brian 'Commodore Stargazer'
    Whitcraft
Bryan Geddes
Candace R. Benefiel
Carol Ann Kukal
Cathy Franchett
Chad Bowden
Chand Svare Ghei chasvag.com
Charles Anchors
Cheri Kannarr
Chris Volcheck
Colin Lloyd
Curtis & Maryrita Steinhour
Dave Hermann
Dave Lewis
David McDermott
David Mortman

Dorothy O'Hare
D-Rock
edward zagadinow
eerian sadow
Erin Penn
Evaristo Ramos, Jr.
Fan of Words
Fran Stewart
Gareth Pendleton
Gavran
Glenn Goldman
GMark Cole
Greg Resnik
Guy McLimore
Hamel Moric
Hiram G Wells
Holly Hunt
Ian Harvey
Isaac 'Will It Work' Dansicker
Ivan Donati
J.R. Murdock
Jakub Narebski
James Chambers
James Rowland
James W. Armstrong-Wood
Janine K. Spendlove
Janito Vaqueiro Ferreira Filho
Jason F. Broadley
Jason Genser
Jason Russell
Jay Zastrow
Jessica Enfante
Jessica Reid
Jiri "Picky" Cerny
John "Shadowcat" Ickes
John G. Hartness
John Green
John Idlor

John L. French
Joyce Ann Garcia from McAllen Texas
Judy Waidlich
JW
Karen and James Henson
Karl Gallagher
Keith Hall
Keith Tracton
Keith West, Future Potentate
    of the Solar System
Kelly Farmer
Ken Mencher
Kerry aka Trouble
Lady Ozma
Lark Cunningham
Lauren Hoffman
Laurie Gailunas
Laurie Hicks
Lennhoff Family
Lisa Kruse
Louise Lowenspets
Louise McCulloch
M A Pugliese
M. L. Falkenstein
M. Menzies
Marc "mad" Winkelmann
Margaret St. John
Mark Knapp Jr
Mark Lukens
Martin Bernstein
Mary Spila
Mat Masding-Grouse
Matt P
Matthew Hieb
Max Kaehn
mdtommyd
Michael Carson
Michael D Blanchard
Michael Fedrowitz
Michael Skolnik
Mike Maurer
Nathan Duby
Nathan Turner
Neil A Ottenstein
Nellie B.
Nicole McPherson
Niki Coppola
Pat Hayes
Patrick Thomas
Paul Ryan
Paul van Oven
Pepita Hogg-Sonnenberg
Peter Thew
Peter Young
R.T. Bryson
Ralph M. Seibel
Raymond Finch
Revek
RK Bookman
Rob Karp
Robby Thrasher
Robert E Waters
Roisin mcCormac
Ross Hathaway
Roy Romasanta
S Ruskin
sam murphy
Samuel Lubell
Scott A Johnson
Scott Elson
Scott Mayanrd
Scott Schaper
Sean McGarry
Sebastian H.
ShadowCub
Shervyn
Sheryl R. Hayes
Silence in the Library Publishing

Simo Muinonen
Simon Clark
Soldier Systems Daily
Stephanie Lucas
Stephen A, Fender
Stephen Ballentine
Stephen Cheng
Suragai
Susan Carlson
Susan R Grossman
Svend Andersen
SwordFire
Tamara Michelle Slaten
thatraja
The loyal minion, Linda
Thomas M. Karwacki Jr.
Thomas Werner
Tina England
Tina Noe Good
Tom Berrisford
Tomas Burgos-Caez
Tony Finan
Tory Shade
Towelman
V. Hartman DiSanto
Vickie B
Wallace MacBix
Wes Rist
William Hughes
William Wiebking

Finally, There's Something We Can All Agree On.

It's something we've all said many times. And it does seem to be one of the few things that Americans unanimously agree on. But it takes more than agreeing with each other. It takes the USO. For more than 60 years, the USO has been the bridge back home for the men and women of our armed forces around the world. The USO receives no government funding and relies entirely on the generosity of the American people. We all want to support our troops. This is how it's done.

Help support our troops.